Crimson Forest

By Christine Gabriel

pandamoon
publishing

www.pandamoonpublishing.com

Jacket design and illustrations © Pandamoon Publishing.

Pandamoon Publishing and the portrayal of a panda and a moon are registered trademarks of Pandamoon Publishing.

Library of Congress Cataloging-in-Publication Data is on file at the Library of Congress, Washington, DC.

ISBN-10: 0990338983
ISBN-13: 978-0-9903389-8-7

To Diane. Though heaven is far away, I would like to thank you for giving me the opportunity to have such a wonderful man in my life. Without his love and patience, this book would not have been possible.

Crimson Forest

Preface

It is said that true love can follow you from one life to the next. It's so powerful it buries itself deep inside the soul, transferring to each new life, carrying with it fragments of memories and feelings, each time renewing hope that one day you'll be lucky enough to find the person you are meant to be with.

Everyone yearns for a chance at true love, seeking it out, praying for the opportunity to be truly happy. I, however, am different. I had never given much thought to how I would find true love, or that I would ever find love at all. I was more worried about being normal, as that was my opportunity at happiness. I wanted more than anything to feel as though I fit in as a regular member of society.

If it weren't for the secrets that lie within the Crimson Forest, I would never have realized that being normal is for people who want to live in the comfort of their safe routines, who want to peer into the world with rose colored glasses and avoid the truth.

This very truth has taught me that fairy tales are real and that there is such a place where true love exists—a place where past lives cross, and happiness can live forever.

1

Nightmares

"Beautiful," I cooed as I ran my hands through the soft crimson-colored moss that crept across the ground and up the old oak tree I leaned against. The crisp, cool air felt good against my flushed cheeks. The light breeze felt like soft fingers running through my long, wild chestnut hair. The sun peeked its head through the tall fall-colored treetops and hit my amber eyes. I smiled and imagined new freckles growing across the bridge of my nose, as that's what seemed to happen every time the sun hit my pale face. I lay my head against the tree's soft mossy coat and closed my eyes. I breathed in the heavy aroma of autumn and allowed the music of the forest to fill me. Every sound was magical: from the sweet song the birds were singing to the rush of water from the nearby river.

Suddenly, I heard a sound that I recognized immediately, and my eyes flew open. A pacifying calmness washed over me like a warm summer rain as I admired the large white-tailed deer that stood directly in front of me. I remained still so that I didn't scare the skittish animal away. Its greyish brown coat glistened in the fall sun, while its muscular body twitched in anticipation of my silent reaction. It took a step toward me, and I noticed something odd. Its large antlers were still covered in soft velvet, which was not normal for this time of year.

I held my breath and slowly reached my trembling hand toward it. Its warm, brown, almond-shaped eyes stared at me calmly. I smiled, gently touching the sharp end of the antler with my fingertip. It snorted and kicked at the ground, its warm breath visible in the cool, fall air. The magnificent animal's demeanor suddenly began to change. Its tail flicked up, showing the soft white color underneath as a warning that something was wrong. Fear replaced the calm in its eyes, and it reared up, letting out an aggressive rattling noise. I watched in sheer horror as blood red moss began snaking its way down the animal's antler, beginning in the place I had touched. It spread like wild fire around the animal's strong body, and, within a matter of seconds, completely engulfed it. The deer fell to the ground and writhed in pain.

"No!" I yelled out as I forced my fear-paralyzed body to move toward it. I put my hands under its head and began to sob quietly. I felt helpless as it looked up at me with sad, unforgiving eyes. It took one last breath, and I felt its body go limp in my hands.

"You did this," a female voice called out from behind me.

I wiped the tears from my eyes and turned around, only to find no one was there. "What do you mean, I did this?" I called out angrily.

I heard a girlish giggle from deep within the forest, "You know exactly what I mean. All you have to do is remember."

"Remember what?"

"Remember who you are, Angelina. Remember who you are."

~ ~ ~

I woke up, sweat drenched and shaking. The nightmares were becoming much more frequent lately, and I didn't know why. Every night, it was the same thing: red moss and death.

I reached for the glass of water on my nightstand and let out a startled gasp as my hand came across something soft like the deer antlers from my dream. It was the velvet picture frame that housed a photograph of my father holding the baby version of me. I treasured that picture. I knew it was there. But I snapped my hand back, knocking over the glass of water. It hit the hardwood floor, and I sighed.

My alarm clock read 6 a.m., time to start my day, so I pushed the covers off me and used ninja moves to hop out of bed and over the mess I had made on the floor. I flicked on the light switch, grabbed a towel from my hamper, and cleaned up the mess.

As I got dressed for the day, I paused momentarily, admiring my womanly curves in the full-length mirror. I supposed I was pretty in a girl-next-door kind of way. I used my slender fingers to push back my long, wavy chestnut hair that hung wildly around my pale, slightly freckled face. My amber eyes peered back at me.

It was going to be a busy day, full of running errands for my mother, dealing with mouthy hunters, and occasionally answering questions for the curious tourist who wanted to know where the red moss in the forest had come from. That was the joy of my life: living next to the famous Crimson Forest.

I had gotten used to people telling me how lucky I was to have grown up in the small town of Buffalo, Wisconsin, home to 657 locals, multiple stray cats, and quite a few drunk hunters. Buffalo was known for the blood-red moss that seemed to make its presence known on every living thing within the dense forest that surrounded our small town. Tourists came in droves to see it, questioning its origin. Multiple environmental scientists had also come, their scientific minds curious as to why Mother Nature would create such an oddity. The source of the moss baffled them. That, of course, caused rumors to spread, which sparked the interest and curiosity within the rest of the human population.

One rumor implied that the spilled blood of the white-tailed deer, slaughtered every year during our busy hunting season, had poisoned the ground, causing the moss to turn crimson, as if it were a constant reminder of our sins against the wild beasts of the forest.

The rumor I found to be the most interesting was one that stemmed from an age-old myth that had been whispered throughout our town for centuries. It told of mysterious creatures that walked the forest during the dark hours of the night, searching for their next sacrifice to sate their thirst for blood. In this story, the blood of humans, not animals, had actually stained the red moss. Some said it was retribution for the many animals murdered by the huntsman that had invaded their habitat.

Regardless of the theories, people came to their own conclusions after seeing the strange anomaly, especially the hunters. They believed the red moss was man made in order to increase the size of the already large animal, which was just silly altogether. However, our town ended up becoming the number one hunting location in the Midwest. Like I said, this was the joy of my life: living next to the Crimson Forest, a place where rumors were made and people were left in constant amazement.

2

Lost Love

I was seventeen, the youngest of the graduating class of 2013. I was envious as I watched all my friends leave for college. They had escaped to bigger and better things, while I was still trapped in Buffalo, mostly due to the fact I wasn't technically an adult yet. So I spent my newly freed-up time helping my mom run the quaint little bed and breakfast she had taken over after my father's disappearance. Just thinking of life without my father saddened me. The memory of losing him was still fresh in my mind, as if it had just happened yesterday.

It was my twelfth birthday, and I was disappointed that my father was going to skip my birthday dinner for the annual hunting trip held in honor of our mysterious forest. That particular evening, as my mother was lighting the candles on my birthday cake, we were surprised by a visit from two plain-clothes police officers.

"Good Evening, Mrs. Adams, I'm afraid we need to speak with you," one of them ordered quietly, avoiding my curious eyes.

"Is everything okay, Jim?" she answered.

"Can we talk somewhere more private?" He motioned toward the kitchen.

I knew that was code for somewhere without me around. I narrowed my eyes at them and watched my mother nod slowly, a frown forming on her pretty face. She set the matches down, stood up quietly, and led the officers into the kitchen. I sat at the table alone, staring at the halfway-lit birthday cake while attempting to hold my breath so that I could hear them better. The only words I caught were "missing" and "woman."

I frowned and picked some of the candle wax off the top of the cake as I tried to make sense of what could've possibly happened. I waited patiently for them to return and, after what seemed like an eternity in kid years, the two gentlemen finally emerged from the kitchen, their heads hanging low in quiet solemnity. I knew by their body language that they were trying their best to completely avoid the fact that I was still at the table watching them. They quickly let themselves out, and I looked at my cake. The candles had finally managed to burn themselves out. "So much for my special day," I muttered quietly to myself.

After a few moments, I realized my mom wasn't coming out of the kitchen. It couldn't be that bad, could it? I poked my head around the corner. Something was terribly wrong. My mother stood trembling, staring out the kitchen window with a blank expression on her face. She gripped the edge of the counter so tightly that her knuckles turned white.

"Mom, what's wrong?" I questioned nervously, hoping she would turn around and tell me it was merely something trivial. Instead, she remained unmoving. I fought the urge to rush to her side as I watched her normally strong stature begin to weaken. She took a deep breath in, and at that moment I knew she was preparing herself to tell me something that was going to be hard for her to say and hard for me to swallow.

"Angelina, today you turned twelve. You're no longer a child, but a young woman." She paused momentarily before finally uttering, "I'm only sorry that you have to find out what it means to be strong so early in life."

"Mom, I don't understand . . ." I stuttered, trying to decipher her body language.

She turned around slowly, fresh tears on her face. Picking up a nearby dishtowel, she quickly dried her eyes and walked over to me. Fearful, I looked up at her and remained silent.

"Your father is—missing."

My heart sank, and warm tears began to fill my eyes. "What do you mean he's missing?" I managed to croak.

She bent down in front of me and took my hand in hers. "There was something—a creature . . ." The look on her face sent chills throughout my small body. "It took him."

"What was it and where did it take him?" I whispered in disbelief.

Her voice trembled. "Honey, they don't know. The group he was with was ambushed. The creature looked like a woman, but . . ."

"But what?"

"They say she wasn't human. They say her eyes glowed an iridescent white, and she was so agile, the group didn't even have the opportunity to protect themselves."

"Is everyone else okay?"

She lowered her head, "A few of them suffered broken bones, but your father—they don't know. She took him with her."

The tears began to spill down my pale cheeks. "No!"

I felt her strong arms instantly wrap themselves around me as she pulled me close to her soft body. "They'll find him, honey. I know they will. We just have to believe he's okay. Your father's a strong man."

I nodded to let her know I agreed. She was right: my father was a strong man, but, from the sounds of it, this creature was much stronger. However, I had to believe that he was going to come home. I had to believe he was going to be alright. I buried my head deeper into my mother's embrace and vowed to never again celebrate another birthday until my father was able to celebrate it with me.

~ ~ ~

I shivered, shaking off the painful memory as I made my way out of the east wing of the bed and breakfast, which was deemed the owner's quarters. I skipped down the steps that opened up to the great room. The mouthwatering aroma of bacon hit me as I joined the hustle and bustle of the busy room. The house was in full swing with hunters preparing themselves for their long day of sitting in tree stands, each one hoping they would be the one to catch the prize deer of the season.

I looked around and admired my charming home with its peeling rose-colored wallpaper and old, worn tables. The stone fireplace popped and crackled delightfully as a few of the big burly men sat in front of it, drinking their hot coffee and reading the morning paper. A few of the younger men were watching highlights from the previous night's football game on a small television. I smiled. I knew my mother had everything in perfect order. She made sure that every guest had a hot meal, clean sheets, and a cozy room to return to.

A sweet song rang out from the kitchen, and I immediately knew she was baking something special. She only ever sang out loud when she was baking. I smiled, secretly hoping she was making her famous cinnamon apples. I listened for a while longer and realized I recognized the song: it was the song my father had won over her heart with when they met. Her rendition of "Brown Eyed Girl" carried her strength in its tune.

I smirked and thought of how she had never remarried. Though she had been propositioned many times by many different men, she would always politely decline. "True love never dies," she would say, "and though my husband may be gone, my heart will always belong to him." She would then give them her sweet smile, thank them for their offer, and add, "One day I will see him again, even if it's only in heaven—I will see him again."

In the kitchen, she stopped singing, so I figured she must've shoved whatever she was baking in the oven. I sighed. It was time to get to work. Tomorrow was the first official day of the big hunt, so I already knew my day was going to consist of checking guests into their rooms and refilling coffee cups.

At the end of the day, just when I thought I was done with my daily duties, my mother walked in and handed me a grocery list. Man, did I hate grocery shopping. I grumbled, showing my discontent as I grabbed my jacket. I headed out the door, silently wondering if I would ever actually get to enjoy being a teenager.

3

Memories

I walked into the little country store and smiled at Mrs. Bailey, the owner, who happened to be a good friend of my mother.

She looked up from what appeared to be a cheesy romance novel and smiled. "Well, hello there, dear."

I gave her a little wave and held up my list.

She smirked. "Your mother must be fretting about running out of things."

"Always," I answered in return as I made my way down an empty aisle. I continued on my horrendous task of shopping, only selecting the things that were on the list, knowing if I picked up one extra item, my mother would throw a fit.

An oddly familiar chill snaked its way down my spine, and I had the overwhelming feeling that someone was watching me. I turned around slowly, half expecting to see someone standing right behind me, and jumped when I saw my own reflection in the surveillance mirror that hung nearby.

I poked my head around the corner of the next aisle and was overwhelmed by relief at its emptiness. I shuddered and attempted to shake off the ominous feeling. I hadn't felt this way since I was a little girl. A memory tugged on the back of my mind, and then it was like someone suddenly hit the rewind button. It was the morning of my seventh birthday, and my mother threw a small party for me with Wonder Woman as the theme since it was my favorite TV show at the time. I ran up the stairs with the red cape my mother had spent hours crafting for me trailing proudly behind my back. I was going to prove to my partygoers that I could fly just like my heroine. I pushed up the white metal window screen and climbed out onto the roof. The cool air whipped my cape back and forth as I stood on the edge. Holding my arms straight out in front of me, I jumped, quickly learning that flying was not on my list of superhero qualifications. I fell head first toward the ground below. I closed my eyes and awaited the impact, disappointed that I wasn't anything more than an ordinary human being. The distance between the ground and me closed in quickly. However, fate had the upper hand as a pair of strong muscular arms miraculously caught me.

I looked up at the mysterious man who had saved my life. My mother had once told me angels existed, but I never believed her until then. The man had a purity about him and a sweet calmness in his beautiful odd colored eyes. In his presence, there was no room in my mind for anything bad, and I was sure the word evil wasn't even in his vocabulary.

I admired his odd features. In his deep-set eyes was an endless ocean of orange that cascaded into a fiery red ring. Messy platinum locks fell over his eyes, which looked odd against his tan skin. His tall, thin, muscular frame towered over me. I cocked my head to the side and, with wonder in my eyes, I asked, "Are you an angel?"

He set me down carefully and smiled back. "No, but that would be pretty neat, huh?"

I kicked at the grass. "Yeah, I thought I was special like Wonder Woman. But I can't fly." I frowned, still disappointed by this new fact. "Now all I'll ever be is boring."

He chuckled and gently placed his hand under my chin, so I would look at him. "Now why would you want to be like this so-called Wonder Woman?"

"Well," I thought carefully, "she's special and everyone likes her. Nobody likes boring people."

"Aw, sweetie, that's not true."

I plopped down on the ground and sank into my cape. "Yes, it is. Everyone thinks I'm weird because I can see things they can't," I answered angrily.

He put his hands on his hips and winked. "Well, I believe you."

"You do?"

"Of course, I do. You can see me, can't you?"

My little eyes lit up. "Wait. You mean you're not real?"

He nodded and held his hand out to me. I eyed it curiously.

"You don't have to be afraid," he reassured me. "You see, sometimes only the most special people are blessed with the ability to see things others cannot." He shifted his weight and bent down so we were at the same eye level.

"So I am special! I just knew it!" I jumped up and grabbed his hand. A warm, loving sensation filled my body, and I was able to see his pure heart shining through his kind soul. I didn't know how, but I knew immediately he had been sent to protect me. From what, I had no idea, but I sensed it was something very bad.

"Are you sure you're not an angel?" I whispered.

He winked and opened his other hand, revealing a beautiful silver locket that had the letter "H" inscribed on the front of it. "I'm something better."

I admired the necklace that dangled from his open hand. "That's so pretty."

"I tell you what. How about if we make a deal?"

"What kind of deal?" I asked, my innocent eyes growing wide with curiosity.

"If you keep my secret, I'll come visit you anytime you want, and we can be friends."

"Really?"

"Absolutely." He nodded. "And whenever you need me, all you have to do is put the necklace on. However, you must promise never to tell anyone about me, or I will have to go away. You don't want that to happen, do you?"

I shook my head no.

"This is very important, okay? Promise me."

"I promise! I promise!" I answered, my pale cheeks flushed with excitement.

"And," he continued, "I get to keep the key that opens the locket."

Disappointed, I asked, "So I can never open it?"

"Well, not yet. But one day, when it's time, we'll open it together. Deal?"

"Yes!" I answered excitedly.

"Oh, and you don't need to worry about how many people like this so-called Wonder Woman."

My smile turned into a frown as I felt my awkwardness begin to settle back in. "Why not? Everyone likes her."

"Because you're more special than she is."

"Do you really think so?"

"Of course, you are, and one day you're going to realize that along with everyone in the entire world."

Comforted by his words, I grinned happily.

"Angelina, I'm always going to be here for you, and that's a promise." He placed his strong hand over mine and smiled. "Our lives are forever intertwined, and once you're older you'll understand."

He stood up and simply patted me on the head before slowly walking away. He stopped momentarily and turned back around, a mischievous look on his face. Raising a finger to his lips he smiled and, with a wink, he suddenly disappeared.

~ ~ ~

I felt a tap on my shoulder. "Excuse me, miss, do you know where the coffee creamer is?"

Startled, I jumped, dropping the few groceries I had in my arms.

"Oh dear, I'm sorry. I shouldn't have scared you." The little old man slowly bent down and began to gather my items for me.

I followed suit. "Oh no, please let me do that."

He stood back up and looked at me curiously. I apologized for my behavior and pointed him in the direction of the coffee creamer. He shook his head and smiled before disappearing down one of the aisles.

I fought back the urge to run out the door. How could I have forgotten such an important memory? I was suddenly curious if this memory had anything to do with my recent nightmares. If the two were somehow connected, what did it mean? I had to find the locket. In fact, if I remembered correctly, I still had it hidden somewhere in my room. I wondered what would happen if I put it on. There was only one way to find out.

4

Secrets

I quickly grabbed the last few items on my list and carried them up to the worn counter, smiling weakly at the old woman as she rang each of them up carefully. Hearing the door open behind me, I turned to see a couple of unfamiliar faces trudge inside. It was obvious they were hunters as they were dressed head to toe in camouflage clothing. They were ruggedly handsome and looked to be around my age, which made me feel instantly shy. I shifted my weight uncomfortably as they walked by.

One of them motioned back toward the door. "We should wait for Tristan."

"Why? He's always late," the other one muttered, rolling his eyes. "I'm going to go find the beef jerky while you wait on him."

Hunters and their stupid beef jerky. I shook my head and rolled my eyes while I continued to wait patiently for Mrs. Bailey to finish ringing up the groceries. A cool breeze kissed my warm skin as the door opened once again. I caught my breath as my eyes fell upon a devilishly handsome man, and for a brief moment his emerald green eyes met mine. Time suddenly stood still.

I was sure my mouth was hanging wide open, and I probably looked like a complete idiot, but at that moment I didn't care. Strange feelings washed over me and I allowed myself to enjoy them. I had never felt anything like this. He smiled as he walked by me, his five-o'clock shadow barely covering the small dimples that graced his well-chiseled face. His thick, muscular body was at least a foot taller than my short five-foot, three-inch frame. His shaggy black hair hung freely over his tan face, almost hiding his exquisite eyes. Feeling somewhat embarrassed I closed my mouth and lowered my eyes toward the floor.

"Come on, man, we've been waiting for you," his buddy exclaimed.

I looked back up and was disappointed to see he had disappeared down one of the aisles. Sighing, I felt my face flush once again when Mrs. Bailey coughed politely to let me know she was still in the room. I smiled sheepishly and searched my pockets for the small wad of cash that my mother had given me. I pulled it out and surrendered it to the friendly old woman who placed it carefully inside her antique cash register.

"How's your mother doing, dear?" she asked, turning her attention back to the groceries as she attempted to strategically place all the items into a single bag.

I shrugged. "Mom's doing her usual thing, you know—pampering the out-of-towners."

Studying her face, I could see life had been hard on her as the lines of old age creased her once youthful skin. I looked into her dark brown eyes and saw sadness. Why it was there, I did not know. She had come to Buffalo alone, never talked about her past, and was rarely seen outside of the small store. Well, with the exception of visiting my mother that is. The frail old lady was quite a mystery, and in a small town people with mysteries are always the topic of discussion. It was rumored that her only son had come here on a hunt and vanished, and that she was possibly still looking for him. Another one claimed she was a widow and had used her inheritance to buy the cozy little store and live life quietly. Though the rumors were intriguing, I admired the fact that she was one of my mother's dearest friends.

Regardless of what the truth might have been I always respected her, as she had been a part of our lives since she had moved here. In fact, my fondest memories consisted of helping her bake pies that she would share with my mother and me. My mother, in return, would always treat her to a cup of coffee and a pleasant conversation.

She nodded. "Well, you tell her I'm ready for that cup of coffee if she's ready for some apple pie."

I nodded as she handed me my change and the one bag she had somehow managed to fit all the groceries into. "I sure will."

"Excuse me, Angelina," a deep voice called out from behind me. "I think you dropped this."

I turned around and came face to face with the handsome stranger that had taken my breath away. My knees grew weak as he smiled at me, his dimples taunting me silently as he offered me a wadded up five-dollar bill.

"Oh, I must've dropped it when I pulled the money out of my pocket," I stuttered, my hands slightly trembling as I accepted the renegade five. I heard a slight cough and glanced up to see a disapproving look on Mrs. Bailey's face. I wondered what the look meant. After all, she and my mother had been trying to set me up for months. I would've thought she'd be tickled pink that I was talking to a guy at all. And a handsome one at that.

"I really should get going . . .," I muttered, managing a slight smile. "Thanks."

"No problem," he replied with a boyish grin, his green eyes sparkling.

I fumbled with the doorknob, opened the door, and then accidently shut it again with the bag. I let out a school-girl giggle as the warmth returned to my cheeks.

"Do you need help with that?" he asked raising an amused eyebrow.

"No, I got it." I giggled again, this time managing to open the door fully. I still felt his gaze on me as I walked outside. The damp, cool air greeted me along with darkness and streetlights. I shivered. I had never been a big fan of the darkness. I had seen enough horror movies to know that a woman should never walk home alone in the dark because big, scary, evil things always hid themselves within it.

I walked quickly down the narrow sidewalk and attempted to let my thoughts drift back to the beautiful man I had met in the store. I smiled at the thought of what it would be like to go on a date with someone so attractive. He had been so honest by giving me back the money I had accidently dropped. I mean, how many people nowadays would do such a thing? When his deep silky voice said my name, I felt as though my heart would beat right out of my chest.

Then it hit me—he had said my name! Questions began swarming around the pleasant thoughts immediately. How could he have possibly known that? I knew Mrs. Bailey hadn't said it, and I didn't know either of the other men he was with. So how did he know?

A loud commotion from up ahead forced me to put away my questions and pay attention to what was up in front of me. While deep in thought, I had forgotten about Tom's Tavern, a small bar that lay on my route home. I cursed at myself as I attempted to avoid the flock of people heading toward it. They were all ready to get their drunk on.

I heard the familiar sound of a police siren coming down the road followed by flashing red and blue lights. It flew past me and came to a screeching halt right in front of the bar. I flinched, as the image triggered another harsh memory.

~ ~ ~

"I have a secret," I whispered to my mom.

"What kind of secret?" she asked. Her arms were wrapped around me.

"Do you remember when I was younger and you would ask me who I was playing with outside?

"Hmm—I believe so?" she answered raising her brow.

"Well, for quite some time, I've had a secret friend—Ialocin."

"Ialocin? What kind of name is that?" She chuckled and shook her head. "I just love your stories, Angelina."

"No, mom, listen. He can do amazing things. I

mean, he might be able to help find Dad," I spewed out as quickly as I could.

My mother was silent for a moment, and I could tell she was trying to absorb what I had just told her.

"Angelina, things like that just don't exist, honey. Invisible friends are make believe."

"No, mom, he's real! I can prove it," I replied, determined to show her the truth. I reached into my pocket and pulled out the silver locket.

Her eyes grew wide with curiosity, "Where did you get that?"

"He gave it to me." I carefully put it on.

We both waited in quiet anticipation. After a few moments, it was apparent he wasn't coming.

I frowned. "I don't understand. The locket has always worked."

My mother placed her hand on my shoulder and smiled, "Honey, I know you miss dad. Let's just let the search party do its job. They'll find him honey. We just have to continue to believe that he's okay."

"But, Mom, it really does work. I swear."

She reached over and kissed the top of my head. "I'm sure it does. Now run upstairs and get ready for bed. It's past your bedtime."

Confused, I did as she requested and ran up the stairs to my room. I flung open the door and threw myself on the bed, bursting into tears. Why hadn't he come when I had put the locket on? He had always come before. I had shared my secret with my mother in hopes that she would believe that he could help find my father. Then it hit me: I had broken my deal with him. I had promised never to tell anyone about him. Dread filled my heart as I realized there was a real possibility that I would never see him again.

The next morning I awoke to voices coming from downstairs. I knew the locals had come to pick up my mother for their daily search in the woods.

Her voice drifted up the stairs. "Angelina, are you coming with us?"

"Not today," I replied groggily, still disappointed by the previous night's events.

"Okay, honey. If you get hungry, there's leftover chicken in the fridge. There are no guests scheduled to come in today, so you should be fine."

"Okay."

"I'll be home soon. I love you."

I heard the front door slam and the house grew quiet—too quiet. I glanced over at the locket, which was lying on my nightstand. Maybe now that everyone was gone, he would appear. I picked it up and put it around my neck, silently praying I hadn't lost him. Once again, nothing happened. Frustrated, I unlatched it and threw it across the room. It slid into a small crevice between the planks of the hardwood floor.

"No," I whispered as I jumped up off the bed. I peered into the darkness and knew it was too late. The locket was gone and so was Ialocin.

~ ~ ~

I shook off the memory and continued walking down the narrow sidewalk. I glanced up and saw two officers breaking up a fight between two drunkards. I shook my head, remembering why I hated this part of the season—it was full of intoxicated "deerstalkers" who bragged about their mighty hunting skills. Afterwards, they would stumble around town until the early hours of the morning before finally grabbing their compound bows to hunt in the forest with all the other drunkards. Safety at its best.

I noticed a small posse of inebriated men standing in the dark shadows near the overly congested beer joint. Cringing, I put my head down and continued to walk past them, acting as if the stench of their alcohol-laden breath and rough appearance were invisible to me. They sucked down their drinks and whistled at me.

"Hey, baby, why don't you bring that sweet little thing over here?" one of them bellowed out.

I ignored him and kept walking.

He began to stumble toward me. "What? Aren't we good enough for you, girl?"

"Just leave me alone," I hissed as I continued down the sidewalk, my heart beating a little faster.

"Just one drink, and you'll want some of this." He pointed to himself. "You know you want to."

"You're disgusting."

He swayed back and forth before letting out a loud snicker. "Oh, the little girl doesn't want to know what it feels like to be with a real man. Well, maybe I'll just show her anyways."

"Don't touch me," I warned through clenched teeth. I quickened my pace to put as much distance between him and me as possible. I noticed a small side street, took refuge down it, and regretted the decision immediately.

The alley, dark and mysterious, sent chilling thoughts running rampant through my mind. My heart raced faster as I fought the fear that had begun to spread inside me. I didn't know which was worse: the repulsive drunkard or what could possibly be hiding in the darkness that surrounded me.

I carried the small bag down the dark alley and tried to ignore the whispers that came from within the shadows. Shuddering, I tried to block the thought that the evil, blood-thirsty creatures of the forest might be watching me. They liked to hide in the dark places, waiting for their prey.

I shuddered once again and pulled my jacket closer to my face. My parents had done a great job scaring me as a child with these stupid fairy tales. The legend of the unnatural creatures had been within the town's history for decades, passing from generation to generation hoping one day the story would be fearful enough to end all hunting. It did the opposite, however, as hunters came in droves, hopeful to be the first ones to catch one of these mystical beings while hunting their white-tailed deer in the thick crimson covered forest.

Occasionally a hunter would run out of the woods claiming they had seen one of the human like apparitions warning them to stay out. Of course, parents took advantage of these myths, telling their children of these terrible things to scare them into coming home on time. For most, it worked.

Breathing a sigh of relief, I made my way toward the brightly lit busy street that lay at the end of the alley. My heart calmed when I saw the soft glow of the bulb under the old broken sign near the door of my home. The delicious aroma of cinnamon apples baking awakened my taste buds as I hurried inside. I set the bag of groceries down on the table and took my jacket off. I looked around the oddly quiet room and realized how much I adored this place. I knew most of the guests were either in bed early because of the morning hunt, or at Tom's, drinking their excitement away.

Temptation filled my taste buds, and I walked over to the warm oven, pulling it open to sneak a taste before my mother figured out I was home. She was always spoiling our guests and me with her wonderful home cooking. There had been many occasions when I would find myself sitting in my room alone, feeling guilty for the immense amount of calories that my body had just ingested.

I felt my mouth begin to water as the delicious dish begged me to be its first taste tester. As I reached inside, a strong arm wrapped around my waist and pulled me away forcefully. Startled, I screamed, burning my finger on the hot wire rack as I yanked it back quickly. The perpetrator wrestled me to the ground and though I attempted to fight back, my strength was no match for his. I closed my eyes and awaited my fate, hoping whatever was about to happen would be over quickly.

5

Promises

Strangely familiar hands ran up my sides and surprised laughter escaped my lips as the perpetrator began tickling me ferociously. I opened my eyes and came face-to-face with my childhood friend Jeremiah.

I narrowed my eyes. "Really?" I grumbled, finally managing to push him off of me. I stood up and nursed my burnt finger.

His blue eyes twinkled in amusement. "Not so happy to see me?"

I held up my damaged finger and glared. "Does it look like I'm happy to see you?"

"Aw, bring that finger here. I'll kiss it and make it all better."

I rolled my eyes while pushing down the little butterflies that began to flutter in my stomach. "Not with where your lips have been," I said, pulling my finger toward my body protectively.

"Hey, now, what's that supposed to mean?" he questioned defensively.

"Well, from what I hear, you've become quite the ladies' man," I commented, a hint of jealousy in my voice.

A slight smile formed across his handsome face. "Ladies' man? I beg to differ."

I rolled my eyes again and sighed. "What are you doing here anyways?"

"What, I can't drop by to just say hi anymore without getting the fifth degree?"

I playfully punched him in his firm arm. "Of course you can. You just scared me, and it's just . . ." I paused, carefully arranging my words in my head so they didn't come out like some crazy ex-girlfriend. "You never drop by to say hi anymore."

My mother walked in to see what all the commotion was about.

"What are you two doing?" she asked picking up the bag of groceries. She took a quick peek inside to make sure I had gotten everything on her list.

I grinned mischievously. "Jeremiah was just telling me how he had stopped by to offer to fix all the broken things around here you've been complaining about lately."

Her eyes lit up. "Jeremiah, what a doll you are. That would be quite wonderful. Do you think you could stop by tomorrow morning, and I'll give you a list of things that need to get done?"

I could tell he was caught off guard as he quickly tried to think of a way out of the mess I had just put him in. He gave up, knowing he was stuck and smiled politely. "Uh, well, Mrs. Adams, the hunt begins tomorrow morning, but I can stop by after that if you'd like." He glanced over his shoulder and gave me a sour look.

I couldn't help but feel sweet satisfaction from the torture I was putting him through. After all, he deserved it for the scare he had given me.

My mother smiled gratefully, and with groceries in hand, she headed back toward the pantry. "Well, thank you, dear. I do appreciate it. It's nice to know we've still got one reliable man around this house." She paused for a moment and turned back around. "You know, it's truly a shame you two never dated."

I felt my face flush instantly. "Mom . . ."

She chuckled. "Yeah, I know. It's none of my business."

Jeremiah coughed innocently, not missing a beat. "Well, Mrs. Adams, I keep asking her, and she keeps telling me no."

I narrowed my eyes at him. "Jeremiah . . ."

"Well, on that note, I'm going to put these groceries away. It looks like you two have some serious talking to do." She winked at Jeremiah. "She's always secretly loved you. Don't wait too long, or you might just miss out."

Jeremiah looked at me in surprise.

I lowered my head in embarrassment. "Oh my God, Mom."

She laughed again and disappeared around the corner.

Jeremiah peered around the corner to make sure she was gone. "Is that true?"

"What? That my mom's crazy?" I asked in disbelief.

"No. That you're in love with me."

I opened my mouth, but no sound came out.

"Because if it is . . ."

"What, you'll drop all five thousand of your other girlfriends?" I blurted out without thinking. I could see the hurt in his eyes.

"All you had to do was say no."

"I'm sorry. It's just that you've made it very clear that I'm more a sister than a girlfriend."

He grew quiet for a moment. "You just think you're so cute, don't you?"

I walked over to one of the old worn chairs

and sat down. "You better believe it," I replied with a laugh. I studied Jeremiah. "You know, regardless of how crazy my mom is, she really does love you."

"Yeah, deep down I truly believe she hoped you and I would live happily ever after with seven kids, two dogs, and a pig."

I laughed. "A pig?"

"Sure, why not?"

"Well, if that happened, then she would really become your mom, wouldn't she?"

He fell speechless, and his face paled. I closed my mouth quickly and kicked myself for bringing up a sore subject. His mother had been known as the town floozy and had abandoned him as a child. She apparently left him and his deadbeat dad for some big burley truck driver she met one night at the local diner. His father was a drunk with no idea how to raise a child, so Jeremiah was an inconvenience to him and nothing more. My mother, being the kind soul that she was, had taken him in as her own. She taught him the ways of the world and helped him learn what it meant to be a good man. Without her, he probably would've ended up just like his loser dad, drinking his sorrows away while hating life.

A big goofy grin spread across Jeremiah's face as he tried to change the subject. "So, Angelina, when are you going to let me take you out on a date?"

My face instantly flushed. I looked down at the ground and muttered. "Sister status, remember?"

His grin faded, and an odd expression fell in its place. Awkward silence followed.

He walked over to the other side of the table, pulled out a chair, and sat down. When his blue eyes met mine, I saw that the twinkle had faded away.

I felt a small twinge in my heart as I studied his handsome face. He had always been a ladies' man, and I blamed that on his mother leaving him. He had never seemed ready to settle down. In fact, I couldn't recall a time when he had even had a serious girlfriend. I knew what girls saw in him: a good-looking, damaged guy they thought they could fix. I knew better. Jeremiah would never change, and I was completely okay with that. He was special. At least he was to me.

I tried not to stare at him as I admired his big, beautiful, blue eyes. They were the color of the ocean—deep and endless—and I could have looked into them for hours. His red, full lips were almost always upturned into a quirky smile, though at that moment they were creased into a frown. His dirty-blond hair was styled into a faux hawk, which was now somewhat messy because he had just run his hands through it. The short stubble around his chin made his boyish face look older, but not by much. He had a baby face, and no stubble could change that.

Feeling as though the tension was once again my fault, I tried to bring up a more exciting topic. "So, are you looking forward to the hunt tomorrow?"

"Ah, yes, the famous hunt. Angelina, I need you to listen to me." His voice was full of warning. He reached across the table and grabbed my hand. Chills ran up my arm, and I looked down. "Something horrible is happening in the forest. I need you to promise me you'll stay away from it."

I pulled my hand back. "Jer, are you really going to try and scare me with those stupid stories?"

"No, Angelina. I'm serious. Something happened that I can't explain." He stammered as he tried to get the words out. "A few of us locals went into the forest yesterday morning to try and get a head start on this year's competition. Something—or should I say someone—found us."

"What do you mean someone found you?"

"I don't know, Angelina. I mean this—thing— threatened to kill us if we didn't leave."

"Jeremiah, you need to go to the police and tell them what happened!"

"No, absolutely not. They'll think I'm crazy. You don't understand. This thing—it wasn't natural."

"What do you mean?"

He ignored my question, stood up, and tried to regain his composure so I wouldn't see the weakness in his eyes.

"Look," I said, "we've known each other since we were children. I've trusted you with all my secrets, so you owe me an explanation. What happened in the forest?"

He cleared his throat and pushed his chair in slowly. "I'm sorry, I didn't mean to scare you."

"Well you've done a pretty good job," I admitted, standing up.

His hands slightly trembled. "That wasn't my intention, but you need to quit being so stubborn and listen to me for once."

My chin began to quiver. "Oh, like the time

you listened to me? The one time I needed you to believe me, and you laughed in my face? Did you happen to forget how scared I had been—being lost in that forest? I was a child at the time, Jeremiah. You're a grown man."

By the look on his face, I knew he understood what I meant.

The night after my father's disappearance, I had snuck into the forest in search of him. It was fall, and the forest looked as if it were on fire. The crimson colored moss snaked its way around the trees, while the fall leaves fell silently around me. The air smelled of wet dirt and death. It was curiously quiet, which gave me an uneasy feeling.

I spent countless hours that day looking for my father, wanting him back more than I had ever wanted anything in my entire life. The darkness secretly crept upon me until I was unable to find my way back. I wandered around for hours, calling for help. But my pleas went unanswered. Exhausted, I managed to find a small cave hidden behind a large waterfall. I wandered inside and sat down, sobbing quietly as I feared I would never again return home.

I buried my head in my hands and thought of how my father had meant the world to me. Memories of past hunting trips flooded my mind, and I could remember begging him to take me with him. He would always smile, grab my hand, place it on his heart, and then place his hand on my heart. He would explain that he was taking a piece of my heart and giving me a piece of his so that when he returned, we would once again be whole. I clutched my chest. A part of me was still missing.

I suddenly realized I was no longer alone. A soft soothing voice rose from within the dark, calmly telling me not to be afraid, that I was special and no harm would come to me.

Looking up, I saw an apparition of a beautiful red-haired woman coming toward me. Her long hair moved with the cool breeze of the night air, her pale skin glowed in the darkness, and her opaque eyes stared at me. The mysterious woman sat down next to me and began caressing my tear-drenched face, promising me everything would be all right. Her presence was comforting, and I soon found myself drifting off to sleep. The next morning, I awoke in the safety of own bed, wondering how I had gotten there. I had almost convinced myself that it was a dream until I saw the dirt from the cave on my hands and knees. Confiding my secret to Jeremiah had been a mistake as he had laughed at me just like everyone else had done my whole life, telling me my overactive imagination had simply played host to a terrifying nightmare.

Jeremiah frowned for a moment, as if he were trying to think of something to say. Finally, with a vague look on his face, he mumbled, "Angelina, I care for you more than you might think, and I don't want you to get hurt."

With that, he stood up, dusted his pants off, and made his way to the door. My curiosity grew even more. He had never kept a secret from me. Was there something so terrible that he couldn't confide in me?

As he turned the knob to leave, I took a step toward him. "Jeremiah, please."

"Angelina, trust me on this. Just this once."

My heart stopped when I saw the pleading in his eyes. I nodded, knowing he was determined to keep whatever secret he was hiding from me. Temporarily satisfied with my silence, he smiled and walked out the door, slamming it shut behind him.

I walked over to where he had been sitting and ran my fingers across the back of the chair pushing it in. The scent of his cologne still hung in the air around me, toying with my emotions. I sighed and pushed my girlish thoughts to the back of my mind. A million other thoughts began to replace them immediately. Why had he seemed so frightened, begging me to stay away? What had scared him out of the woods? Could it have anything to do with my father's disappearance? I knew deep down the only way to get the answers was to go looking for them myself.

"Angelina, sweetie, could you tell Jeremiah not to slam the door the next time he leaves," my mother said as she walked back into the room. "It's already about to fall off its hinges."

I walked over to her and kissed her cheek tenderly. "Yes, mother, I'll make sure he gets the message."

She smiled and put her cool hand on my cheek. "Thank you dear, I do appreciate it."

"I'm going to go out for a little while. It's stuffy in here."

"Are you sure that's a good idea with all the people out tonight? You know tomorrow is the first day of the hunt."

"Mom, I'll be eighteen in a month. I'm practically an adult."

Sadness crept into her tired eyes. "I just worry

about you. You're all I have left."

I felt a stab of guilt and smiled. "I know, mom, but I'll be fine. I promise."

"Okay, well, take this flashlight, because Lord knows it's dark out there. Oh, and don't forget your cell phone. You left it on the table again." She pulled it out of her pocket. She walked back over to me, put her arms around me, and gave me a light squeeze. "Please, just be careful."

I hugged her in return. "I always am."

"I love you, Angelina."

I smiled. "I love you too, Mom."

As she walked out of the room she began humming "Brown Eyed Girl" again and I was reminded of what a wonderful person she was. She had always been so strong. Even when my father disappeared, she never displayed her emotional struggles in front of me. I could only hope that I had inherited her strength, so that when I finally moved out on my own into the big world, I would be able to use those traits to become as successful and caring as she was.

6

Secret Warning

The smooth handrail followed the winding staircase to the endless hallway of doors. I was grateful for the moment that the guests were either sleeping or away from their rooms. Silence was rare here, so when it was quiet, I always took advantage by reading a book or sitting on my bed in deep thought, enjoying the endless questions that were locked away in my head and the silent answers that would eventually follow.

My mother and I stayed in the East Wing, which was known as the owner's quarters. Guests were not allowed down the East Wing. But one would occasionally wander down it, which prompted me to make my mother install an insanely large lock on my bedroom door. I figured I would rather be safe than sorry.

I unlocked the door to my room and went inside, smiling at its quaint comforts. Within its lavender walls, sat a twin-sized bed that hadn't moved from its location since I was a little girl. An antique dresser sat perfectly in the corner covered with all my girly necessities. The picture of my father and me occupied the nightstand next to my bed. It may not have been much, but it was all I needed.

I sat down on my bed and ran my hand over the worn comforter, enjoying its softness. My parents had never had a lot of money. But since I was their only child, they had tried to spoil me with whatever small amenities they could afford. Now that I was considered an adult, I was responsible for buying my own items with the little bit of money that I earned helping my Mom. One day I would leave this place, but for right now, I knew my mother needed me. Plus, the fact that I was only seventeen didn't help my cause.

Sighing, I stood back up and grabbed the backpack that was a constant fixture on the small hook inside my closet door. I quickly filled it with a change of clothing, the flashlight my mother had given me, and a small pocketknife that I had hidden in my closet just in case some drunken idiot decided to break into my room and try something stupid.

I shut the closet door and noticed something small glistening in a beam of moonlight near my bedroom window. My breath caught and my hand trembled as I bent down and picked up the small silver trinket I thought I had lost forever. It was just as beautiful as I remembered.

I ran my fingers along the thin silver chain and around the dainty locket that was attached to it. A lump formed in my throat when I felt the small engraving of the letter "H" that was etched into the front of it. How strange it was that the locket hadn't appeared until now. After spending hours looking for it the night I threw it across the room, I was positive I'd lost it.

I turned it over to examine the small keyhole. My heart ached as I recalled who had the key. I swallowed the lump in my throat and carefully opened the fragile clasp to secure the chain around my neck. I held my breath, wondering if

Ialocin would appear. After a few moments, I shook my head. I was silly for expecting him to show up after all these years. I turned back toward my closet and caught a glimpse of myself in the full-length mirror. The locket hung loosely around my neck to just above my cleavage and complemented my pale, freckled skin. I admired the image in front of me. My birthday was a month away and I would be eighteen—an adult. The image in the mirror, however, didn't remind me of an adult. With my bright, youthful skin and innocent, amber eyes, I still looked very young for my age. My mother always said it was a gift, but I had always considered it to be a curse because most of the guests, who adored my mom, looked at me like I was nothing more than a simple child.

My mother would disagree with me. Though she always had a special way with the guests who stayed at our little bed and breakfast, she would say it was because of me that they returned. It was as if I had some sort of magical aura that attracted people to us. Too bad it didn't help in the boyfriend department. Sure, I had been asked out on plenty of dates, but for some reason I could never bring myself to say yes to any of them. I had always had an odd feeling that there was someone out there waiting for me to find them.

I shuddered as that oddly familiar feeling crept over me again. Why, all of a sudden, were all these old feelings returning? I brushed it off, walked over to my desk, and turned on my laptop. An instant message popped up reminding me of my dinner date with my best friend Marie.

"Crap," I muttered knowing there was no way she would condone my going into the forest alone. I didn't feel too bad breaking our plans. Figuring out what Jeremiah had told me now seemed more important than gossiping about girls and laughing about which boys we thought were cute. I typed out a quick reply stating that something important had come up and I would be out for the night. I figured she would probably start blowing up my cell phone with questions and switched it over to vibrate mode so I didn't have to hear the annoying beeping noise it would make with each message.

I moved the mouse to the power button and heard the familiar sound of my instant messenger letting me know I had received a new message. It was probably Marie with a slew of questions asking me what was going on. An eerie feeling crept over me as I realized it was from an unknown contact.

It simply read:

He is coming for you. Get out, now.

Another message popped up:

Go to the forest. You'll be safe there.

I shook my head in disbelief. What kind of deranged person would . . . Another message popped up, and another, and another . . .

Get out now.

Get out now.

Get out now.

Get out now.

Run to the forest NOW!

Message after message, all repeating the same things. What a sick joke, I thought to myself as I slammed my laptop shut. Some people had such twisted imaginations. My phone vibrated, and I pulled it out of my pocket. A new text message had arrived and I frowned at the unknown number that flashed across my screen. Fear filled my heart as I read the message:

Knock, knock, knock.

As if on cue, I heard loud knocking coming from the front door downstairs. The phone fell out of my hand and skittered across the hardwood floor as my heart dropped into my stomach. I moved to the window and inched the curtain open just enough to see a dark figure standing at the door. It knocked again, and, this time, with such force that I could feel the vibrations through the wall.

I heard the front door creak open and my mother greet the stranger with a cheerful voice. Then chaos broke out. Something thudded on the floor, and my mother's scream rang through the paper-thin walls. The commotion grew louder, and I imagined a small tornado wreaking havoc downstairs.

My mind raced. What was happening? Why had my mother screamed? Who was destroying my home, and why? Then it hit me, this thing was most likely coming for me next. I coaxed my weak, shaky legs toward my door where I turned the lock. The lock may have been insanely huge, but it was cheap and most likely wasn't going to keep whatever this thing was out. I fell into a panic and began frantically looking around my room for a way out. The small beam of moonlight that had shown me the necklace earlier gave me an idea as I ran back over to my window.

I grabbed my backpack and slung it over my

shoulder. As quietly as I could manage, I lifted the window and carefully climbed onto the ledge. A vague memory of wearing a red cape crossed my mind. I shook it off and concentrated on what I was doing. I was alone, and if I were going to die, I was going to die trying to get away, not by the hands of some crazy person.

Carefully placing one leg onto the tree limb, I used perfect balance to push over the rest of my body, holding onto the trunk for support. I began to lower myself down toward the ground.

Just a few more feet. *We can do this*, I thought to myself.

Hearing a loud noise coming from inside my room, I looked up to see a man with blood-red eyes staring back at me. He growled, revealing his razor sharp teeth.

"Stay away from me," I croaked, my voice weak and unsteady.

"It's time for you to come home." He growled again, reaching for me as I held onto the tree limb.

I inched away from him. "No, get away from me!"

Realizing I was out of his reach, he began to come out the window after me. "You can't get away that easy."

I watched in horror as another dark shadow came up behind him and yanked him back inside. I heard a loud, angry shriek and the sounds of a fight. Thank my lucky stars I left when I did. I didn't want to be in that room with whomever or whatever else was in there.

My heart stopped when the window slammed shut and my room grew dark. I held my breath, debating what I should do next. All of a sudden, one of the dark figures flew up against the window and shattered the glass, sending large shards flying toward me.

"What the . . .?" I gasped, lost my grip on the tree limb, and fell the last few feet to the ground. A sickening thud engulfed my ears and immense pain snaked its way up my leg.

"Oh my God!" I screamed, reaching for my ankle. Tears made their way down my cheeks and I found myself silently praying the creature chasing me wasn't from the forest. The fear creeping through my body paralyzed me. A loud shriek rang out, bringing me back to my senses. I knew I had to get away from the house as fast as possible, so I took a deep breath and scrambled to my feet, wincing at the pain that continued to shoot up my leg. I could deal with the injury later. Right now, I knew I had to get to a safe haven. The messages had been right about the intruder, so they had to be right about the forest.

Mustering the strength I had left, I hobbled down the sidewalk, hoping I had made the right decision, occasionally looking behind me to make sure I wasn't being followed. Every noise made me jump as I fought back the paralyzing fear I had felt lying on the ground. Up ahead, I saw what looked like a large dog slink behind a car that was parked on the side of the road. I stopped momentarily, waiting for it to reappear. I felt the heavy thud of my heart beating against my chest. I shook my head and blamed my imagination for playing tricks on my fragile mind.

I kept my head down and continued walking down the narrow sidewalk. I passed by the busy tavern and attempted to ignore the vulgar things the drunken hunters yelled at me. One of the burly drunkards stumbled forward and grabbed me by the arm pulling me close to him. I screamed out in pain as my ankle twisted sideways. The pain was mind numbing as I reached into the side pocket of my backpack and grabbed the pocketknife.

"Well don't be scared, pretty thing. I will make it all better," he slurred, alcohol heavy on his breath.

"Let me go!" I raised the hand that held the small knife.

"Aw, and what are you going to do with that little blade?" He laughed as he pulled me closer to him. Adrenaline pumped through my veins as I reached up and felt the blade slice the rough skin across his cheek. He instinctively let go of me and put his hand over his wound.

"You little bitch!" he yelled jumping toward me.

I heard a loud growl and turned to see a large black wolf standing in front of us.

"Whoa, nice puppy," the drunkard coaxed, backing away slowly.

The animal crouched and bared its razor-sharp teeth. Drool dripped down its dark face as it stared menacingly at us.

"Hungry? Eat this!" the man yelled, throwing me to the ground as he turned around to run.

I slid across the rough concrete and felt the skin tear away from my hands and arms. The large beast growled again. I closed my eyes. When I heard screams in the distance, I opened my eyes and saw that the wolf had jumped over me and was in the process of ripping the man to shreds. More screams followed once the crowd realized what was going on. People began running in all different directions, which allowed me time to scramble to my feet.

I headed toward the forest, silently begging the pain in my ankle to subside. I hobbled up the stone steps that led to the tree line. The ground was covered in patches of crimson moss and I knew I was close to safety, or at least I hoped so. According to the messages, I would be safe here. But Jeremiah had warned me to stay out. I hoped with all my heart he was wrong about the things he had told me, and that I was able to find answers to the many questions I had held onto for the past five years.

A single tear fell down my cheek as I came upon the great Crimson Forest. Over my shoulder, I took one last look at the small town I had always called home. Figuring this was the lesser of the evils I now faced, I turned back toward the dark forest, and tried not to be fearful of what could possibly be hiding inside. Trembling, I stumbled through the thick brush not knowing who or what I would find, or who or what would find me.

7

Stranger Danger

The night sky was alive with a million magnificent little stars, each one trying to outshine the other. They were the only things that lit the way through the pitch-black forest. I shuddered at the terrifying noises that surrounded me and could only imagine what monsters watched me as I stumbled toward the only welcoming noise I recognized. It filled me with hope, and I continued to push my way through the thick branches and brush until I came upon the familiar sight of Fox River. The river was the only fond memory I had of this wretched place. I remembered spending countless hours on its sandy shores with Jeremiah skipping rocks. We laughed like two innocent children who knew nothing of the monsters that went bump in the night.

The moon illuminated the clearing so that I was able to find a suitable place to rest my throbbing ankle. A few moments later I found myself leaning up against a large boulder. I slid down its cool surface slowly and thought of the mess that I had somehow managed to get myself into. How I wished for the comfort of my warm bed and my mother's kiss goodnight. The tears filled my eyes as reality slowly started to set in. I had no idea if she was okay, and the thought of losing her scared me to death. She had always been a good, honest woman. A life without her was impossible to imagine. A warm tear fell down my cheek, and I wiped it away angrily with my dirty hand. No time for crying. I had to keep moving.

I coaxed myself to get up and stumble over to the shoreline, carefully placing my ankle into the river's icy waters. Shivering, I was pleased by how much it eased the pain. I sat down on the sandy edge and allowed my foot to soak in the rushing water as I gazed up at the stars, admiring each one's beauty. My mother had explained that every star had been placed into the sky for each person that had passed from this life into the next. I was curious if my father was up there. I really wanted to believe he was still alive, and the thought of him watching over me relaxed me. I smiled at that thought and pulled my numb ankle out of the frigid water. I grabbed my backpack and stood up, wondering what I should do next. Looking around, it was probably best to follow the river south. I knew it would lead me toward the old cave that I had found as a child. There had to be some answers there, after all, that's where I had seen the beautiful red-haired lady.

Time seemed to move slowly as I followed the rushing water under the bright moonlight. My eyes begged me for sleep and I soon concluded it was time to find a place to rest. Taking advantage of the moon's bright light, I scanned the edge of the forest. An abnormally large fallen log covered in thick red moss lay near the edge of the forest. I went over, encouraged by the fact that it was hollow. I bent down and breathed in its earthy aroma. It was most certainly dead and I cringed at the thought of bugs crawling around inside of it. Still, bugs were better than wolves or red-eyed monsters. I shrugged off the thought and reached for the flashlight inside my backpack. I switched it on and shined the light down inside the dark hole. It looked just big enough to fit my small frame and would suffice to hide me until morning.

I pushed my backpack into the hollowed-out log and crawled in behind it. There wasn't much room to move, so I lay my head on the crook of my arm and sighed. This was definitely a first for me. If Jeremiah could see me now, I thought sadly. I was curious what he was doing, and I wondered if he would come looking for me once he realized I was gone. Something slithered across my leg, and I let out a soft shriek as I attempted to reach my hand down to swipe away whatever it was. It was going to be a long night. I clutched the flashlight against my chest and tried to concentrate on how the soft crimson moss felt against my tired body. My weary eyes finally gave in and a few moments later I found myself dreaming of the lady with the red hair.

Smiling, she caressed my face with her cool hands. "We will be together soon," she whispered quietly.

I looked into her odd-colored eyes, confused by her statement. "We will?"

"Yes, my child. Soon. I promise." Her perfect white teeth showed beneath her ruby-red lips.

I awoke in the pale dawn, startled by the odd hallucination, and my hand instantly went to where she had caressed my cheek.

I attempted to stretch, but my arms hit the soft moss that hung a few inches away from my face. As I crawled out of my makeshift shelter, I noticed my ankle felt better. I tried walking on it and found I could do so quite comfortably. I sat down on the log and carefully rotated it back and forth. I realized that it had completely healed itself.

"No way," I said, shaking my head in disbelief.

"What's happening to me?" I wondered out loud. I shook my head, grabbed my backpack from inside the log and walked over to the river. I contemplated what had happened to my ankle while I was asleep. Could the red-haired woman have healed it, or maybe it was aliens?

I took advantage of the cool water and washed the sleep from my face. I looked down at my mud-caked, tattered shirt. A quick dip couldn't hurt. I pulled my shirt off and threw it next to my backpack. Just as I unbuttoned my pants, I noticed a nice flat rock, and couldn't resist the urge to skip it across the water. The frigid bath could wait.

"Nice skip," a deep male voice behind me complimented.

My heart stopped momentarily, and I quickly reached for my shirt that lay on the ground.

I could hear the smirk in his voice.

"Go ahead, put your shirt back on. I won't watch."

Fear set in as I dropped the tattered shirt and reached my trembling hand inside my backpack for the clean one I brought with me. I quickly pulled it over my head and bent down, allowing my fingers to secretly begin searching for something I could use to defend myself.

"Now, I wouldn't do that if I were you," the

deep voice warned.

I stood up cautiously and turned around. For a moment, I thought I was having an out-of-body experience, as my soul seemed to touch his. I stared in awe knowing he was one of the most beautiful creatures I had ever come across. He was the man every woman on earth dreamt about being with and who all men wanted to look like. He could only be described with one word—perfection.

I studied him, debating whether or not he was actually human. He possessed certain characteristics that would allow him to pass for a regular bystander, but then there were the other qualities that I just couldn't deny, like his steady, unmoving eyes. They were the color of the sunset on a warm fall day, deep orange with a hint of crimson red around the edges. His facial features were sharp and distinct. His jet-black hair was a chaotic mess, each strand looking as though it were fighting for a place of its own. The sun kissed his olive skin while his rippling muscles fought anxiously against the white cotton t-shirt that fit his well-built body to a tee. He smiled, revealing perfect white teeth and a charming dimple on his left cheek.

I felt embarrassed and attempted to compose myself. "I'm sorry, and you are . . .?"

"Why don't we start with who you are and what you are doing in my woods?" he replied raising an eyebrow, his wonderful little dimple taunting me with each word that came out of his mouth.

"Well, sir, for your information, I'm simply camping, and the last time I checked, the State of

Wisconsin owned this forest, not you." I nervously smoothed out my wrinkled clothes.

"Camping?" He laughed, amused by my suave demeanor. "You're really roughing it with that backpack, aren't you?"

As he crossed his muscular arms, my eyes were drawn to a long jagged scar that ran from his elbow to his wrist. I tried not to make my staring obvious, so I averted my eyes toward my backpack and smiled snidely. "Yep, just me and the backpack."

He shook his head and winked. "My, you're quite intriguing, Angelina. They were right when they said you were a feisty one."

My mouth instantly fell open. "Wait, I never told you my name."

"Well, you see, I know a lot of things about you, my dear. More than you even know about yourself." He leaned toward me and offered his hand, which I eyed cautiously. "There's no need to be afraid," he said. "There are many other creatures much scarier than I."

"Yeah, you're not kidding." I frowned at the image in my mind of the red-eyed creature. "You know, I was always told to never talk to strangers."

"Ah, but I'm no stranger."

I was confused by his statement but reached my hand out slowly, debating whether or not to accept his. "I don't know . . ."

"Angelina, I promise no harm shall come to you while you're with me."

"Fine, but if something does happen to me, I'm going to come back and haunt you as a ghost," I answered, finally giving in to him. An odd expression crossed his face, and I wondered if I had said something I shouldn't have.

"It was just a joke," I mumbled, feeling relieved as his expression began to change back to normal. In what seemed to be an inhuman move, he was suddenly next to me, and I felt as though his body was going to swallow me whole.

"I would never let anything happen to you," he whispered, putting his face close to mine.

I felt my face grow hot. "What's your name?" I whispered.

He spun me around carefully and smiled, "My name is Nicolai, and I suppose we're not strangers anymore now, are we?"

The butterflies fluttered around in my stomach as I tried to come to terms with my body's strange reaction to him. Oddly enough, I felt comforted by his presence and, for some reason, I believed him when he said he would protect me.

Looking into his unusual fiery eyes, I blushed. "I suppose not."

"Then we should be on our way." His eyes glanced toward the dense forest.

"And where do you suggest we go?"

"To find your father, of course."

I looked at him with sheer surprise. "Did you just say to find my father?"

He winked. "I sure did."

My heart began to beat a little faster. "How do you know my father?"

"Let's just say he and I are old friends."

"Friends? He's been missing for years!" I felt as though I was about to lose control of my emotions. "Do you know where he is? Is he okay?

When can I see him?"

"Whoa, calm down, Angelina." He put his hand on my shoulder. "You'll get all of your answers. But, for now, we must go."

"Wait. Why can't you just tell me how you know him?"

He glanced back into the forest nervously. "We need to go. If you want your answers, then you need to follow me." With that, he disappeared into the forest.

"No, wait!" I called out after him, but it was too late. How could this man know so much when I had told him so little? I was intrigued by his words, and hopeful for answers, but what if I was wrong about him? What if he was, in fact, more deadly than he appeared to be? I knew if I left this spot, there was a very good possibility I would never find my way back. It reminded me of something my father had once told me: "Angelina, if you ever lose your way in the forest, stay in one place and know that I will find you." Oh how I wished he were still there to make those words come true.

I looked back toward the rushing water and noticed my backpack on the ground. Suddenly, I had an idea. If I left the backpack behind, then anyone who came looking for me would know where I had been. It would at least leave a clue and maybe they could track me from there. I felt a twinge of hope, wondering if Jeremiah would come looking for me and if he would be the one to find it. After all, he was a tracking master.

I peered into the woods wondering if I was too late to follow my handsome companion. Small butterflies churned in my stomach when I saw Nicolai's dark hair glistening in the sun as he waited patiently for me in the distance. Some risks were worth the reward, and my father was one heck of a reward. I was finally going to find out what happened to him, and this beautiful stranger was going to help me. Perhaps it was pure luck, or maybe it was karma holding me in its good graces for my many years of good deeds. Whatever it was, I was going to take full advantage of it. I not only had someone to protect me from whatever lurked within the forest, but I now had someone who could help solve the mysteries that had brought me here in the first place.

8

Risen

I admired how the crimson moss snaked its way up the tall trees as we traveled south along the river's edge. The autumn leaves fell silently around us while the sun embraced us in its warmth. I wiped the beads of sweat from my forehead and pushed my damp hair away from my face. All those years of being pampered by my mother's home cooking didn't help as I struggled to keep up with Nicolai.

"Getting tired?" he asked, noticing my pace had slowed down.

Breathing heavy, I came to a stop. "Oh, you know, just haven't worked out in a while." He stopped with a surprised look on his face. "Wait, you work out?"

I let out a hearty laugh. "Um—no."

He smirked. "You're right. I would've seen that."

"What did you say?"

"Oh, I said you should have seen that."

"Seen what?"

He hushed me and pointed toward a young fawn that cautiously emerged from the thick brush in front of us.

"Oh, how beautiful," I cooed.

"Angelina, hold out your hand," he whispered as he bent down and coaxed the deer to come toward us. Amazingly, the animal did as it was told.

He put his cool hand on mine. "Steady."

He slowly guided my hand to the animal's soft body. Its warm brown eyes watched me intently and soon relaxed as I ran my hand over its smooth, grey fall coat. Nicolai's gaze suddenly shifted to something unseen.

"Angelina, don't move," he commanded, a deep authority in his voice.

"Why? What is it?" I questioned nervously as I moved closer to the fawn.

"No, don't move," he ordered again.

I didn't move a muscle. In fact, I quit breathing altogether.

Nicolai's body tensed as he continued to stare at something in the forest. My eyes followed his gaze, but all I could see was a plethora of crimson colored moss and tall trees.

The deer began to tremble next to me, and I smiled weakly, deciding it was best to move from my motionless position to calm the animal. I ran my hand down its back and tried to reassure it that everything was going to be okay. My weak smile faded once I realized Nicolai was no longer next to me. I quickly scanned the area as panic began to set in. He was nowhere in sight.

The fawn let out a loud grunt and kicked at the ground. I bent down and wrapped my arms around it.

"It's okay. We're going to be okay," I reassured it, trying to believe my own words. Then, as if I were caught in one of my recurring nightmares, it looked up at me, its big, almond-shaped eyes filled with anxiety. I swallowed the lump that had begun to form in my throat and looked at my fingertips to make sure there wasn't any crimson moss sprouting out of them.

Finally, out of the corner of my eye, I saw what Nicolai's gaze had been focused on. I turned my head and watched in awe as the apparition of a women strode toward us at a surprisingly fast pace. The closer she got to us, the more the small fawn trembled in fear. It kicked at the ground and grunted loudly. I couldn't ignore the feeling that something bad was about to go down.

The crimson moss made the woman stand out with her abnormally pale white skin and long, wavy blond hair. Her eyes were cold and unfriendly as she stared at me, their icy blue color full of hatred and spite. Her pace slowed as she walked past me, unsmiling and barefoot, to the river.

Bending down, she chuckled and swirled her pale fingers in the rushing water. "I see you've found your way back to us, Angelina. The wait has been far too long."

"How is it that everyone here seems to know my name?" I asked annoyed by the sarcasm in her voice. "Is there a name tag on my back or something?"

"Oh, Angelina, everyone here knows who you are," she waved her hand toward the forest, "including that succulent little deer."

The deer cowered behind me as the woman stood up and walked over to me. She caressed my cheek, and her cold touch instantly reminded me of the red-haired woman that had come to me in the cave when I was a child. I pulled away from her and frowned. I already knew she and I were not going to be friends.

She patted me on the head. "Now, why don't you make this easy on all of us and come with me," she ordered.

"I don't think I'm too keen on that idea, and please don't pat me on the head like I'm some small child."

She snickered. "Well if you don't want to be treated like a small child, then maybe you shouldn't act like one."

I felt my face getting hot. "I don't know who you think you are, but I can tell you right now I won't be going anywhere with someone who's as much of a bitch as you are." I covered my mouth and looked up in surprise. Had that really just come out of little old me?

Her icy eyes filled with anger. "I don't think I like your attitude. Let me rephrase this so you understand a little more clearly: either you come with me of your own free will or I will make you come with me."

"Well, I don't know how you think you can make me come with you, so I'm going to kindly refuse."

Shrugging, she smiled wickedly. "I guess that's your answer, then."

The frightened deer had finally had enough. As it turned to run into the forest, I watched in horror as the blue of the woman's eyes brightened. She raised her right hand toward the deer and crimson moss began snaking its way across the ground toward the frail animal. It reared up and let out a loud rattling noise.

"No, not this time," I yelled, throwing the weight of my body into her. It caught her off guard, and we both fell to the ground. The terrified animal ran into the depths of the forest while it still had the chance. She threw me off her, and I slid across the rocky shore.

"You think you can stop me?" she growled, pointing in my direction.

Immense pain instantly rose within my abdomen. The pain spread like a fast-moving infection throughout my body and was soon in my chest. I struggled to breathe as the air escaped my lungs and I attempted to scream, but no sound came out. Tears began running down my cheeks as I prayed for the pain to subside. As if my prayers were suddenly answered, the pain disappeared. I looked up with relief to see Nicolai's worried face peering down at me.

"Where the heck did you go?" I managed to croak.

"I told you I would protect you,' he whispered to me. "I had to make sure she was alone."

"Of course, I'm alone. I'm the only one Ctephanyi needs to get this job done," the woman retorted.

Nicolai turned around and warned, "Laurana, you should leave before this gets ugly."

"Oh, Nicolai, you were always the outcast within our people, weren't you?"

"Well, you know me. I like being different."

"Who are you?" I asked, my voice still hoarse.

She cocked her head, "Oh, she's alive. Pity."

"You can't kill her. Ctephanyi wouldn't allow that," Nicolai hissed.

She laughed, her blue eyes glowing. "Ctephanyi may not allow me to kill her, but I can still play with her."

"You didn't answer my question," I remarked,

my voice steadying. "Who are you?"

"I'm your worst nightmare."

"No, you're not," I smirked, recalling my recent nightmares. Curiosity ran through my mind as I stretched my hand out toward her, barely touching her bare foot.

She looked down, annoyed by my gesture. "You silly human. Do you really think your mere touch can harm me?"

I smiled. "We'll find out in a moment."

She let out a hearty laugh, which quickly turned into a gasp. "Impossible."

The surprise on her face matched my own. My nightmares were coming to life right before my very own eyes. The crimson moss snaked its way around her foot and up her ankle. She pulled at it feverishly, a bewildered look on her pretty face.

Nicolai grabbed my hand. "Angelina, no! You can't do this."

"I don't even know what I'm doing," I answered, shocked by the scene in front of me.

Laurana screamed in confusion as the crimson moss wound itself tightly around her leg and pulled her small body toward the ground.

"Angelina, please, you have to stop this," Nicolai urged, placing his hand on mine.

"I don't know how!" I yelled.

"Close your eyes, and focus on my voice."

I did as I was told, and a warm calmness washed over me.

"Calm down. You're not that person anymore. You're special."

His voice was soothing, and I felt myself begin to smile as my heart calmed itself.

"Now, stop the moss."

My hand subconsciously touched her again. My eyes flew open and I watched in amazement as the moss loosened its grip on her. She pulled herself free and backed away from it, fear in her cold eyes.

She shook her head. "That's impossible, how can she . . .?"

Nicolai stood up. "Nothing's impossible."

I remained on the ground, shocked by the revelation that I had controlled the crimson moss. I looked at my hands, and they looked normal. So where the heck had it come from?

"She's different, Laurana. You can't take her to Ctephanyi."

"I can't go back empty handed," Laurana replied. "You know that."

"I couldn't care less about how Ctephanyi feels about anything, to be honest with you," he replied, the fire in his orange eyes beginning to grow.

"What a pity. You would give your life for this woman, for this half human?" Her hair began floating around her pale head.

The shock subsided. "Half human?" I questioned, looking up at the both of them.

They ignored me as they continued their argument. Nicolai's face was full of surprise. "Ctephanyi doesn't realize what she's done yet, does she?" he asked as he pointed toward me. "She is something more, so much more than another risen soul."

"Impossible. She's nothing more than another half-human that we are yet again left to dispose of."

"Ctephanyi will soon see what she's done, and

you'll all wish you had taken more of an interest in this half-human, as you call her.

I stood up and brushed off my pants, briefly looking down to make sure there was no moss growing on them. "I would really appreciate an explanation of what's happening to me."

Nicolai looked over at me, sympathy in his beautiful orange eyes. "Angelina . . ."

"She doesn't even know what she is herself, does she?" Laurana asked. Very interesting. This could be useful information."

Nicolai turned back toward her sharply. "No, Laurana, Ctephanyi must never know."

"Can't you see that I don't give a crap about this half human? Ctephanyi will find her talents very useful."

"I don't know who this Ctephanyi is that you keep talking about, but I really couldn't care less to meet her," I yelled out unnoticed.

"Laurana, you can't tell her. If she finds out Angelina can control the crimson moss . . ." He looked down and shook his head.

"Ctephanyi will know of her abilities. Angelina may control the crimson moss, but she does not control me."

My chest tightened again as the agonizing pain washed over me. I fell to my knees and gripped my chest.

"Well, now, you've gone and done it," Nicolai vented through clenched teeth.

While I struggled to breathe, he jumped toward the wicked woman and grabbed a fistful of her long, blond hair. She screamed in agony and attempted to pull herself from his firm grip.

"Grabbing a girl by her hair?" She growled

menacingly, finally ripping herself free. Long blond strands hung from Nicolai's clenched fist.

He grinned. "Release your spell on her, or else."

She spun around and glared. "Never."

I fell to the ground and stared up at the sky. I saw my mother's face and smiled. I raised my hand to touch her. "It's not your time yet," she whispered. "You have much left to do."

"Mom, don't go," I pleaded quietly.

Nicolai realized what was happening and turned around. "Angelina, no! Don't go!"

Laurana seized her chance. She grabbed him by his shoulder and, using her inhuman strength, threw him into a nearby tree. It splintered from the hefty blow, sending chunks of wood everywhere.

My mother's voice grew faint. "Remember who you are, honey. Remember who you are."

"No, please don't go," I begged.

She touched my lips with her ghostly fingers, and my airway magically opened. "I love you," she whispered, slowly disappearing in front of me.

I sat up and gulped for air. A tear trickled down my face, and I wiped it away angrily with my dirty hand. My mother was gone. The monster that had broken into my home had murdered her. What if—no! My head snapped toward Nicolai, and the anger welled up inside of me. What if he were the monster?

9

Friend or Foe

Nicolai stood up, brushed himself off, and rushed toward Laurana, grabbing her around the waist and holding her high above his head. He used his mighty strength to throw her to the ground, which trembled with such force that I had to steady myself.

Laurana, breathing heavy, lay motionless on the rocky ground for a few moments before managing to pull herself up. She looked rough. There were numerous cuts on her arms and legs. She had a defeated look on her face and knew she had no chance of winning the battle against Nicolai. Like a dog with its tail between its legs, she slowly stood and stumbled back into the forest. She paused, turned her head, and glared. Pointing a long, pale finger at the both of us she hissed, "Nicolai, you've made a mistake. Ctephanyi will not be happy about this. And as for you, Angelina, we shall see each other again soon. That, my dear, is a promise."

She took one more look at us and disappeared into the dense brush. I could feel the bile from my stomach begin to rise up, and for a moment, I felt as though I was about to be sick. I stood there quietly, wondering what other horrors I would encounter. What had they meant by half-human? Who was Ctephanyi and what did she want with me? Were the stories of the unnatural creatures true? I closed my eyes. Maybe I was dreaming. Maybe it was all just a bad dream.

"Sorry, love. I hate to break it to you, but you're not dreaming," Nicolai interrupted.

"Wait a minute." I snapped my head up to look at him. "How did you know what I was thinking?"

He shrugged, a blank expression crossing his face as he shoved his hands into his pants pockets.

Angry tears filled my eyes. "Oh no, you're not getting off that easy. You need to answer my question right now. How did you know what I was thinking?"

He looked down and kicked at the ground. "This world we live in is full of mysterious things we're unable to explain."

I glared at him. "I think I deserve an explanation."

He sighed. "You're right, you do. Sometimes we connect with other people in a special way." His beautiful fiery eyes met mine. "With those few, I can sometimes hear their thoughts and feel their emotions."

I stared at him in disbelief. "So you're saying you and I are connected in some weird way, and, therefore, you can read my mind?"

"Yeah, it's kind of like that."

I shook my head. "That crosses a line into some privacy issues, don't you think?"

He laughed. "I suppose it could."

"Do me a favor, don't read my mind again," I snapped, feeling completely violated.

"I didn't mean . . ."

I raised my hand to stop him. "My thoughts are my own."

He nodded. "Okay, I get it."

I lifted my eyebrows and stared at him. "I mean it."

He chuckled. "I get it. I won't do it again. I promise."

Dear Lord, I thought to myself. Was anything safe from these people? Would I make it another day in this evil place? Nicolai smiled and picked me up carefully. I wrapped my arms around his neck and rolled my eyes. "Oh, so now you're going to carry me?"

"I figured since you said you've been slacking in the exercise department, you could use a little rest."

"My hero!" I cheered sarcastically.

He smirked. "Hero, eh?"

"Every girl needs a little saving at some point in her life."

"You're right, and I hope one day you realize that I truly want to be your hero."

I looked up at the sky, remembering the vision of my mother. "I only wish you could've been there to save my mom," I whispered.

He continued on in silence, and I began to wonder if he had anything to do with her death. "Nicolai, can I ask you something?"

"Of course."

"Last night, I was attacked by something inhuman. Do you happen to know anything about that?"

He stopped and looked at me. It was hard to read his face at that moment, which scared me.

"Angelina . . ."

Angry tears brimmed at the corners of my eyes. "Did you kill her? Was it you?"

He lowered his eyes. "No, it wasn't me."

"Then, who was it?"

His voice was heavy with sadness. "I don't know. I wish as much as you that I could've been there."

I searched his beautiful face for answers. "Are you lying to me?"

His eyes met mine and I knew it wasn't him. I didn't know how, but I saw something familiar in his eyes and just knew.

"I would never lie to you, Angelina. You have always been the only . . ." He paused. "You are my . . ." He looked away.

"I'm your what?"

He continued walking. "Never mind."

The silence was thick and unbearable, but I was afraid to ask him anything else. I looked up into his odd-colored eyes and noticed something I hadn't seen before. There was unmistakable pain and suffering hidden within them. I wondered what had happened to him to make him so tortured. I hoped in time I would be able to figure it out. He was most certainly a mystery. Something began to tug at the back of my mind, some memory I couldn't quite recall. I pushed it away and lay my head against his shoulder while he carried me deeper into the forest.

"No more following the river?" I asked.

"No, it's not safe anymore. Laurana may come back, and if she does she won't be alone."

"So who is this Ctephanyi?"

He scowled. "She's a very bad person."

"Why does she want me? I mean—did I do something to offend her?"

"No."

"Then what?"

"She hates humans, all of them."

I was confused. "But, didn't Laurana specifically say she wanted me?"

He grew quiet, and the look on his face told me not to bring it up again. I let him scowl for a few moments before changing the subject. "So, how do you know where to go? This forest is huge."

His eyes livened up a bit. "I've lived in this forest for a very long time. I know my way around."

"How old are you?"

He laughed. "Let's just say, I've been around for awhile."

"Fair enough." I smiled, relieved he was talking to me again. I caught a whiff of his earthy scent and breathed him in. It reminded me of a smell I had come across as a child. My mind was too exhausted to place it, so, instead, I pictured his smiling face. Could one person really be this perfect? I closed my eyes and found myself drifting off into a peaceful sleep. I knew he would protect me as we continued on with our journey. Not only was he slowly turning out to be my own personal hero, he also was turning out to be my own Prince Charming. At that moment, I felt like the luckiest girl alive.

10

Truth Be Told

I opened my eyes and wondered how long I had been asleep. Once I realized my head was still lying against Nicolai's chest, I smiled mid-yawn and ran my fingers along his bulging arm muscles. I couldn't help but wonder why he was so protective over me.

Without thinking, I blurted out, "Why are you here?"

He stopped walking for a moment and smiled at me thoughtfully. I could feel the uneasy flutter of butterfly wings in my stomach again as he answered quietly, "I told you. I'm here to protect you."

"That's a cop-out answer."

He laughed.

I raised my eyebrow. "Nicolai, you hardly know me."

A disappointed look fell over his face. "Hardly know you? Angelina, there are so many things you don't know, and so many things you don't want to know." He set me down, grumbling, "Hardly know you . . ."

My frustration was beginning to confuse my thoughts. "How do you know I don't want to know? Please tell me. I need to know what's going on. I feel like people are trying to kill me every chance they get. Can't you at least give me the courtesy of knowing why? I think I deserve that."

He sighed and stopped walking. Setting me on my feet, he said "Alright, if you must know."

He walked over to a nearby tree and leaned up against it, crossing his arms in defeat. "Angelina, do you know what I am?"

I answered him honestly, "Well, I have an idea."

"Oh, then please, do tell." He smirked, thoroughly amused by my answer.

I turned around. I was afraid to face him. His eyes were such an unusual color, his speed was remarkable, and his strength was undeniable. My imagination ran wild and I wondered if maybe the scar on his arm was from a battle with a terrified hunter that he had found and dragged into the forest.

"You're what people have nightmares about," I finally whispered. "You're the miscreation of mankind that has been in our town's folklore for centuries. Your kind wander into our town late at night, staying until dawn, then retreating back into the forest with a terrified human—revenge for all the hunters who have invaded your precious land." I trembled slightly as I turned back around to face him. I looked directly into his eyes. "You're a vampire."

Just saying the word made my skin crawl. Deep down, I was afraid. In fact, I was scared to death. I could only imagine what he was truly capable of.

He let out a hearty laugh. "Well, dang, you make me sound quite terrifying."

I looked at him dumbfounded. He was laughing at me!

"I'm sorry, it's just that you humans have such

imaginations. That's something I've always enjoyed about your species."

"My species?"

"Now, don't get me wrong. I consider what you said a compliment and, though I hate to be the bearer of bad news, or good in your case, you happen to be quite wrong."

"I am?"

He laughed again. "Yes, I'm sorry to disappoint you."

I stared at him in silence.

Sensing my confusion, he continued, "Angelina, vampires do exist and, though I'm not one of them, I will say I've met a few in my time, and they're quite exciting creatures."

"Well, if you're not a vampire, then what are you? There are so many similarities."

"Hmm. I suppose there are, though I believe they have little white fangs," he replied. "Most vampires are so overly dramatic and old fashioned. We're a little more modern day."

"Do you drag humans into the forest at night?" Did I really want to know the answer to that question?

Before I could get an answer he was next to me, wrapping his strong arms around my waist. "Angelina, we are a species that came along well before the vampire race. I won't lie to you. There are some of us who torture humans purely for sport, but most of us try to live quietly. We are, however, without a doubt the most lethal creatures known to man." He gently placed his hand under my chin, prompting me to look up at him.

"Most lethal creatures known to man? What

else is out there?"

He bent down and put his lips close to my ear. "There are hundreds of species humans are unaware of living on this planet. Most are extremely deadly, however, I do believe I've only ever met one creature more lethal than I."

His warm breath caressed my face and began to distract my train of thought. "Is that even possible?" I uttered quietly.

"Of course," he continued, his lips now teasing my neck. They were so close I could feel the pronunciation of his every word on my delicate skin. "You're it, Angelina. You are more deadly than anything I've ever come across. The day I saw your face was the day I understood the meaning of my existence," he whispered moving his face closer to mine. "I would willingly give up my life if I could be the man that steals your heart and takes your breath away with a kiss."

He pulled me close to him and his lips met mine. Surges of electricity ran through my body, making me tingle from my head to the very tips of my toes. I felt as though I had just been struck by lightning. His kiss was hungry, with a hint of love, and lust. He tenderly caressed my cheek with his hand, sending shivers down my spine.

An image of Jeremiah's face flashed through my mind and guilt ate away at the tender moment. I was surprised by the sudden switch in my emotions, and I pulled away shamefully. My eyes filled with tears. What was I doing? I cringed at the old feelings I thought I had buried for Jeremiah. In fact, I didn't even know why they still existed.

"Nicolai, I'm so sorry." A warm tear fell down my cheek. "I just don't think I can do this."

His eyes filled with disappointment, and the hand that had so lovingly caressed my cheek fell limply to his side. He walked over to a fallen log and sat down. He ran his strong hands through his black hair and sighed. "Angelina, I have dreamt of this moment for years. You don't know how long I've waited for you."

I shook my head. "Nicolai, I don't understand."

"I was there the night you were made. I saw what happened, and I know who and what you really are. I've waited so patiently for you to come back to me."

"You're not making any sense," I whispered in between tears.

"Don't you see? Don't you understand?" He turned to face me, the pain in his eyes visible.

I sobbed, "No, I don't see, and I don't understand a word you're saying to me. I beg you to tell me, to help me understand."

He looked at me with a blank expression on his face, stood up and began walking away.

"Nicolai, where are you going?" I choked through tears.

He turned around, and the look on his face broke my heart. "Angelina, everyone in the entire world, regardless of their species searches for a love like ours. Our love has survived thousands of years, crossed boundaries it shouldn't have been able to, only to be brought back here." He pointed toward the forest around us.

I shook my head, unable to process what he was saying.

He sighed. "I know my words don't make any sense now, but they will. This I promise you."

Without another word, he turned and ran into the forest. I didn't want it to end this way, so I came to my senses, wiped the tears from my eyes, and ran after him, but I was no match for his inhuman speed. I stumbled blindly over broken branches, tripped over hidden vines, and even got smacked in the face by a few rogue briar bushes.

I had to face the ugly truth. I was lost, and Nicolai was nowhere in sight.

I slumped down next to a moss-covered tree stump and put my head in my hands. It was starting to get dark, and I was utterly alone. I didn't even have my backpack anymore, so there was no telling what was going to happen to me. I had no flashlight, no weapon, and no exceptionally handsome man to protect me from the evils of this mystical place.

I lay my head against the soft crimson moss and touched my lips with the tips of my fingers. I was instantly reminded of Nicolai's kiss. It had started out so wonderful and welcoming, but how could I ever fall in love with someone I had just met? He seemed so sincere and charming. The way he had caressed my cheek, the way he had sent those wonderful little chills down my spine, the way he had protected me against Laurana—they were truly admirable traits. What was underneath all that? Knowing my luck, he had probably planned to take me back to some fierce monster for supper.

My heart began to ache, and I could feel my eyes fill with tears again. I was so lost. What I wouldn't give for my mother to be here right now.

She would have told me not to worry and that a warm cup of tea solved all of life's problems. I sighed and pulled a pile of leaves closer to me so I could lie down. Who knew what would happen to me now? Thoughts of Laurana coming back for me crossed my mind. Maybe this time she would get what she wanted and kill me. After all, she was pretty ticked off when she left. Maybe this so called Ctephanyi would find me, or perhaps it would be the red-eyed monster that had killed my mother. Either way, I was too tired to care anymore.

I hugged my knees and tried to think of the better times, when I was happy. I smiled as an image of Jeremiah and me hiding in my closet crossed my mind. We were so young and innocent. After he had laughed at my story of the red-haired woman, he had snuck into my room to apologize. He held me close and caressed my hair while I sobbed at the fact that I would never get to see my father again. How could one so young be so caring? The guilt once again returned. I had been in love with Jeremiah since the day my mother took him in as her own, though he had made it very clear he didn't feel the same way. To him, I was just the sister he never had, and there was no seeing past that. Still, thinking of him made me happy. Smiling, I fell asleep and dreamed of skipping rocks with my childhood friend in the crimson forest that, at the time, had kept us safe from all the unknown evils of the world.

11

Love's Embrace

I awoke startled by the smell of bacon cooking over a campfire. Realizing I was no longer alone, I sat up and rubbed the sleep from my eyes. I blinked a few times and stared in silence. Sitting right across from me was Nicolai.

"Well, good morning, my dear. How did you sleep?" he asked, avoiding my eyes.

"Where did you go? You left me all alone," I managed to say as I attempted to push down the knot that had begun to form in the back of my throat.

"It was time."

"Time for what?"

He turned his head, and I followed his gaze to a fallen log a short distance from where we were sitting. Another person had joined our little party. I rubbed my eyes again, fearful that maybe I will still dreaming, and pinched myself to make sure I was awake. The man in front of me was real.

He stood up and, though my legs were weak and shaky, I followed suit. We stopped within inches of each other. With tears falling down his weathered cheeks, he placed his hand on my heart and said, "Now, we're whole."

I threw my arms around my father's malnourished frame. He looked different but yet the same. Wherever he had been had taken its toll on his strong body. Small scars covered his arms and a shaggy, unkempt beard hid his face. Though he had lost quite a bit of weight, he still had the unmistakable twinkle in his beautiful blue eyes. That twinkle was meant for me, and it was the one thing I knew no one could take away from him.

After a few more hugs and kisses, we walked over and sat down beside the warm fire.

"Your mother, how is she?" He asked the one question I didn't know how to answer. I looked down and attempted to hold back my tears.

"Ahh, I see," he said, his voice quivering. He coughed and swallowed his sadness. "Angelina, things like this happen."

"She loved you so very much." I choked back the tears that begged to fall. "She never gave up on you."

He wrapped his loving arms around me. "I know that honey. Don't you worry. I will see her again. Even if it's in heaven, I will see her again."

I smiled, a single tear escaping down my cheek. "You know, she used to say the same thing about you."

He chuckled. "Smart woman."

I nodded. "Yeah, she sure was."

We sat in bittersweet silence, reminiscing about our past life. Though I missed my mom, I was happier than I had been in days, and there was only one person responsible for my newfound happiness.

I looked over at Nicolai. A thoughtful look crossed his face, as he stirred the embers in the fire with a long jagged stick. I caught another glimpse of the scar that ran from his elbow to his wrist. For some reason, it stood out more prominently today than it had before, and I wondered why. Maybe I just hadn't looked that closely at it before.

I touched my father's face gently. "I've waited a long time for this moment," I said, standing back up, "and I have one person to thank."

I sat down next to Nicolai and put my hand on his shoulder. He ignored my touch and continued stirring the embers inside the fire. I bent down in front of him and cupped his cheek with my other hand. He finally stopped and looked up at me. His eyes now matched the color of the embers. Looking deeper, I saw his soul laid out in front of me. I could see the pain, hurt, desperation, fear, and love. They were all there, and they were all there because of me.

"Oh, Nicolai . . ." I gasped. I finally understood. The memory that had been tugging at the back of my mind became crystal clear. He had always been there. He had been my best friend, my confidant, and my hero.

"I couldn't tell you," he muttered quietly, "you had to figure it out for yourself."

"My secret," I whispered.

"I've waited so long for you."

"My friend."

"The day you let our secret be known was the day I had to let you go."

I shook my head in disbelief. "I waited for you for two days, but you never came. You said you would always be there when I needed you."

"There were rules. I had to follow them."

I put my hands on his face and pulled him closer to me. "Ialocin. That was your name."

He nodded. "That was the name I gave you to call me."

Realization set in. "Wait, Ialocin—isn't that Nicolai spelled backwards?"

"There were rules that needed to be followed."

"I understand everything," I whispered, before pressing my lips to his. He pulled me closer, and I could feel my cheeks flush with excitement. His embrace was so hungry, and he kissed me with such ferocity, I thought my lips were going to explode. He wrapped his strong arms around me, and I knew I couldn't fight it anymore. I let all the guilty feelings go. This was the man I had waited my entire life for. My mom had been right —Jeremiah had waited too long. I had fallen head-over-heels in love with Nicolai. It was destined from the moment he saved my life as a child. Finally, something in my life seemed to make sense.

I heard my father cough awkwardly behind me. Slightly embarrassed, I pulled away, my face still flushed from excitement. I looked back into Nicolai's amazing eyes and saw nothing but pure love. Smiling, I turned around and plopped back down next to my Dad.

He put his arm around me and pulled me close to him. "I've missed you. You don't know how much I longed to see you again."

"Oh, me too! I missed you so much," I croaked trying to fight back the lump that had returned to my throat. "We all thought you were . . ."

"Well, for a short period of time, that's how I felt," he patted my leg, "and then this strange fella over here saved me."

I grinned in Nicolai's direction. "Yeah, he's a regular ol' Superman, though I still think Wonder Woman could take him."

Nicolai held a finger to his lips and winked.

My father looked down solemnly. "I was in a very bad place when he found me."

"Well, old man," Nicolai replied, sitting down next to us, "that's the past, right? Now you've got something to start living for again."

"You're right about that." I winked.

"Angelina, make sure you eat something this morning. We have a long hike today," Nicolai urged, pushing some of the freshly cooked bacon toward me.

My stomach growled at his offer, and seeing how I couldn't remember the last time I had eaten, I took him up on it. "Thanks." I managed to say through a mouthful of bacon bits.

"We need to try and get out of the woods by nightfall. I have a feeling something bad is coming very quickly."

"What is it?" I frowned up at him.

"I don't know. I felt something this morning that I haven't felt in a long time." For a moment, his voice trailed off. "The last time I had that feeling I lost you."

My appetite suddenly disappeared. I mean, how was I supposed to eat after hearing something like that? I stared into the fire and picked at the leftover bacon I was still holding. Frustrated, I threw the bacon into the burning embers, stood up, and looked around. It was hard to believe that such evil monsters could be in such a beautiful place.

A cool, crisp breeze began to blow casually throughout our small makeshift camp causing crimson colored leaves to fall down lazily around us. Everything seemed so peaceful, even the crimson moss, but I knew the truth—it was all just a grand illusion.

My mind wandered back to the previous day's events. Who would've thought something like this could ever actually happen? I mean, when you watch a scary movie, you always laugh away the fear that follows you afterwards. It's rare that what's behind the fear actually becomes reality.

My mind continued wandering, and I soon found myself thinking of the small town I had called home. I missed my mother. I knew my best friend Marie was probably sick with worry, and poor Jeremiah was most likely cursing at me for not listening to him. My heart began to ache as I realized the place I had wanted to leave so badly wasn't really that terrible after all. If anything, it certainly wasn't boring anymore.

A warm ray of sunshine beamed down on my face from a small opening in a cluster of trees. I looked up at the sky and smiled, knowing my mother was watching over me. It was as if she were sending me a sign to let me know everything was going to be okay. She knew I was in good hands, and I wouldn't let her down.

My father laughed, and I glanced back toward the campsite. He put his hand on Nicolai's shoulder and smiled. The way they acted toward each other gave me the feeling they had some sort of history that I didn't know about and for some reason it didn't surprise me. In fact, nothing surprised me anymore. I watched them intently and felt the ache that had been in my heart beginning to dull. Love took its place as the two men continued to laugh and joke with each other. They were all I had now, and I would do whatever it took to keep them safe. I had lost enough in my life to know I couldn't afford to lose anything else.

"Angelina, it's time," Nicolai pointed out, narrowing his eyes at me.

I nodded and studied the troubled look on his face. Something was wrong. Reality had just turned its ugly head in our direction, and I didn't like it one bit. Sighing, I walked over and kissed him on his cool cheek.

"Don't worry, love. Everything is going to be okay," he encouraged leaning his forehead against mine. "I will keep you both safe, I promise."

"I know. I trust you," I replied, this time kissing his lips.

He kissed me back lovingly and grabbed my hand.

"Shall we?" My father said with a wink, allowing Nicolai to lead the way.

~ ~ ~

My legs silently ached as we walked for what seemed like hours. I was beginning to think the forest was under some sort of wicked spell that made it go on forever. Why had it seemed so much smaller when I was a child? Wasn't it supposed to be the other way around? Exhausted, I finally gave into my aching legs and sat down on a fallen log. I had to take a break.

"Angelina, we have to keep moving. We don't

have much time before dusk is upon us," Nicolai urged. "We can't say in the woods any longer."

I attempted to catch my breath. "I know. I'm just so tired."

I fumbled with the locket that hung loosely around my neck. It had completely slipped my mind that I was wearing it. I ran my fingers over the dainty letter and realized I kind of enjoyed the mystery of not knowing what was inside. I liked that it had begun to feel as if it were a part of me, like it had always been mine.

"What've you got there?" Nicolai asked, noticing my fingers fumbling with the necklace that hung perfectly around my neck.

I wrapped my hand around the locket protectively. "Oh, it's nothing," I replied with a smile.

He came toward me slowly with a look of curiosity in his ember eyes. "Nothing, huh?" He looked down and unfolded my fingers gently. "You found it." He gasped. "Why didn't I notice this earlier?"

Surprised by his reaction, I wrapped my fingers back around it. "Yes, and it's mine."

"Angelina, it's okay," he whispered, startled by the fierceness in my voice. "It is yours, but I have to admit, you kind of sound like that ugly gremlin from *Lord of the Rings*."

I looked at Nicolai, surprised. "You watch movies?"

"I wasn't born under a rock—oh wait." He laughed, and I stared at him in confusion.

My father laughed and mocked me. "My precious."

I laughed along with them and apologized.

"I'm sorry. I didn't mean it to come out so forcefully."

Nicolai wrapped his strong hands around mine and with tears forming in his eyes he smiled. "It's a puzzle piece that will help you solve who you really are."

"Wait, do you still have the key?" I asked, my heart beginning to race.

"I don't. The day I left you, the key disappeared."

I frowned.

He squeezed my hand. "Don't worry. When it's time and you're ready, you'll see what's inside."

I ran my hands over the dainty letter "H" again and slowly looked back up at him. He smiled, a hopeful look on his face.

From the corner of my eye, I noticed my father turn his head toward us sharply.

"What does the letter H have to do with me?" I muttered.

"You see, there are rules I must follow, and I was hoping you would remember what that letter meant to you."

I was frustrated by the riddles that continually appeared in our conversations. "Rules for what?"

"In time, you will remember. I promise."

He stood up, dusted the debris from his pants, and continued on into the woods. My father walked over to me and held out his hand. I grabbed it and he pulled me up, my frustration still gnawing at my usually calm demeanor. I carefully tucked the locket back under my shirt and sighed.

My father smiled reassuringly. "You know he doesn't tell you certain things because he is disallowed from doing so."

"I know. It's frustrating."

He patted me on the shoulder and guided me through the forest. This whole time I thought the rules I had at home were strict. Whatever rules Nicolai had to follow had actually begun to scare me. All I could do was hope that the mysteries surrounding me would come to light and preferably sooner rather than later, because the emotional roller coaster I was riding was almost too much to bear.

12

Fearful Thoughts

Dusk came quickly, and I could see the worry on Nicolai's face growing. I guess I hadn't realized how deep into the forest we actually were. He stopped abruptly and scanned the forest. He clenched his fist and began pacing back and forth while running his other hand through his messy black hair. The frustration and confusion could be seen in his eyes as he muttered incoherently under his breath. I went to him and smiled lovingly. I wrapped my arms around him and he looked down at me. "It's going to be okay," I said, trying to reassure him. He nodded, and I ran my hand down his smooth arm.

A strange sensation came over me as I ran my fingers gently over his jagged scar. A memory flashed before my eyes: I was wearing a long white dress, and my long chestnut hair floated around my pale, freckled face. I was chilled and unable to move. Beside me, I heard a familiar voice, but weakness made my body heavy. Oddly enough, as I began to feel my frail human body fade away, the voice grew stronger. I turned my head slightly and grew alarmed by the significant amount of blood that surrounded me. My dress was no longer the color of purity, but instead the deep crimson color of death.

Using the minimal amount of strength I had left, I looked for the familiar voice. Tears formed in my amber eyes as I realized it was Nicolai, and he was holding his arm. Blood cascaded from a deep, jagged laceration that seemed endless as it ran from his elbow to his wrist. I turned my head a bit more and noticed three dead bodies scattered around him. The puzzle was slowly coming together.

I looked back at Nicolai and could see angry tears running down his grief-stricken face as he begged for mercy from another very familiar face —the red-haired woman. I felt utterly helpless and wanted to run to him to tell him that everything was going to be fine. Feeling the darkness stealing the very breath from my lungs, I uttered his name.

He crawled over to me and held my head in his arms. "Please, baby, please don't leave me."

He looked up with pleading eyes at the red-haired woman. "Please help me, I will do anything."

I smiled a weak smile and put my hand on his cheek. A warm tear hit my face as he continued to beg her. I wiped away his tears and took his hand to place it against my quivering lips. I kissed it gently and looked up at him. "Death is not the end, but only the beginning. A love like ours can never truly be taken away." I closed my eyes.

He put his head on my chest and listened to my fading heart as he sobbed quietly, knowing there was nothing he could do to save me. His strong fingers caressed my hair. The time had come, and I allowed the darkness to carry me away to the one place where pain and fear were only memories of a world that thrived on the suffering of others.

Gasping, I opened my eyes to the forest and took a step back. Nicolai was looking at me with questions in his eyes, and I just shook my head in disbelief.

"What just happened?" I whispered.

He caressed my cheek. "Angelina, there are forces at work that are more powerful than anything you could ever imagine."

"How is that even possible?"

"All things are possible. As you said a very long time ago, a love like ours can never truly be taken away."

I opened my mouth to say something, but he just put a finger against my lips to hush me and kissed my forehead lovingly. I wished I had known everything that had happened, as my life had become one large, confusing puzzle. If only I had had all the pieces, I could have made sense of it.

Nicolai caressed my hair, and it reminded me of how he had caressed my hair in the vision. Sighing, I kissed his cool face and walked over to my father and hugged him. He looked at me with an odd expression. I did a double take and realized he looked as if he had grown younger over the past few hours. I stepped back and opened my mouth to question him, but he lifted his hand in protest.

"Angelina, the answers are everywhere. You just have to find them."

I threw my hands in the air. "Where? You both speak in such riddles."

"Honey, you must be patient. When your mind is ready, it will allow you to remember."

"Remember what?!"

"Who you are," he simply said and walked away.

Nicolai followed my father without saying a word. I was so confused by the vision I had seen. I just wished everything around me wasn't such a secret. My mother had always told me that curiosity would one day get me into trouble, that one day it would bestow a painful learning experience upon my inquisitive nature. It looked like she was right, and that time was now.

13

Secret Love

Jeremiah looked around the quiet tavern. It was unusual for it to be this quiet during the busiest time of the season. Tonight, however, everyone seemed to be in deep thought. He was pretty sure they were all thinking about the same thing—the creature they'd come across in the forest.

Jeremiah shook his head and looked back down at his empty glass. He felt bad for not telling Angelina the truth, as he had always been honest with her. He sighed and pushed his empty glass toward the bartender.

"Another one, eh?" the bartender asked.

He nodded. "Yeah, fill it up."

The bartender grabbed a can of Coke and filled the glass. "Rough night, bud?"

"You could say that," Jeremiah muttered, putting the glass to his lips.

Tonight, he would drink away his sorrows, maybe even pick up a woman to help get thoughts of Angelina off his mind. He smirked at the idea and took a drink. He ran his fingers across the smooth edge of the glass and sat back to look around the small little bar. This place was familiar to him. He was reminded of the many nights he had come here to drag his drunken father home after a long night of drinking his sorrows away. The bottle had been his father's best friend and Jeremiah knew it. He could recall the look on Angelina's face the first time she saw him drag his father out of the bar. She had given Jeremiah a slight smile as if to say it was going to be alright. Then, she had simply put one shoulder under his father's limp body to help lift him.

He stood up and pushed the glass back toward the bartender, pulled a few dollars out of his wallet and threw them on the bar. The bartender gave him a nod, and he walked over to the door. It opened and Benjamin, his hunting partner, walked in. They looked at each other in quiet surprise.

Benjamin's jaw clenched. "Don't go into the woods tomorrow. It's not worth your life."

Jeremiah put his hand on Benjamin's shoulder and nodded before continuing outside. Bright lights flooded the dark street. Loud sirens and voices filled the air. The street was crammed with police officers and paramedics. He looked around and covered his mouth in disgust. There were pieces of what appeared to be a human spread around the ground. Fights were pretty common during this time of year, but this was ridiculous.

He pushed his way through the curious crowd, shoved his hands in his pockets, and turned down the alley. He saw more flashing lights coming from around the corner. Not surprised, he continued walking. He figured it was probably just another rumble in the streets caused by some drunkard. His heart stopped once he turned the corner and saw the flashing lights were outside Angelina's house. His adrenaline began to race, and he jogged over to the crowd of people that had gathered out front.

He pushed his way through. "What

happened?" he demanded.

Angelina's best friend Marie emerged from within the doorway. He could see her eyes were red and swollen from crying. The fear in his heart grew as he put his arms around her.

"Oh, Jeremiah, something terrible has happened!" she sobbed.

He scanned the crowd. "Marie, where's Angelina?"

"They can't find her," she stammered through the tears, "and poor Mrs. Adams is . . ."

"Is what?" he asked firmly.

Marie pointed toward the doorway. Jeremiah looked over and could make out the image of a crumpled body leaning against the stairway. His arms went limp, and he let go of Marie to push his way through the crowd. He recognized the officer at the door and ran up to him.

"Joe, what happened?"

"Jeremiah, you need to stay back. We've got a crime scene on our hands."

"Crime scene? Where's Angelina?"

"I don't know. They haven't found her yet."

"You have to let me in."

"You know I can't do that."

"I'm the best tracker in Buffalo. You know I can find her."

The officer glanced around. "It's pretty gory in there."

Jeremiah nodded. "I've seen worse."

"I don't know about that," the officer mumbled. "County's on its way. If they catch you, you're going to become a suspect, and I'm going to be out of a job."

Jeremiah pushed past him. "I got it. Thanks,

man."

"Don't thank me quite yet," the officer called out behind him.

He was right. As soon as Jeremiah entered the room, he felt sick. The once welcoming bed and breakfast was now covered in death and destruction.

The walls were coated in a thin blanket of blood. The old tables and chairs sat in pieces around the room. Large scratch marks ran across the once beautiful rose-colored wallpaper.

Mrs. Adams's body lay crumpled against the stairway. He only recognized her by her shape and clothes because her head had been ripped clean off.

He bent over and held his stomach, swallowing the bile that had begun to make its way up. Something in the fireplace caught his eye, and he steadied himself and walked toward it slowly. He narrowed his eyes at the object sitting on top of the perfectly placed logs.

"Oh my God, no." He fell to his knees. "No, please God, no." He ran his hands through his blond hair and shook his head. He looked up again in disbelief. The bile rose up once again and this time he couldn't stop it from coming out. He gave himself a moment to gather his composure and stood up, wiping his mouth with the back of his hand.

He went to Mrs. Adams's body lying against the stairway and picked up her bloody hand, holding it against his chest one last time.

It felt cold and clammy, but he knew this was the last time he would ever feel her touch. A single tear fell down his face as he carefully placed her hand back on the wood floor. He glanced back toward the fireplace and cringed. Her head sat perfectly on the logs she had once used to keep her small home warm. Feeling sick again, he looked away. What kind of monster would do such a horrible thing? She was too good a woman to die like this.

He knew what this place meant to Angelina and her mother. It had been their fresh start. After the disappearance of Angelina's father, her mother had decided this would help the both of them move on. Now, for the second time, devastation had hit them.

He cautiously made his way up the stairs, attempting to avoid the blood that was smeared along the walls. Sour memories plagued him as he made his way up to Angelina's bedroom. He remembered following Angelina up these same stairs, sitting on her small twin-sized bed, and listening to her while she confessed her love for him. He had been a coward and had lied to her. He had felt the same way. In fact, he was pretty sure he loved her more than he had ever loved anything in his entire life, but he had been unable to muster up the courage to tell her that. That was the day he had broken her heart by telling her they were like family and nothing more.

He frowned as he sidestepped her bedroom door, which had been pulled from its hinges. So much for that insanely huge lock, he thought to himself as he walked through the empty doorway. He tried to imagine what kind of man or creature was capable of such destruction. Tracking mode set in, and he got to work. He started with her closet. Her clothes had been pulled out and shredded, and lay strewn throughout the tiny room. He knew he had to hurry, so he concentrated on the most important things first. He reached his hand above the doorframe and felt around for her knife. He was pleased to find it gone. The hook where she kept her backpack was empty. He turned around and walked over to the shattered window, avoiding pieces of her broken bed. He examined the remaining pieces of glass that somehow managed to stay within the wooden windowpane. He hoped for any clue as to what could've possibly happened, and that's when he noticed a clump of what appeared to be dark fur hanging from one of the glass shards. He pulled it off carefully and rolled it around his fingertips, allowing his senses to determine what sort of animal it could've possibly come from. It almost felt like wolf hair but that was unlikely, as wolves didn't normally visit the Buffalo area.

He stood back up and scanned the room for more clues. There had obviously been some sort of struggle between this animal and something or someone else, and it was apparent the animal had been thrown against the window, shattering the glass. He could only hope that Angelina was not the other person involved. His mind wandered back to the night of the hunting party, and he wondered if perhaps it had something to do with what he had seen in the forest.

He continued to walk around the room looking for anything unusual. His eye caught something shiny lying on the floor near where her dresser had once been. Bending down, he picked up a small golden key and examined it closely. There was a small letter carved into the front of it.

"H," he whispered out loud. This key had to be a clue. He tucked it into the front pocket of his jeans and took one last look around the room. Sirens blared in the distance and he knew it was time to leave. He hurried out of the room and down the steps, pushing past Officer Joe.

"You okay, kid?" the officer called out from the doorway.

"I'm going to look for her," Jeremiah said.

"Leave the real work to the cops, kid."

"You and I both know I'm the best for this, Joe. I can track her better than any cop on the force, and your guys will just mess up my clues." Officer Joe didn't say anything. He merely nodded and continued to keep the curious bystanders at bay.

The cops pulled up in front of the house. Jeremiah knew his fingerprints would be all over the place, but that wasn't uncommon, and he knew Joe would have his back.

Officer Joseph Smith had been like a second father to him. His wife had died while giving birth, so he was a lonely widower. He had nobody else, and Jeremiah felt that was why Joe had taken him under his wing.

On the nights Jeremiah's real father didn't come home he would call Joe, who would take him to his house, feed him, tell him a story, and put him to bed. Joe had taught him how to track animals and people during their many hunting trips in the Crimson Forest. So, when Jeremiah said he was the best tracker in town, Joe knew it.

He thought back to when Angelina had mentioned her fear that something was coming for her. Even in their younger years, she had felt she was being watched by something unseen. Now, he knew her fears had come true. He hoped she had successfully escaped whatever had come for her.

Marie ran up to him, puffy eyed and frantic. "Did you find anything?"

"When's the last time you talked to her?" he asked her calmly.

She looked up at him with fresh tears in her eyes. "She sent me an e-mail a few hours ago saying she had to go take care of something."

"What could she possibly have had to take care of this late at night?" he questioned, bending down to look for clues. His keen eyesight caught a faint blood trail in the grass that edged the sidewalk and he followed it. He touched it lightly with his fingertips. "Less than an hour old," he mumbled to himself, following the trail a little farther. He shook his head, realizing where it was leading him. He should have known. She had always been so stubborn. "Out of the frying pan and into the fire," he cursed under his breath. "Damn it, Angelina, I just got out of the forest. Now I have to go back in and search for you."

He looked back toward the house and saw Marie's shadow stumbling down the sidewalk toward him. He shoved his hands in his pockets and leaned up against the nearby streetlight.

"Did you find anything?" she asked, her eyes still red and swollen from crying.

"Marie, have you told anyone else what you've told me?"

"No, I haven't said anything to anyone except

you," she insisted, a fresh tear falling down her tan cheek.

"Good, let's keep it that way, at least for right now."

"What are you going to do?"

"I'm going to find her."

She reached over and hugged him. "Bring her back, Jeremiah, please."

He nodded. "I will. I promise. Look, I'll be right back. I've got to take care of something." He jogged back toward the bed and breakfast arriving just as the county officers were pushing past Joe to investigate for themselves what had happened. A few of them covered their mouths in disgust while the others jotted down notes.

He nodded toward Joe, who motioned him to come closer.

Jeremiah stood at the edge of the crowd. "Woods," he said.

"Tracks?"

Jeremiah nodded. "Time?"

"Not much. Will do what I can."

Jeremiah nodded again and disappeared into the crowd. He loved how they had their own secret lingo. He knew Joe wouldn't be able to buy him a ton of time, but he wasn't going to let Angelina down. He knew what he had to do, and he knew he had to do it alone.

14

Tracking Memories

Jeremiah crept down his driveway cautiously with the distinct feeling that he was being followed. He quickly unlocked his front door and went inside. He relocked it behind him and looked around his home before taking comfort on his old worn out sofa. He held his head in his hands and tried to quiet the guilt that plagued his thoughts. Angelina crossed his mind, and he was immediately reminded of how he loved everything about her, from her long, wild chestnut hair to the softness of her pale skin. Even the way she blushed when he joked with her and the curve of her beautiful apple red lips when she smiled at him made him as giddy as a school boy. Dang it, why hadn't he just told her how he really felt? He loved her.

Warm tears slid down his cheek and he shook his head. This was the most he had cried in years, and it was definitely a new experience. Wiping the tears away, his mind wandered back to the morning of the hunting party. Everyone had been so excited about the contest they were going to have to see which one of them could bring back the largest deer, and he had every intention of winning.

They had split up into groups of two before heading into the thick forest. Jeremiah paired up with Benjamin, an old farmer, and he felt pretty lucky with his partner choice because he knew

Benjamin had hunted these woods before and would know exactly where to go. They had crept silently through the woods, setting up cover under a large hollowed-out oak tree by the river. Luck continued to be on their side as a large white-tailed doe emerged from the edge of the forest. It walked toward them cautiously, thirsty for the cold water the river offered.

Jeremiah silently raised his bow and eyed his target. Smiling, he aimed directly for the doe's heart and let the arrow fly. But his smile disappeared quickly as a flash of red flew in between him and the animal. Surprised, he dropped his bow. He was astonished by the creature that stood in front of him. She looked human with her pale skin and long red hair, but her other features suggested she was something else. She had icy white eyes, and she appeared to be floating a few feet above the ground. His jaw dropped once he noticed she was holding the arrow he had just shot. She broke the arrow in half and threw it at his feet. "This will be your only warning," she hissed. "If you come into my forest again and hunt my animals, I will steal the life from your puny human body." She was gone as fast as she had appeared. He turned to see Benjamin running out of the forest as quick as his old legs would carry him. Jeremiah retrieved his bow and hurried to catch up.

After that, fear had weighed heavily on poor Benjamin and getting him to talk had been a challenge. The other groups had also witnessed similar occurrences. Strange, beautiful beings mysteriously showed up, threatening to take their lives if they didn't leave the forest and its animals alone. This sent a ripple of fear throughout the entire hunting party.

He shook off the image of the red-haired woman and stood up. He went over to his utility closet and grabbed three items: his bow, a backpack full of hunting gear, and a large Buck knife. He then headed to his bedroom where he opened his dresser drawer and took out his most prized possession. It was the first flat rock he had found while skipping rocks with Angelina. It was different than all the other rocks he had skipped because this particular rock was heart shaped. Angelina was so excited when he found it lying on the muddy shore of the river. It had always brought him good luck, and if there was anything he needed right now, it was good luck.

He shoved it in his pocket and continued rummaging through the drawer until he found a small photograph of him and Angelina. He smiled at the small image of her in her homemade Wonder Woman cape. It was her seventh birthday, and he remembered it fondly. She had disappeared for a short period of time, and he had gone to look for her. He had found her outside talking to something unseen and had merely dismissed it as being an invisible friend. Now he wondered if maybe there was someone there after all. He tucked the picture into his front shirt pocket and closed the drawer.

Back in the living room, he took one last look around before slowly unlocking the door. He turned the knob and sighed knowing he had no idea what he was up against. However, he knew Angelina was worth it, and he wasn't about to let her down. He would bring her back. He had to.

He walked out the door unafraid. He was a man with purpose and nothing was going to stop him. Once he found her, he would make it right and ask her to marry him. He would confess his love and never again make the mistake of letting her go.

~ ~ ~

Tracking Angelina into the crimson forest hadn't been easy. In fact, most of her tracks had been covered up, and he could tell they had been covered up on purpose. He had followed the river south toward the mountainous area of the northern highlands. There he had lost her tracks completely. It was as if she had disappeared into thin air.

Disappointed, he sat down on the edge of the river's sandy shore and admired the rushing water. This place had always been a retreat for him where he'd spent hours skipping rocks and just thinking about life. Many of those occasions also consisted of thoughts about Angelina. He remembered sitting for hours trying to talk himself out of telling her how he really felt. If he would've just been honest with her, he could've protected her from all this mess. He was the only man in her and her mother's lives, and he had failed both of them.

He picked up a rock and skipped it across the river. "One skip, two skips, thr . . ."

A female voice chimed in behind him, "Three skips."

He cursed under his breath for momentarily letting his guard down. He turned around and found himself face-to-face with the red-haired lady he had seen on the hunting trip. Her bare feet hung perfectly suspended just a few inches above the jagged rocks. He instinctively reached for the knife that was tucked into his belt, but found he was no match for her inhuman speed. She quickly pinned him to the hard rocky ground. She laughed in amusement as he tried to push her off of him.

"My, you're a handsome man."

"Get off me," he demanded. She currently had the advantage over him, so fighting her from this angle would be almost impossible.

"Aw, but that wouldn't be fun," she said with a smirk. "I kind of like this position."

"Yeah, well, I'm not a fan."

"I tell you what. I'm in a good mood today, so I'm going to offer you a deal, and I believe you'll agree, seeing how I know what you're looking for." She stood up and moved to the river.

His blue eyes widened. Could she really be talking about Angelina? He jumped to his feet and narrowed his eyes. "How do you know what I'm looking for?"

"I can see it in your heart. You ache for her." She entered the frigid water.

He studied her momentarily, noticing how her long, red hair lay perfectly across her pale shoulders and her icy white eyes looked almost translucent as the sun beamed down on her small frame. She turned and smiled at him, showing off perfect white teeth under her ruby red lips.

This is impossible, he thought. How long could these creatures have walked the earth unnoticed?

"Impossible? Not necessarily." She chuckled.

"You read my mind?"

"You humans are always so inquisitive," she stated, going deeper into the water. "Now, as I said before, I will make you a deal."

"What kind of deal?"

"I need something and only you can get it for me. I don't usually put this much faith in your kind, but your determination in this quest is quite impressive."

"If it gets Angelina back for me, I will do anything you ask."

She turned and looked at him. "Anything?"

"Yes, anything. I will do whatever it takes," he promised. His cheeks flushed, as he had never before had to beg a woman for anything in his life. It didn't matter. Angelina was worth it.

"What an interesting human to give up so much for such a simple thing as love." Her slender fingers rippled the surface of the water as her eyes glowed even brighter. "That is truly something I envy about your species."

"Why be envious? Love has caused me nothing but pain and suffering."

"Yes, but your heart feels much differently. Your brain may be angry at your circumstance, but, in the end, your heart always wins. That will be humanity's entire downfall."

She waded further into the glistening river and disappeared momentarily under the rushing water. He wondered what she was. Surely, she couldn't be a vampire because she didn't burst into flames from the sun or have pointy fangs. At the moment, he didn't really care. If she could help him get Angelina back, she could be an alien for all that mattered.

She stood up and brushed her wet hair back with pale hands. She rose up out of the water, dripping wet, and raised her arms over her head. Her eyes were now iridescent and an evil smirk graced her blood-red lips. "The deal shall consist of this. You will bring me a man named Nicolai. He will be a challenge for you, but, if you bring him to me, I will show you where your dear Angelina is. However, if you fail, I get to keep both of you. Do you agree?"

He nodded. "It sounds fair enough. Anything to get her back."

She clapped her dainty hands together. "Then it shall be."

The ground began to tremble and he watched in fascination as she floated over the water toward him. She stopped in front of him and took his left hand in hers. Her fingernails were bright, iridescent white. She lightly touched the palm of his hand with her index finger, illuminating it and causing an immense burning sensation to spread throughout his hand and into his arm. He grew dizzy from the excruciating pain. His stomach twisted and he fell to his knees. His vision blurred, and the throbbing in his head became almost unbearable. She finally let go of his hand and laughed in amusement.

"What have you done to me?" he growled.

"Our deal is now bound into a pact. However, I've added a little something extra to help you in your quest."

As the burning pain finally subsided, he breathed a sigh of relief. He closed his eyes and Angelina's face, so beautiful and innocent, appeared before him. He would do what was asked of him. He would do it for her.

He opened his eyes and blinked a few times. He held his hand up in front of his face and was amazed by what he saw. He could see every line, every freckle, and every hair on his hand. He focused on the forest in front of him and was able to see every line on every leaf, every twig on the ground. It was truly amazing. The red-haired woman had given him the ability to find the hidden tracks of Angelina and the man known as Nicolai.

The red-haired woman smirked and snapped her fingers. "Only because you amuse me, I'm going to give you an idea of who you'll be looking for."

An image flashed in his mind of a tall handsome man with jet-black hair and orange eyes walking next to Angelina. Ah, so this was the man he was in search of. He knew just from the quick vision that he wasn't going to like him. He felt a twinge of jealousy and wanted this man out of the picture.

"One more thing," the woman added, throwing a backpack toward him. "I found this bag here. Does it happen to look familiar?"

He caught it and smiled. He knew who this backpack belonged to—Angelina. He looked up to thank the woman, but she was already gone. Inside the bag was a dirty, bloody, tattered shirt. His heart skipped a beat. Angelina was injured. He threw the shirt to the ground and continued to riffle through the bag. He found her small knife and shoved it into his bootstrap for safe keeping. He tossed the bag into the rushing water and slung his own bag over his broad shoulders.

He bent down and moved some of the fallen leaves, which revealed a set of footprints leading into the forest. He knew where to go and was ready to do whatever it took to bring her back with him—even if it meant killing the strange man that traveled with her.

He jogged through the dense forest, following the newly highlighted trail. This wasn't going to be an easy fight, but he was ready and nothing was going to hold him back—not anymore.

After several hours of following their tracks, the sun began to dim behind the tops of the crimson leaves, and he figured it was time to find a place to set up camp. He found a fallen log and enough kindling to make a decent fire.

Returning to the log, he reached into his front pocket and took out the picture of him and Angelina. He admired her sweet face and smiled as the warmth of the flames comforted his mind and relaxed his body. His eyes grew heavy and he leaned back, holding the picture to his chest. Exhaustion from the day's events set in and he finally gave in to much-needed sleep.

He found himself dreaming of the red-haired woman. She pointed at a door that magically appeared in front of him.

"What's behind it?" he asked.

"I don't know. This is your dream," she answered, her icy white eyes glowing.

He cautiously turned the knob and opened it. He found himself staring at a room full of people dressed in formal dresses and suits. He was in awe as he realized he was back at his high school prom. He wasn't sure why she was showing him this but he knew there had to be a reason buried in this memory somewhere.

Prom night was meant to be special for everyone—the last dance before the big goodbye. He looked up and saw Angelina standing in the doorway. She had looked amazing that evening in a long, black gown that hugged her every curve with her long hair flowing freely around her pale face. Her full lips had been painted a luscious red, and her beautiful amber eyes were highlighted by a hint of makeup. He frowned as he watched her walk in alone. She had always been alone and that bothered him. In fact, he couldn't remember the last time he had seen her with a boyfriend, if ever.

She walked in and every head turned her way, yet she never noticed. She simply walked down the auditorium steps with a beautiful smile on her face and ran her nervous eyes over the crowd. He could tell by her posture that she was looking for a reason to turn around and walk right back out that door. He smiled and politely excused himself from his date. He grabbed Angelina by her delicate hand and pulled her out onto the dance floor. Her cheeks flushed red with embarrassment as he twirled her around, but she smiled and looked at him lovingly. At that very moment, he had wanted to kiss her, but he didn't want to let her down. He didn't want to hurt her.

He felt a light tap on his shoulder and turned around to see his date looking at him with a disappointed look on her dolled-up face. Angelina, looking even more embarrassed, politely excused herself, and made her way back toward the exit. He reached out for her, but she ignored him.

As she ran up the steps, a tall figure, pale and muscular with jet-black hair, held the door open for her. He seemed to be engrossed in her every move.

Jeremiah felt an annoyed tug on his hand from his date and turned around, confused as to what he should do. She put her arms around his neck and provocatively nibbled on his ear. He smiled and spun her around, as the stranger seemed to magically disappear from his mind and, for a brief moment, so did Angelina.

Laughter woke him and he jumped to his feet. He looked around his campsite, ready for a fight, but soon realized he was alone.

The stranger with the jet-black hair—how had Jeremiah forgotten him? Surely he'd seen him the night of the prom, but something or someone had hidden it from his memory. He knew the red-haired lady had shown him this memory now, and he knew why. How long had this stranger been following Angelina?

If Jeremiah had just paid enough attention to her, like he should have, he would've seen the warning signs a long time ago. He could've stopped the stranger who, he now knew, was the one and only Nicolai.

15

Secrets Unlocked

Jeremiah bent down and grabbed a handful of leaves. He rubbed them between his dirty hands and frowned. There was now a third set of tracks. By the size and shape of them, he knew it had to be another man. He already knew Nicolai was going to be a challenge for him, so having another man in the mix wasn't ideal. He sighed and stood up. He could tell they were at least half a day ahead of him by the staleness of the tracks. If he wanted to catch up with them, he would have to pick up the pace.

With no time to waste he ran through the woods, dodging the occasional small plant, and jumping over broken branches. He had been given a great gift, and he wasn't about to take it for granted. His heart raced a bit faster as his heightened senses warned him that something or someone was nearby. Keeping the same pace, he acted as if he hadn't noticed the strange creature and slowly reached for the knife tucked carefully into his belt holster. He gripped the handle and prepared himself.

The creature jumped out at him from behind a tree and knocked him to the ground. He pulled the knife out and stabbed the air blindly, trying his best to wound his attacker. The creature's scream told him he had hit his mark. He rolled over and jumped up, coming face to face with another pale woman, only this one had long blond hair and eyes bluer than the sky.

She held her wounded shoulder and glared. "You humans—you are such a waste."

"You know what, whatever you are, whoever you are, I'm only going to warn you once: I'm on a mission and it's best if you stay out of my way," he snarled back.

"I don't care what kind of bull crap mission you're on. All I know is that I'm going to break every single one of your puny human bones and leave you here for the vultures to feed on." She lurched toward him.

He braced himself for her attack. "Try me."

She came at him full force and swung her fist toward his face. He barely dodged the blow and sliced her cheek with his blade. She screamed again and jumped on him, wrapping her pale arms around his neck. He swung her around and managed to slam her up against a tree. She cried out in pain as the tree splintered. Like a human leech, she held on, but when her grip around his neck loosened, he knew he had weakened her.

"Usually, girls don't want to wrestle like this with me," he grunted as he continued to try to pry her off his back.

He spotted a large rock a few feet away and fell to his knees. If he could get to it, he could use it as a weapon. She bit down on his shoulder and clawed at his face.

He smacked her hands away and, through clenched teeth, he growled. "Woman, you are more annoying than a hungry mosquito in the middle of June."

He thrust his body toward the rock. Wrapping his strong hand around it, he raised it over his head and used every bit of his strength to hit her with it. Fresh air rushed into his lungs. The woman lay motionless on the ground with her pretty blond hair turning red from the injury to her head. He knew he had to act quickly before she woke up, so he reached for the coil of rope that was in his backpack and bound her hands and feet, checking the knots every few minutes to make sure they were tight enough that his womanly foe had no chance of escaping.

He studied her features and realized she resembled the red-haired woman. They both had pale skin, odd-colored eyes, and amazing strength. He holstered his knife and took a long drink from a bottle of water he had stashed at the last moment. The forest he had loved so much was turning out to be nightmare. He was amazed anyone in his town was still alive with all the odd creatures that lived nearby.

He set the half-empty bottle on the ground, ran his hands through his blond hair, and watched the strange woman's chest move up and down slowly. He was glad to see she was still breathing because he had some questions he needed answers to, and he needed them now. He hoped she had some information as to where Angelina and Nicolai were heading. He grabbed a nearby stick and started poking her in the side. She began to stir, so he bent down to move bloody strands of hair from her face. She opened her eyes and looked stunned to find herself bound up by a human.

"Untie me now, or you'll truly regret the day you were ever born," she growled.

"Lady, please, my father made me feel like that

years ago." He smirked. "Now be a pretty little girl and tell me who you are and why you attacked me."

"You don't need to know who I am, and you don't know the meaning of attack. It's only a matter of time before I kill you."

He sat down in front of her and smiled. "Well, we'll see about that now won't we?"

They stared at each other for a moment, testing each other in silence. She finally gave up and let out a long drawn-out sigh.

"You're not going to untie me, are you?"

"Nope."

"You're pretty determined, aren't you?"

"Yup."

"Well, then. What are you doing here? You said you were a man on a mission."

"I'm looking for someone—a woman with long, dark hair. She's traveling with a man who's like you."

He watched as a look of surprise crossed her face.

"Would her name be Angelina?" she asked raising an eyebrow.

"Yes, that's her," he said, returning the surprised look. "The man she travels with is to be returned to a red-haired lady that is also of your kind."

"Red-haired lady?" she questioned.

"Yes, we made a deal. However, she made it a point to say she wanted the man brought back to her."

"Untie me. I can help you," she urged.

He laughed and stood up. "Right, because that's a smart idea. I'll untie you, and we'll have round two of who's going to kill who."

"No," she replied looking up at him, "I'm being quite serious. I can help you. I know the red-haired lady you speak of. Her name is Ctephanyi, and I'm also on a very similar quest."

He narrowed his eyes at her and wondered if she had the ability to tell the truth. What was the worst that could happen? He would have to kill her? The reward of her helping him was definitely worth the risk.

"I tell you what. I'll untie you if you promise to help me. But if you try anything stupid, I'll make you regret it."

She nodded in agreement.

He bent down in front of her and, with one swift movement, cut the rope off her bound wrists. With a flash, she jumped up and rubbed at the red marks on her wrists. He watched in amazement as the marks began to disappear.

"Well, human, what are you waiting for? We've already wasted too much time messing around."

He picked his bag up. "You're right." In an attempt to show her good faith, he held out his free hand. "I'm glad you realize I'm a human, but I would much rather you call me by my given name."

She looked at his hand and smirked. "Well, human, what would your given name be?"

"Jeremiah."

"Well, Jeremiah, I am Laurana," she answered with a firm handshake.

He wasn't surprised by the strength of her handshake. Frankly, nothing surprised him anymore. The last few days had proven to him that there were definitely unexplainable things in the world.

"Shall we be on our way then?" she asked, her blue eyes sparkling.

Looking ahead, he could see faint tracks in the leaves. "Looks like we're heading this way" he stated, following the tracks through the forest.

She walked next to him in silence. His mind began to wander and he was curious as to what she was. Looking at her pale features, he noticed she looked mostly human like the other woman. However, there were slight differences such as her strength, the way she seemed to float over the ground when she walked, and her eyes. He had never seen a color more amazing than the color of her eyes. They reminded him of a snowstorm over the ocean—frigid and frightening. When he fought her, they became a bright, beautiful translucent blue. He knew it wasn't humanly possible to have eye color such as that and wondered if she hid them with contacts when coming in contact with normal people. Laurana turned to look at him. Feeling embarrassed, he turned his head toward the trees.

"Don't be embarrassed," she said with a laugh.

He lied, "I'm not."

"I get looks such as yours often. It's in your nature to be curious about creatures that are unknown to you."

"What exactly are you?"

Smiling, she looked up at the sky. "I'm a very old species that has long since been forgotten."

"Are you, like, a vampire?"

She laughed again and looked at him. "We get mistaken for them often. Vampires are very similar to our kind, but we are much older than they are. Plus, we don't have fangs."

"Wait—so vampires do exist?"

"Oh yes, and so do many other mythical creatures that your race writes books about. We often laugh at how close to the truth you really are. You don't even realize that when you're walking down the street, you could be right next to one of us, or something just as deadly. Your race is so caught up within itself that ignorance is truly bliss."

"Well, I suppose you're right in that respect. Now, I know a man should never ask a woman this, but I feel as though I have to."

"What question would that be?"

"Well, you say you're a species that has long been forgotten. Just how old are you?"

She looked thoughtful for a moment, "Do you remember the story of Vlad the Impaler?"

"Wait—you mean Count Dracula?"

She laughed at the reference. "I was the archer that killed his first wife."

"Hold on a minute. I remember that story. Didn't she jump from the tower?"

"Ah, historians do love making up their own stories when they don't have all the facts. What's even more amusing is you humans believe every word."

He did the math in his head. "That was over 500 years ago!" he exclaimed, trying his best to hide the look of utter surprise on his face. "Well then, I must admit, you look great for your age."

He thought he saw her face flush.

"Thank you, I think," she answered quietly adding, "There are others much older than myself."

"Older than you? Do they all look as great as you do?"

"Well, we all have very similar features. You can tell us apart by our eye color. The older you are, the lighter your eyes become."

"So, this Ctephanyi, how old is she?" he asked.

"She's the oldest of all of us. She was one of the first creatures to ever arrive on this godforsaken place. She's very powerful."

"You sound like you're afraid of her."

She looked down at the ground. "I do not cross her. She has a very unforgiving nature and holds no sympathy for any creature."

"What about this Nicolai?"

She frowned and looked at him. "Nicolai is Ctephanyi's son."

Jeremiah swallowed hard. "Her son?"

Laurana nodded.

Great, he thought to himself. Not only was the man that had Angelina an inhuman species with an immense amount of power, he was also the son of the wicked red witch he had met earlier. Things had just gotten very complicated.

16

History Lesson

Laurana could see the torment on Jeremiah's face and continued on with her story. "You see, Nicolai was banished many years ago from our home for falling in love with a human. We are not allowed to speak of him when we're in her presence."

"So it's forbidden for your race to fall in love with any other species?"

"Yes, especially humans."

"So Nicolai basically did the teenage rebellious thing and defied his mother's wishes."

"No and yes. You see Ctephanyi had sent him to retrieve a human sacrifice. She believed that sacrificing a human every one hundred years would keep the powerful Goddess Hecate happy and keep our race alive. During his task, Nicolai came upon a young girl in the woods. She was picking berries with her father when a large black bear came upon them. Her father fought the best he could, but both her father and the bear ended up severely wounded. Nicolai stood nearby and watched as the young girl cried over her father's broken body. She laid her hand upon his motionless chest and begged for his soul to return. However, it was too late for him. His soul had already traveled to the other side. After a brief moment of saying her goodbyes to her father, she crawled over to the wounded bear, which was still alive, and placed her hands over its wounds. The bear groaned in pain and kicked its legs in protest as she ran her hands down its body, encouraging it to be still. In between heavy breaths, the bear let out a low growl and began to stand up. She nodded at the bear with an angelic look upon her face, and it walked away.

"So she healed it?"

She nodded. "That's the story at least."

"So, how did Nicolai actually meet her?"

"Well, he was so amazed by what he had seen that he let his guard down, and she saw him. He claimed that he had never laid eyes on such a beautiful human in all the hundreds of years he had been alive. There was something special about her, and he wanted to keep her all to himself. He had, as you humans call it, fallen in love at first sight. From that moment, he knew he could never let any of our species know of her special talents. He decided that day that he would become her protector, and would keep her safe from all harm, including his own mother. However, Ctephanyi found out, and it angered her so much that she banished him."

Jeremiah was intrigued by the story. "So they lived happily ever after?"

"No. Though she was only seventeen, she accepted his marriage proposal, and they were married the following fall. That following spring, a woman his new wife considered to be a mother figure came down with a mysterious illness. This upset his wife greatly. She tried to heal the woman, but, for some reason, her magic failed, so she begged Nicolai to let her go into town to get some traditional medicines. Though he didn't like the idea of his new bride wandering around alone, he agreed this one time to stay behind and keep the woman safe. His wife assured him that she would be fine on her own. Time ticked away slowly, and he began to worry as minutes turned into hours with no word from her. When he finally couldn't take it anymore, he went in search of her and was horrified by what he found."

"She was with another man?" Jeremiah joked.

Laurana didn't laugh. "Not quite. When she was nearly to town, she came upon three men whose carriage had a broken wheel. She offered to help them, and they took advantage of her kindness. They attacked her and dragged her broken body into the woods. By the time Nicolai found her, she was almost gone. The men happened to still be there, and he had made them all pay dearly, though he now carries a large scar on his arm."

"So, he lost her." Jeremiah felt a moment of sadness. He couldn't imagine losing Angelina forever.

"Temporarily."

"What do you mean, temporarily?"

Laurana gave him a mischievous smile. "Nicolai summoned his mother and begged her to save the life of his human bride. Ctephanyi refused, which angered him and, that very moment, he made a promise to kill every one of our species off until she agreed to do it. She laughed at him and left him there with his new bride. For months following his wife's death, he sought out his revenge by killing his own kind. He had the gift of silence, allowing him to surprise his prey. Finally, when Ctephanyi felt enough blood had been spilled, she decided it was time to make him a deal. She would bring his wife back to life under certain conditions. When she was old enough to be on her own, he had to bring her back into the woods to be turned into one of us. Ctephanyi would not allow her to stay human, as it was our greatest law."

"Did he do it?"

Laurana nodded. "He agreed. But to make him suffer even more, Ctephanyi sent him on a task. He had to find a newborn soulless child whose parents were so grief stricken they were willing to do anything to have their child back. "

"Why a baby?"

A wicked smile fell upon her face. "As a punishment for killing their own kind, Ctephanyi was going to make Nicolai watch his young wife grow up again. She wouldn't remember who he was, and he would have to make her fall in love with him all over again."

"That's pretty harsh." Jeremiah almost felt pity for the poor guy—almost. "So did he ever find anyone like that?"

"Yes, he did. In his search to find the perfect couple, he became a doctor in a maternity ward."

"That's clever."

"Well, when you've been around for thousands of years, it's easy to become anything you want to be. We are an intelligent species after all."

He snickered. "I'm seeing that."

"One night, as he was delivering a child, the mother had severe complications which made the delivery very hard. The mother survived, but the baby girl did not."

"So, what happened?"

"Nicolai made a deal with the father of the

child. The mother was still drugged and had not yet been told of the child's demise. He told the father that he could make his baby girl come back to life, and that the father would get to raise the child as his own for twelve years. After that time, she would have to go with Nicolai into the forest. The father, being completely grief stricken, agreed."

Realization set in as the words came out of Jeremiah's mouth. "So Ctephanyi put the soul of Nicolai's wife into the stillborn baby?"

"Yes. And to further punish her son for his sin, she cast a glamour spell over him so that when his wife was old enough to see him, he would look different to her. That way, memories of her past life wouldn't be triggered by his unique features."

"Wow, that's terrible."

She looked at him, expressionless. "Is it?"

He shrugged. "So, whatever happened to this child?" he asked, ignoring her question.

"Well, it seems you're looking for her right now."

"You mean—Angelina is . . ."

"Yes, that's exactly what I mean."

"So, what now? What happens when Ctephanyi gets Nicolai back? What does she plan on doing with him?"

Laurana shook her head. "Nicolai has disappointed his mother again, and this time, she isn't going to be so forgiving."

"What could he have possibly done to make her even angrier than being with a human?"

"When Angelina wasn't returned as promised, Ctephanyi claimed her father's soul instead. She tortured him daily, promising to make him pay for not honoring their bargain. One night, as she was preoccupied with another business matter, Nicolai snuck in and freed him. He's managed to keep him hidden as well."

"So, now Nicolai has both of them."

"Yes, but not for long. You see when you're as powerful as Ctephanyi is, you can make anyone do anything you want." Laurana looked down shamefully.

Jeremiah suspected Ctephanyi had probably made Laurana, along with many other species, do her dirty work. The more he learned about Ctephanyi, the more he hated her. After he returned Nicolai, he had every intention of taking Angelina and leaving. He knew what Ctephanyi was capable of, and he didn't want any part of it.

They continued to walk in silence. Occasionally, Laurana would point out a track or look at him with a weird expression on her face. He was curious what was on her mind. He wondered about the other creatures he probably walked by every day. That thought scared him, especially after meeting this particular species. It amazed him that the stories of the creatures in the forest were, in fact, true. All the years of hunters running out of the forest claiming they had seen things that would change them forever, and now he knew he would be one of them. How could anyone be the same after such an adventure, especially after the things he had seen? That's what scared him the most. His soul felt hardened by the things that had happened in the last few days. A little part of him liked how he now felt; the other part missed the innocence he no longer had.

The sun finally set and darkness surrounded them. Jeremiah stopped briefly to check for fresh tracks. He looked up and smiled once he realized they were only an hour behind Angelina and Nicolai. Jeremiah knew they would be asleep soon and that would give him the perfect opportunity for a surprise attack. He was pleased by his new ability, and having Laurana with him gave him more confidence about his confrontation with Nicolai.

Laurana looked down at him. "We're close."

"Yes, about an hour to the east," he replied. "They've most likely stopped for the night. This gives us a huge advantage."

"You're right. We will sneak in while they're asleep."

Jeremiah grinned. "They'll never see us coming."

She peered into the dark forest. "We're close to town."

"How close?"

"Close enough," she replied vaguely.

"Well, then, I suppose we should pick up the pace." He stood back up and began jogging down the path.

He felt Laurana beside him, and his heart jumped at the thought of being reunited with Angelina. He didn't care if she had been Nicolai's in the past. She was different now. Nicolai had had his chance to protect her, and he had failed. Now it was Jeremiah's turn to prove to her that he was the better man, and that's exactly what he planned to do.

17

Darkness

I had hoped that we were done spending the night in the wretched forest. However, we ended up settling down to yet another campfire. The air was crisp, and the moon was a bright beacon over the dark treetops. I lay on my back staring up at the sky, and wondered what Jeremiah was doing at that very moment. I missed my friend, and I was sure he was devastated by my disappearance. I was curious if he had sent out a search party to look for me, and I was sure they had found my poor mother. I wondered how my life would change once we were able to get out of the forest and return to town. So many things had happened to make me a different person than I was, and I wasn't quite sure I was ready to deal with the aftermath of my new life.

I glanced at Nicolai and saw a look of worry once again plague his handsome face. For the last hour, he had been going on that something or someone was coming after us. Once my father decided it was time to camp, Nicolai protested. Perhaps he was afraid Ctephanyi or Laurana would find me and, in his mind, that was not an option.

The flames licked the air angrily, and I could see my father had fallen asleep next to his hero. I was curious if Nicolai ever slept. Probably not. He was definitely a unique creature.

As if he had been listening in on my thoughts

again, I felt a cool hand on my cheek. "Well, hey there, beautiful. Admiring the stars, are we?"

I put my hand over his. "Them and, of course, you."

He kissed my forehead and lay down next to me. I cuddled up next to him and lay my head on his chest, surprised by the emptiness of a nonexistent heartbeat.

"Your heart. It's not beating," I exclaimed.

He laughed and ran his hands through my hair. "I know."

"How are you still alive?"

"Anything is possible, my dear. There are so many things about this life that you do not understand. Once we get out of this place, I will tell you anything you want to know."

I kissed his smooth chin. "Anything?"

He returned the kiss to my lips. "Absolutely. I have waited a lifetime to tell you about the world."

I loved the way he kissed me. His lips were so soft and cool, so full of passion and love. I wanted to spend the rest of my life just kissing him.

I cuddled closer to him and nuzzled his neck. "Will you tell me just one little thing about myself that I don't know?"

He was thoroughly amused. "Oh, so you think you can bribe me with these wonderful little kisses into telling you things you need to learn on your own?"

"Of course. Is it not working?" I offered another kiss, this time to his cheek.

"I don't know . . .," he teased.

"Well then, I suppose I shall have to keep

trying." I kissed the tip of his perfect nose, and then reached over to kiss his eyebrow and forehead. The little butterflies made themselves known by fluttering around in my stomach as he wrapped his arms around me. My hair fell into my face, and he delicately pushed away the fallen strands. I stared into his beautiful eyes and smiled. I couldn't believe I had found someone so perfect.

"Please?" I begged, kissing him one more time.

He laughed and propped himself up with his elbow. "My, you're a little devil, aren't you?"

"Only when I'm with you," I answered innocently.

"Fine, I will tell you of our wedding day."

My eyes widened. "What? I'm only eighteen. I've never been married."

"You see, sometimes past lives cross each other and, my dear, we were definitely married."

"Married?" I whispered, astounded by the news.

"Oh yes, it was the second best day of my existence."

"What was your first?" I questioned, raising an eyebrow.

"The day I met you."

"Good answer." My heart melted. "Well, let's hear it then. I mean, after everything I've been through, I just want to know who I am and solve this puzzle before I go crazy."

"Fair enough," he said with a nod. "It was a warm fall day. The leaves were their beautiful crimson color, and we had decided to have an evening wedding so we could watch the sunset through the trees. We had invited a few close friends and the woman who had cared for you as a child. Everyone was so happy for us, especially the woman. In fact, she didn't even mind that I wasn't human." He winked.

"So, she knew that you weren't like us?"

"Oh yes. The woman was very different. She had a sense about people, and the first time you took me to meet her, she just knew. Now, don't get me wrong. She did warn you that I was a dangerous, sexy creature, but she could see the love in my heart, and she knew I would never let any harm come to you."

"Sexy, huh?" I rolled my eyes. "Go on, tell me about our special day."

"Well, the woman spent countless hours making you the perfect dress, and you looked absolutely beautiful in it. When you appeared at the end of that flowered aisle and began walking toward me . . .," his eyes wandered up to the sky, "I felt as if the gods had given me my own personal angel."

"Nicolai?"

"Hmm?"

"What did I look like?" I asked quietly.

Smiling, he turned and put his hand on my face. "You actually looked very similar to what you look like now. The only difference is that now you've been given some of your parents' genetic traits, like your mother's figure, and your father's freckles.

"Do you think I'm just as beautiful?" I looked down, afraid of his answer.

He put his hand under my chin. "They say beauty is in the eye of the beholder, but how can anyone look at you and not know how incredibly perfect you are?"

My heart skipped a beat, and I sighed. Things were beginning to make sense, and I felt as if I finally had a purpose—to make Nicolai happy. He lay on his back, and I put my head on his chest, which he kissed lovingly.

I could feel myself slowly starting to fall asleep. "Nicolai?"

"Yes, my dear?"

I closed my eyes. "Please don't leave me."

"Angelina, not a soul on earth could move me from your side."

With that, I fell into a peaceful sleep, dreaming of my past, hoping for a much better future with the man I had come to love more than life itself.

~ ~ ~

I awoke with a jolt and instantly knew something was wrong. Nicolai was no longer next to me. So much for the whole "not a soul could move me from your side" speech. I stood up, somewhat shaky. The early morning air was still crisp, and the wetness from the dew had begun to settle on the ground. I crept quietly over to my sleeping father and gently woke him.

"What is it?" he replied, startled.

I put my fingers to my lips to quiet him. "Listen."

We both listened to the stillness around us and, sure enough, I heard a twig break in the distance. We both jumped when Nicolai suddenly appeared in front of us.

"We must go now. They're near," he urged, taking my hand.

"Who?" I questioned, fear causing my heart to beat ferociously.

"No time for questions. We must leave now." He pulled me gently. "Town is closer than I thought. We need to head south."

Sensing the urgency in his voice, I nodded and grabbed my father by the hand. We stumbled blindly in the early morning darkness. My father quietly cursed behind us as Nicolai led the way through the thick brush. Suddenly, there was a deafening thud, and my father's hand was ripped away from mine. I cringed at the sound of something heavy being dragged away from me through the fallen leaves.

I stopped dead in my tracks, "No!"

"Angelina, we must go!" Nicolai persisted, pulling me toward him.

I ripped myself free from his grasp. "No, I can't lose him again. I turned around and tried to follow the heart-wrenching noise. Nicolai was behind me, but for the first time, I surprised myself by being faster than he was.

The forest grew eerily quiet, and I fell to my knees, frantically searching for my father's fallen body. Though fear gripped my heart, my instincts kicked in, and I managed to find a small branch. I held it firmly with both hands and waited for whatever monster was coming for me. As if I had been blessed with a psychic sense, a strong hand grabbed my arm. I swung that small branch with every bit of the anger and hatred that had built up within my body over the past few days. The hand let go. I jumped up, and another hand grabbed my leg. Screaming, I looked down and saw my father's bloody face staring up at me.

"Angelina, they're here to take you. Go on without me," he begged.

I bent down and pulled him up. "No, I won't lose you again."

I heard a loud commotion nearby and knew Nicolai had come in contact with what was after us.

Tree limbs suddenly began falling down around us.

"Come on, let's go!" I yelled to my father.

As we stumbled through the forest, I noticed a light coming from up ahead. My heart leapt as I realized it was the edge of the forest. We ran toward the tree line as the limbs continued to fall around us.

"No," I gasped, and, for the second time, my hand was empty.

"Run, Angelina, run!" my father yelled through muffled cries.

The decision was mine: keep running, or stop and try to help. I took a deep breath and turned around. I was nothing without Nicolai or my father, and I would do whatever I needed to do to keep them safe.

I dropped to the ground and searched for something I could use to protect myself. Clenching a medium-sized rock in my trembling hand, I tried not to panic as a shadow moved toward me from within the darkness. I braced myself.

It was Laurana and, this time, I faced her alone.

"Well, Angelina, looks like we meet again,"

she said with a smirk.

The rock in my trembling hand seemed like a pebble in comparison to the power she held, and I fought the temptation to throw it at her and run.

She grinned evilly. "I told you we would meet again, only this time I brought a friend." She looked toward the forest.

"I'm quite surprised you have any friends." My nerves began to settle as anger built up inside me.

"Oh, you're such a funny little girl, aren't you?"

I rolled my eyes. "Yeah, I'm such a comedian."

"I tell you what. I will give you one more chance to come with me, only because I find you to be quite amusing."

"Well, I hate to let you down again, but my answer is still no."

She shook her head and began walking toward me slowly. "What a shame."

"Want to see what's shameful?" I replied, waiting for the right moment.

Intrigued, she stopped right in front of me. "Enlighten me. What's so shameful?"

"This." I swung the hand that held the rock and hit her square in the jaw. The surprise on her face was priceless, and I took the opportunity to run. I wasn't fast enough and winced at the pain as she grabbed my arm and squeezed. Bones snapped, causing me to fall to my knees and warm tears to fall down my cheeks. Laurana let go and laughed.

Her blond hair blew wickedly in the cool breeze. "Did you think you were really a match for me, human?"

She suddenly flew backwards. I looked up and saw Nicolai's bright orange eyes peering at me through the darkness. I winced in pain as he picked me up and began to run back toward the edge of the forest.

"Did she hurt you?" he demanded.

I held my arm close to my body. "I think my arm is broken."

"We need to get you to a hospital."

The bright lights at the edge of the forest gave me hope. I prayed we would get out alive, but I feared for my father.

I peered into the darkness over Nicolai's shoulder. Maybe my father had gotten away. Laurana would be after us shortly, and I knew if she caught up to us, she wasn't about to play nice.

"Don't worry, I will get you out of here," Nicolai reassured me.

I smiled weakly in return. "I trust you."

I lay my head against his shoulder and enjoyed the cool air rushing against my flushed cheeks. I tried not to think of the horrors that awaited me, or the throbbing pain from my broken arm. Instead, I concentrated on Nicolai and his determination to get me to safety.

Without warning, Nicolai yelled out a slew of words in a language that I had never heard before. He stumbled forward, and I flew out of his arms and slid across the harsh ground, somehow miraculously missing a tree. I was stunned. What had just happened?

Something whizzed past my face and nicked my cheek. My hand instinctively went to the fresh wound as warm, wet blood ran down my face. I rolled over onto my stomach to put myself as close to the ground as possible and used my good arm to crawl toward the edge of the woods.

I knew it couldn't be Laurana. It had to be the person she brought with her, and the thing that had nicked my cheek had to be an arrow. I didn't know where this potentially dangerous marksman was, but I had to move as fast as I could to get out of there. Someone grabbed my ankle, and I turned over kicking whoever it was in the face. I heard the muffled groan of a man. This was it, my chance to get away. I stood up and ran. Even though I was now a perfect target, I had to take the risk. If I continued to crawl, I would never make it out alive.

Tears of happiness began to fall as I stumbled out of the woods and onto a paved road, followed by insane laughter once I realized the forest continued on the other side. This was just my luck. I wiped away the tears with dirty, trembling hands, and ran down the road hoping a car would stop and save me from the monsters in the darkness.

I heard a noise behind me and turned around just as a male figure made his way out of the forest a few yards away. Bright lights caught my attention, and I turned back to see fast-approaching headlights. I stumbled down the road, waving my good arm in the air in an attempt to get the driver's attention. The man yelled something behind me but I ignored him, as the car got closer.

"Stop!" I begged as the car began to slow down. As I stumbled toward it, something caught my eye in one of the tall pine trees. I looked up and watched in horror as it jumped out of the tree and landed on the hood of the car. I put my hands over my ears to muffle the sound of metal crunching and tires popping. The dark figure turned around and smiled. Laurana. Amusement played across her pale face as she jumped off the crushed car and, with one hand, pushed the vehicle into the ditch. I felt sick to my stomach knowing that someone else had become injured because of me.

She smoothed out her shirt. "Shall we quit playing games now? I'm beginning to get annoyed."

I looked past her and could see another car coming toward us. It was as if a little light bulb turned on over my head. "You know, when I was a little girl, my mother told me if I couldn't say anything nice then I should say nothing at all."

"Well let's not disappoint her then. Oh wait, she's not here to disappoint anymore now, is she."

Her comment stung, and my hatred for her grew even more. My eyes focused on the oncoming headlights. The timing had to be perfect, otherwise my plan would fail.

"I'm not afraid of you."

"You should be," she replied, reaching for me.

I shifted my weight and threw my body into her, causing her to stumble right into the path of the oncoming car. The sound of her body hitting the metal frame was bone chilling. I closed my eyes as the car came to a screeching stop. I heard footsteps behind me, and my eyes fluttered open. It was too late. Something hard bashed into my head, and I fell to the ground with blood running down my face. My vision blurred as I tried to identify my attacker. The male figure stared back at me. He looked oddly familiar.

"Please. No," I begged.

He raised the object in his hand and hit me again. My eyes dimmed as the blood began to pour out of the deep gash on my forehead. I lay on the pavement and wished for death. Life had a funny way of repeating itself. I envisioned myself in the white dress with Nicolai by my side, my blood soaked hair floating around my face. I reached up and touched the shadow of a memory. My hand fell limply to my side as the darkness wrapped its satiny black blanket around me and took me to a place I had been before, a place I never wanted to return to.

18

Misguided Trust

Jeremiah brushed away the torment his heart felt from hitting Angelina, but he was afraid if he hadn't knocked her out, Laurana would have done something much worse. He knew the evil Laurana was capable of. He turned around and stared into the darkness. The forest beckoned him to finish what he had started with Nicolai. He had left him in the woods, wounded by an arrow that he had shot into his shoulder. After a fierce struggle, he managed to shoot another arrow into Nicolai's leg, though he almost hit Angelina in the head with a misfire. There was not a doubt in his mind that Nicolai could magically heal himself. He knew it was only a matter of time before he was looking for them.

He heard the sound of metal being pushed across the road and looked up. Laurana emerged unscathed from underneath the crushed car. He frowned at the thought of her still being alive. He didn't like the fact that she cared so little for humanity. If she had it her way, she would much rather watch humans suffer than be happy.

He bent down and pushed Angelina's blood soaked hair out of her face. She looked pitiful, so battered and broken. Her arm was bent at an odd ankle, and he assumed it was broken. She had bruises on her pale skin, along with numerous cuts on her arms and face. He lightly touched the spot he had nicked on accident with his arrow.

Her head was bleeding heavily from where he had hit her. He had never meant for her to hurt like this.

He carefully picked up her limp body and sighed. If she were to find out he had worked with Laurana to find her, she would never forgive him. However, now that he had her, he wasn't about to let her go. He had done what he came to do. Now he just needed to get her home.

"Where do you think you're going?" Laurana asked smugly.

"I'm taking her home. I helped you get Nicolai. He's out in the woods waiting for you," he replied calmly as he turned to walk down the road toward town.

Laurana laughed wickedly. "Oh, you just thought I was going to let you take her and that was going to be it?"

"We had a deal, and I had a deal with Ctephanyi. I've kept to my part. Now, you keep to yours."

"I'm afraid that your part of the deal has not been kept. You promised to take Nicolai back to Ctephanyi."

Jeremiah stopped and turned around to face her. She was right. He had promised to take Nicolai back to Ctephanyi. He felt as if this nightmare would never end.

"Well, where did you leave him?" she asked.

"He's just before the edge of the woods. He's wounded and I'm sure he's going to be angry."

"Now, that sounds like a fun time. Shall we go get him?" She winked.

He nodded and pulled Angelina's limp body closer to him. He wasn't going to let her out of his sight again. He also knew if he didn't keep to his part of the bargain, they would take her from him and most likely end his life. That wasn't something he was going to risk.

~ ~ ~

Nicolai pushed himself up against a tree, grabbed the arrow that was lodged in his shoulder and, as he bit down on a broken branch, slowly pulled it out. He broke it in half and threw it into the darkness. He took a deep breath and concentrated on the second arrow that was stuck in his leg. This one proved to be more of a challenge because it was lodged deep inside his thigh muscle. Thoughts of Angelina falling into Laurana's hands crossed his mind as he grabbed the end of the arrow. He used the anger that came with the vision to fight back the pain as he pulled. He broke the arrow in half, but, this time, he saved the arrow tip. He put pressure on his leg and hoped it would heal fast enough that he could save Angelina. He was certain she would only be able to defend herself for a short period of time. The human traveling with Laurana was familiar, and Nicolai was curious why he was so eager to help her.

Anger welled up inside him. He wanted to make them both pay for the suffering they had brought to him and Angelina. He had suffered long enough without Angelina in his life, and it was their turn to be happy. He had endured watching her grow up before his very eyes and had waited so patiently for the day to come that he could make her his again.

Something had happened during the night of the soul rising. Angelina had come back with her powers embedded inside her new body. They had somehow transferred themselves from her previous life. He knew if his mother were to find out, she would want to change her immediately. Anyone more powerful than she was a threat.

Angelina's past life had been hidden from her for a reason. It was only after they took their vows that she confessed her most valuable secret to him—who and what she really was. He now knew his mother had been tricked into raising this particular soul, and if Angelina recovered any remnants of her past life—he shuddered at the thought. When he told her that she was the most lethal creature known to man, he meant it.

His body tingled as it began to heal itself. It was only a matter of time before he could stand beside his true love and defend her. He lay his head against the soft, red mossy tree and closed his eyes. He smiled at the memory of Angelina thinking she could fly like her heroine. He still remembered the anxiety he felt when she climbed out onto the edge of that roof. She had jumped off, flapping those tiny little arms like a new baby bird learning to use its wings for the first time. He had never moved so quickly in his entire life. He barely caught her in time. Then she looked up at him with those big, beautiful chestnut colored eyes. It was in that moment that he saw her old soul trapped within her new body, and it had given him the hope he needed—the hope she would one day remember who he was. That very moment, he knew they were destined to be together forever. Fate had played its part, and now it was time Nicolai played his.

Keeping her safe had definitely been a challenge because she had been such a curious child. Everything seemed to intrigue her. In the span of five years, he had saved her more times than he had fingers and toes. His heart still ached from all the mini heart attacks she had given him.

There was the incident with the rare Massasauga Rattlesnake. While playing in the woods, she saw it lying under a rock and thought it would make a great house pet—until it bit her. Then there was the time she climbed to the top of an old oak tree in order to see heaven. All was fine until she jumped up to touch the bright yellow dot in the sky and fell out of the tree.

He shook his head and smiled. He remembered the conversation her father had with him.

"Nicolai, I know she's meant to be yours, but for right now, she's mine. Now, I don't mind you coming around and keeping her safe and all, but know that, as a father, I still have my eye on you."

Nicolai laughed to himself. Typical father, he thought. The smile left his face as he recalled the day her father disappeared because he refused to give up his only daughter. That was the day Angelina told her mother about Nicolai, and he lost his ability to be with her. He had continued to watch her from afar. The night he left her side was the night he had gotten word her father was being moved, and he knew it was his chance to rescue him. But, it was all a trap. The moment Nicolai left, something took advantage of the opportunity. If he had only been there . . .

A tear slid down his stern face. He had let them down. He wiped the tear away and tried to think of something more pleasant. An image of Angelina dressed in a black gown crossed his mind. She begged her mother to let her stay home the night of her senior prom, but her mother simply smiled and handed her a bag from Lillian's, one of the most expensive boutiques in the area. Nicolai had left the room with her mother, deciding to meet Angelina at the dance hall. The moment he saw her in that floor-length, black silk gown with the plunging neckline, all innocent thoughts left his mind. She was breathtaking.

She walked into the prom so nervous, not having any idea of how incredibly beautiful she looked. All eyes were on her as she scanned the crowd in front of her. That's when Nicolai stepped forward. Jealousy had cut through him like a hot knife through butter when he saw that Jeremiah, the only man he considered to be any kind of competition, was dancing with her. He had watched Jeremiah grow up with Angelina and knew about the feelings he hid from her. Nicolai had kept his distance as they danced and couldn't help but feel pure satisfaction at her early departure. She left quickly, and he followed her to the moss-covered steps that lay at the edge of the forest. How badly he had wanted to console her as she threw herself down on the soft red moss and cried.

Nicolai sighed, opened his eyes, and gasped. The one person he least expected to see was standing right in front of him—his mother.

19

Love Endures

"Mother?"

"Well, look at you," Ctephanyi replied calmly. "You're a mess."

"I wouldn't be a mess if you would've called off your hounds."

"If you wouldn't have fallen in love with a human, all of this could've been avoided."

His eyes met hers. "I love Angelina, and I've suffered a long time for her. When will you realize that I will continue to do so? She is my soul mate, and you, of all people, should know that."

Ctephanyi frowned, and he knew he had hit a sore spot. She was still very bitter from her own soul mate leaving her at one of her most desperate times. She sat down next to Nicolai and placed her hand on his open would. It began to glow an iridescent blue and new skin formed over it within seconds.

She nodded. "There you go. All healed."

He looked at her with a question in his eyes. "Mother, why do you hate humans? They've done nothing to us."

She avoided his eyes. "Fine, perhaps it's time I told you. After all, you're my only child, and it's only fair that you know the true reason behind my hatred for the human race."

He was surprised by her answer. He studied her face and noticed that she seemed to have aged, which was almost impossible for their species. Her long red hair had light gray streaks in it, and she had dark bags under her beautiful pale eyes. How had he not noticed this before?

"A very long time ago I met a man who was the same species as us. He was such a beautiful man," she said smiling to herself. "We fell madly in love and got married. Soon after, I found out that I was pregnant with you, and we were both so very excited. One night, as we were enjoying a quiet dinner together, you, being the impatient child that you are, had decided to meet the world earlier than planned."

"Yeah, that sounds like me." He grinned.

She didn't return his smile as she continued, "He rushed off to get a few items we would need to make sure you had a safe delivery. On his way to town, a caravan of men ambushed him . . ." Her voice trailed off.

He knew where she was going with this. Her eyes filled with tears, and he finally understood.

"They killed him," Nicolai stated matter-of-factly.

"Yes, they killed him, and I had to give birth to you alone."

He picked up her hand and held it against his chest, "I'm sorry mother. I didn't know."

She looked at him, sadness in her eyes. He had forgotten how much he actually loved her. While she intimidated most, he knew she was just trying her best to keep them safe. Now, he understood why she had given him such a hard time about falling in love with Angelina. Angelina was human, and humans had killed Ctephanyi's true love. He knew the extent of her magic. Bringing back one of their own kind was impossible. When one of their species died, its blood was fed into the earth. The blood of their ancestors ran through the crimson moss, giving it life as it grew throughout the forest. It was a constant reminder of those who had fallen before them.

He turned and looked at her. "Mother, what's happened to you is not so different from what happened to me. My wife was murdered by her own race. How do you think I felt when that happened to me?"

"Nicolai, humans are evil. It runs in their blood, and it has since the day they set foot on this planet. They are selfish creatures only looking out for what's in their best interests."

"No, they're not all the same. I mean, look at Angelina. She's different," he pointed out. "Mother, if you would just give her a chance, you would see how wonderful she is. Her heart is pure and she's special."

"Special?" she asked, intrigued.

The sound of heavy footsteps rustling through the leaves made them both look up. Nicolai jumped to his feet while his mother remained seated. Laurana's cold eyes met his.

"Long time, no see," she said with a smirk.

He ignored her as the anger began to well up inside of him. "What is he doing with her?"

He clenched his fist as Jeremiah carried his beloved Angelina toward them.

"Aw, Nicolai, what's the matter?" Laurana snickered. "Jealous much?"

"What are you looking at, orange eyes?" Jeremiah frowned, pulling Angelina closer to his body.

"I'll show you what I'm looking at." Nicolai jumped toward Jeremiah, but Ctephanyi put her arm out protectively.

"Mother, move," he hissed.

"Nicolai, no."

"But, he's the one who helped Laurana . . ."

Ctephanyi interrupted. "He helped Laurana do as I asked."

Laurana snickered again. "Surprise!"

Nicolai felt utterly betrayed. "You asked them to do this?"

He watched his mother walk over and lightly touch Angelina's face. "She's alive, barely." Ctephanyi motioned for Laurana to join her. "We don't have much time. Take them to the Soul Stones."

Laurana nodded. "Come on boys, it looks like we're about to have a party."

"Wait, what do you mean we don't have much time?" Nicolai asked, studying Angelina's broken body. She lay limply across Jeremiah's arms. She had been badly wounded. He could see by her chest movement that her breathing had become shallow. He stared at Jeremiah with pure hatred.

"Stop looking at me like that. I did it to save her."

"Save her from what! Your selfishness?"

Laurana stepped in between them. "Boys, please settle down. We need to be on our way, or neither of you will ever get to see your pretty little Angelina again."

Nicolai returned his attention back to his mother. "How could you do this to me?"

She placed her dainty hand on his shoulder, but he shrugged it away. "My son, I've waited a very long time for this. Now, go with Laurana before it's too late."

Nicolai had no choice. If he didn't get Angelina underground, she would die, and then she'd be lost to him forever. He looked up at Jeremiah and frowned. "Let's go, pretty boy."

"I'm not going with you," Jeremiah retorted.

"Oh yeah? So, you're just going to let her die then, are ya?"

Jeremiah looked down at Angelina's blood-streaked face. No matter how much he didn't like it, he knew they were right. He had no idea where they were taking him, but wherever it was, meant life for Angelina.

Laurana smiled wickedly. "Yeah, not much of a choice, is there?"

Jeremiah glared at her. Though she was beautiful, her snide little attitude was beginning to piss him off.

Ctephanyi's curious eyes scanned the forest. "Where's her father?"

"I took care of him." Laurana answered proudly.

"You did what?" Jeremiah and Nicolai asked together. They glared at each other momentarily before returning their attention to Laurana.

"What? He was dead weight." She laughed. "Get it? Dead weight!"

Neither of them looked amused.

"You need to go. Her time is very short," Ctephanyi ordered, concern showing on her pale face. "Laurana will show you the way."

Laurana motioned for them to follow her, blowing them each a kiss before she turned around.

Nicolai glared at Jeremiah. "Give her to me." he demanded.

"Not a chance. I think you've brought her enough sorrow."

"Me? What about you? You've practically killed her." Nicolai pointed to the numerous wounds on her fragile body.

His words stung. "I was trying to protect her from Laurana," Jeremiah muttered quietly.

Nicolai snickered. "Well, you did a really good job and got her father killed in the process."

"If you would've just stayed out of her life completely, none of this would've happened."

Nicolai's eyes burned brightly. "If I had stayed out of her life, she wouldn't even be here."

Jeremiah conceded. Nicolai was right. He knew their history thanks to Laurana. Without Nicolai, Angelina would've been nothing more than a mere memory hidden within the mind of the man who had to let her go.

20

Envy

They walked side-by-side in awkward silence. Jeremiah kept a watchful eye on Angelina's breathing as they followed Laurana through the dense forest. He was curious where she was taking them. As she strode farther ahead of them, he began to imagine some giant, hollowed out tree that led to some dark dungeon.

Nicolai let out a hearty laugh, "Not quite."

Jeremiah looked at him and raised an eyebrow. He had forgotten they could read minds.

"We don't really prefer living in trees," Nicolai said, amused by the look on Jeremiah's face.

"Surprising," he retorted.

Nicolai turned to look at him. "Oh? Why is that so surprising?"

"I don't know," he answered, "I guess I just thought people who live in the forest would live in the trees." He shrugged.

"I'm not Tarzan."

"Yeah, well, you kind of look like him."

"I'll take that compliment." Nicolai scoffed.

"Compliment?" Jeremiah looked at him sarcastically. "I meant as in acting like an unintelligible ape."

Nicolai raised an amused eyebrow. "Ape, huh?"

He nodded. "Yeah, you kind of look like one too."

Nicolai laughed again. "Well, in that case, I

know what Angelina's favorite animal is."

Jeremiah cringed. Nicolai had won with words, but suddenly he had an idea. He smiled at Nicolai mischievously.

"What's that look for?"

"No reason," he answered, thinking back to the night he had convinced Angelina to go skinny-dipping with him and a group of their friends in the river. He let the image of Angelina's naked body form in his mind. That night he'd actually only seen her naked for a brief moment, but that brief moment was enough to burn an image of her beautiful body into his mind forever.

He concentrated on the way the moonlight made her pale, freckled skin glow. He envisioned wrapping his strong arm around her bare waist as her long, wavy hair fell carelessly down her back. He pictured kissing her slender shoulders and smooth neck.

Nicolai stopped, a disgusted look on his face. "You've seen her naked?"

"Obviously."

Laurana reappeared. "That's enough gabbing, girls. We're on a time constraint."

Nicolai bent down and picked up a moss-covered log.

"And what are you going to do with that?" she asked, a smirk on her pretty face.

He glanced at Jeremiah and threw it. Jeremiah ducked just in time, as it flew inches over his head, splintering into another tree.

He rolled his eyes. "Scary."

Nicolai, irritated, charged ahead without saying another word.

Laurana laughed, surprised by the altercation. "What did you say to piss him off?"

"I didn't say anything." He grinned.

"Mmm hmm."

Jeremiah watched her jog ahead of him, an amused look on her face. He sighed and followed behind her.

Nicolai continued walking in silence as Laurana led them to their destination. The sun was beginning to make its way into the sky and the fall leaves made their color known once again. The crimson moss snaked across the ground and up the tall trees.

Jeremiah gazed into Angelina's face and saw she was still out cold. Her breathing was becoming more shallow, and he began to worry they wouldn't make it in time. He was regretting hitting her. He knew he had hit her hard, but he didn't think it was hard enough to kill her.

The scenery around them began to change the farther they walked. Jeremiah looked up and noticed the trees were beginning to look barren, and not because of the season. The tops of them were gnarled stubs with their lower branches drooping like ghostly fingers. The crimson-colored moss was no longer its bright color, but instead an ashy black.

Nicolai noticed his confusion and bent down, gently touching the moss. "It's dying."

"Why?"

"In order for there to be life, there must be death." He broke off a piece of the moss and threw it to the ground. "Life is not guaranteed, but death always is."

Jeremiah remained quiet as Nicolai stood back

up.

"There are no birds," he noticed, silence filling his ears.

"Nothing lives here."

"Except you."

Nicolai frowned. "We're here," he said, pointing to two large rock structures.

Jeremiah held his breath in awe. He saw Laurana a short distance ahead. She was leaning up against one of the structures, arms crossed, and a scowl on her face.

"Welcome home, boys."

"Some home," Jeremiah commented, confused by the structures. He looked up. They had to be at least twelve feet tall, if not more. They were about as wide as an old oak. There were odd symbols carved into each one, and they stood about three feet apart.

"What's the scowl for?" Nicolai asked, turning toward Laurana.

"They're not ready for you yet," she said.

He sighed. "What do you mean they're not ready?"

"Hey, I'm just relaying a message," she said with a yawn. "She said for you to take her home."

Jeremiah's heart filled with hope. "We can go home?"

"Not your home," Laurana interjected. "His home."

Jeremiah's eyes darted back to Nicolai. "Your home?"

Nicolai nodded at Laurana and continued on into the forest.

"Wait? Where are we going now?" Jeremiah asked.

Nicolai didn't turn around. "You heard the girl."

Jeremiah shook his head, and suddenly Nicolai was in front of him. They stared at each other momentarily.

"You know, she will never go back with you," Nicolai hissed, a troubled look on his serious face.

Stunned by his sudden mood swing, Jeremiah pulled Angelina closer to him. It scared him to think Nicolai was right. How could she ever forgive him for what he had done? No, he thought. He would find away, he would be the hero, not this—creature.

Adrenaline began pumping through his veins, as he looked Nicolai right in his fiery orange eyes. The hatred he'd built up finally erupted, allowing the venomous thoughts he'd kept to himself to come cascading out of his mouth. "And she's going to go with you? Look at what you've done to her. She's lost every single person in her life except for me. I came here to rescue her and take her back to a normal life. Do you even know what that word means? Apparently not, because if you did, you'd let her go. You wouldn't let this sorrow continue to follow her. All she's ever wanted to be was normal. You were so blinded by the thought of your dead wife that you forgot about this girl." He looked down at her and pushed the hair away from her face. "Angelina may have someone else's soul, but she is her own person now. If she goes with you, she is sure to find only misery and will eventually grow to hate you for holding her back from the normal life she deserves."

Nicolai opened his mouth, but nothing came out. He turned around and walked away without saying another word. It was probably a good thing they didn't continue with their battle of words, because Jeremiah was sure it would've gotten physical. He was still exhausted from the previous night and wasn't too keen on trying to prove himself at that very moment.

They walked a short distance before coming upon a quaint little cottage that was tucked away in a small clearing surrounded by woods. It was a welcoming place with creeping rose bushes, a small pond, and a garden full of fall vegetables. A trellis archway begged them to walk under it as it graced them with the sweet smell of flowers hanging from within its small openings. Butterflies fluttered through the yard while bees sucked the nectar from the distant flower garden. The birds whistled their sweet songs as small rabbits gnawed on the garden-fresh lettuce nearby.

"What is this place?" Jeremiah asked, envisioning the Garden of Eden.

For the first time in hours, Nicolai smiled as he made his way up the cobblestone pathway. "Why, home, of course."

21

Home Sweet Home

Nicolai turned the hand-carved doorknob and pushed open the door. Jeremiah walked past him, went inside, and stopped in the middle of what he assumed was the dining room. Nicolai walked in and pointed toward one of the closed doors.

"Put her in there. We'll wait here for now. When they're ready, they will come for us."

Jeremiah nodded. He fumbled with the doorknob, careful not to drop Angelina from his arms. Finally managing to turn the knob with his index finger and thumb, he pushed open the door and looked around. An old four-poster bed sat beneath a delicate row of dried yellow roses that matched the sunset-colored walls. A hand-stitched quilt lay neatly over it, along with four overstuffed pillows. He lay Angelina down in the middle of the bed, gently placing her hands in the middle of her chest. She took a deep breath and smiled.

"Angelina?" he whispered, disappointed when her eyes remained closed.

He sighed and shoved his hands into his pockets, slightly rocking back and forth on his heels as he debated what he should do next. He envisioned Angelina dancing around the room in her past life, picking out colors, and laughing as she stitched the quilt together.

An old silver-lace picture frame caught his eye. It sat on the corner of the walnut dresser across from him. He reached over and picked it up, eyeing it curiously. His hand began to tremble when he recognized the couple in the picture. Without a doubt, the man was Nicolai, with his dark hair, serious face, and stern eyes.

Jeremiah's breath caught once he laid his eyes on the woman. She had long, wavy, brown hair, kind eyes, and a radiant smile. In many ways, she resembled Angelina with her pale, freckled skin and petite frame. After all the years he'd known her, it was hard to believe she was once someone else.

He set the frame back down and peeked his head inside the small closet by the door. A row of hand-sewn dresses hung neatly beside a row of white t-shirts and slacks he assumed were Nicolai's. He quietly closed the closet door and went into the dining room where he was met by Nicolai's stern gaze.

"Is she okay?" he asked, seriousness in his voice.

"She's still alive, if that's what you mean."

Nicolai tapped his finger on the wood table, "This is the best place for her." He sounded as if he were trying to reassure himself.

Jeremiah pulled out a chair and sat across from him. "If you say so."

Awkward silence followed. Finally, Nicolai broke the silence. "This was our home, you know, before she became who she is now."

"You've kept it quite nice," Jeremiah complimented, looking around. Nicolai had probably left everything in its exact order since the day his wife died.

Nicolai bent over and ran his hands over the

smooth hardwood floor. "Well, I knew one day I would bring her back here. She loved this place. We built it together."

Jeremiah couldn't have cared less about how much she loved this place, but he humored Nicolai anyway. "That must've taken some time."

"Yes, it took over a year, but it's perfect."

No doubt Nicolai was proud of the place they had built together. It had been built out of love, but that was in the past and this was the future. He couldn't picture Nicolai in a place like this, and it was too simple for Angelina.

"How long before they're ready for us?" Jeremiah asked.

"It will be a little while, so you might as well make yourself comfortable," Nicolai replied, his eyes fixated on the door to the room Angelina was in."

"Why so long? I thought they were in a hurry to get this over with."

"They have to ensure that everything is prepared properly. We have kept our home a secret for thousands of years, and the proper precautions must be taken."

"Understandable, I suppose."

Nicolai stood up and walked toward the front door. "You might as well get some rest. You're going to need it."

Jeremiah followed suit, pushing his chair in. "Where are you going?"

Nicolai frowned. "I'm going for a walk."

"Haven't you done enough walking for one day?"

Nicolai stared at him. "I'll be back shortly. Don't try wandering away. You won't get very far." He slammed the door shut behind him.

Jeremiah rolled his eyes. Nicolai was so dramatic. He looked around the small dining room and ventured into the kitchen. If he were going to be there a while, he might as well see what other secrets this little cottage held.

The kitchen cupboards had no doors on them, which he found odd. He ran his fingers over the tiny hand-painted pink daisies that graced the edges of the smooth wood trim. He envisioned Angelina's alter ego with a tiny paintbrush in her dainty hands. He smiled at the thought of her covered in pink splotches from wiping away mistakes, because everything had to be perfect.

He eyed the white china that sat in perfect rows of five. In fact, every cupboard was set up the same way. Five rows across, five dishes deep. "Weird," he muttered to himself as he walked out of the kitchen and back into the dining room.

There were two other doors beside the bedroom door he had gone in. Curious, he went to one and turned the knob. Locked. How odd, he thought to himself. He walked across the room and tried another door. Locked. Why would there be locked doors in a cottage tucked away deep in the woods, he wondered.

A loud groan came from Angelina's room. His heart raced as he flung open the door.

"Angelina?"

His blue eyes widened as he stared in amazement at the sight in front of him. A golden aura covered her body protectively as she levitated a few feet over the hand-stitched quilt. The bruises began to fade on her pale face, and the cuts on her arms began to heal. He stared, open-mouthed, as he moved slowly toward the rocking chair beside the bed. His legs gave out from underneath him and he plopped down in the chair. It rocked back and forth a few times from his sudden movement.

He moved her hair away from her forehead and studied her face. The gash he'd given her was gone. Was this what Nicolai meant when he'd said how different she was? She most certainly wasn't an ordinary human. In fact, he wasn't sure if she was human at all.

He continued to watch in awe as the aura around her body brightened. He was afraid to touch her again but curiosity took control of his hand, and he touched the bright light. Every muscle in his body twitched, and his skin tingled. It reminded him of when his feet fell asleep from sitting in the same hunting position for hours on end. He turned his hand over and gasped. His own bloody scratches and bruises began to magically disappear.

"Impossible," he whispered.

He sat back and rocked for a few moments, so he could give his mind time to analyze what he'd just witnessed. Angelina had the ability not only to heal herself, but others around her. Nicolai was right. If Ctephanyi or anyone else were to find out about her abilities, he would never see her again. She was a threat and a temptation, all wrapped into one being. At that very moment, he made the choice to protect her secret at all costs, even if it meant giving up his life for her.

The aura around Angelina's body began to dim, and her body lowered itself back down. He knew he didn't have much time before Nicolai returned, and he had to get her out of there before Ctephanyi claimed her soul.

He stood up and slid his arms under her. Using his amazing new strength, he picked her up and held her close to his chest. He pushed her hair behind her ear and whispered, "It's just you and me, Angelina. It's always been just you and me."

Her head rolled and rested against his chest, and he kissed her forehead before heading for the door. He peeked his head around the corner. The coast was clear. He went to the window and glanced outside. No sign of Nicolai. This was going to be a challenge, but if it meant their freedom, then it was worth it. With that, he pulled open the door and ran toward the tree line.

22

Beautiful Scenery

"Where do you think you're going?" a voice demanded.

Jeremiah stopped dead in his tracks and turned around. His arms went limp, and he felt Angelina begin to slip out of them.

He stared at the ghost in front of him. "You're supposed to be dead."

"Now, boy, don't you drop my daughter," he threatened, motioning toward Angelina.

Jeremiah regained his composure and steadied his weak arms. "How are you here, and where did you come from?"

Angelina's father glared at Jeremiah. "More importantly, why are *you* here, and why do you have her?"

"I'm taking her home. Nothing good will come to her if she stays here with them. All they bring her are sorrow and death."

"And what do you bring her?" the man asked. "I saw you with the blond-headed devil woman."

"I made a deal with her to get Angelina back. I've come to the realization that she's the one thing my life has been missing, and I will do anything to protect her," Jeremiah answered honestly.

Her father nodded. "Well then, son, we should get out of here before they come back."

"Yes, sir. No arguments here."

It was like watching a ghost return from the

dead as her father limped toward him and squeezed his shoulder in approval. Jeremiah cringed, expecting a cold touch from a spectral hand, but it had warmth to it.

"You're really alive," Jeremiah questioned, still shocked.

He laughed. "Well, I believe so."

"Everyone in Buffalo thought you were . . ."

"Yeah, that's what I've been hearing." He motioned for Jeremiah to keep moving.

Angelina's father stumbled blindly through the forest. It saddened Jeremiah knowing Ctephanyi and Nicolai had something to do with his disappearance. Angelina had missed out on a major part of her life—having a father figure. She never got to see what it was like to have her father wait by the door for her after a date, or clean his shotgun in front of a boy she liked. She never got to cry on his shoulder when a boy broke her heart. She had missed out on all of that because of Nicolai.

He felt tension begin to build in his broad shoulders. His hatred for Nicolai grew even more. He prayed the day would soon arrive that he would be able to give him a taste of just how badly he had hurt her.

"Come on, boy, you're slacking," Angelina's father called out from a short distance ahead.

Jeremiah nodded and picked up the pace. Even with Angelina's father injured, they managed to keep a decent pace through the thick forest.

The sun began to set. Jeremiah was unfamiliar with this part of the forest and knew it was too risky to continue traveling in the dark, so he decided to find a safe place to camp. He was sure

Nicolai knew of their disappearance by now and was out scouring the forest for them. His species had proven themselves to be great trackers, so Jeremiah had to outsmart them by setting up camp in an inconspicuous place.

He stopped momentarily, and handed Angelina's body over to her father so he could get his bearings. From the rocky terrain they had traveled into, he knew the cliffs were nearby. He bent down, closed his eyes, and listened to his surroundings. He smiled once he heard the faint sound of running water.

"Okay, the river's close by," he said, standing back up. "Let's head toward it."

Angelina's father nodded and handed his daughter back over.

After a short distance, they stumbled upon a large waterfall.

"This is an old waterfall," Jeremiah commented, admiring the large amount of water that rapidly cascaded over the edge of the cliff.

"How do you know that?'

"You see how small that channel is up there?" He pointed toward the top of the gorge. "You can see the edge of the rock shelter."

Angelina's father stared up at the gorge. "Rock shelter?"

"Yeah, over time, the splash back of the water erodes the rock behind the falls, creating a kind of hidden cave."

"Oh, I get it," her father said, nodding. "Is there a way to get behind it?"

"See the path?" Jeremiah pointed it out. "It's pretty faded, but it's there. If we can get up to it, we should be able to get behind the falls."

"Well then, let's make it happen, captain."

Jeremiah flung Angelina over his shoulder, so he could use his free arm to navigate up the steep rocky terrain. Her long hair swung back and forth lazily over his back as he began the treacherous climb.

He heard her father's footing slip. "You okay back there, old man?" he called out behind him.

"Old man? You're only as old as you feel," he grumbled, pushing forward.

Jeremiah stifled his laugh, losing his own footing on the loose gravel. He was at a bad angle to do so, and he knew it. As he slid toward the edge of the gorge, he tried to grab onto a large rock but missed it by inches and went careening over the edge.

"Jeremiah!" her father called out.

"Apparently, I'm the one who's getting old," Jeremiah yelled back. Her father's face peered over the edge, and Jeremiah looked up at him helplessly, barely clinging to the large tree root protruding out of the rocky surface. Angelina dangled like a rag doll from his other hand. "I can't even manage to climb up a hill anymore."

"Oh my," her father gasped. "What do you want me to do?"

Jeremiah looked down at Angelina. "I'm going to have to swing her up to you."

"Is that even humanly possible?" her father asked, judging the distance between them.

"Anything's possible when you're not quite human," Jeremiah called up to him, his eyes beginning to brighten.

"Jeremiah, what—what happened to you?"

Angelina began to slip from his sweaty hand.

"Ask questions later. Let's worry about her first."

Her father nodded. "I'm ready."

"On the count of three, I'm going to swing her toward you. All you have to do is catch her."

"You're sure about this?"

Jeremiah nodded. "One." He began swinging her steadily. "Two." He looked up and, using the new strength Ctephanyi had bestowed upon him, swung her upwards. "Three."

Jeremiah cried out in pain as he heard a sharp snap in his shoulder from the strenuous throw. He struggled to hold onto the branch. "Did you catch her?" he called up, sweat pouring down his face. Silence followed. A few pebbles trickled over the edge past him. "Hello?" he called up again.

"I got her," her father called out breathlessly. "I got her!"

Jeremiah let out a deep sigh of relief.

"Your turn," her father called out.

"I think I dislocated my shoulder."

Worry creased the lines of her father's face. "Well it looks like I'm just going to have to break a few rules."

Jeremiah looked up at him confused. "What?" He felt his grip loosening.

"You see, son, there are forces on this earth stronger than you and me," he said, raising his arms above his head as he looked up at the sky. "And there are some species, like myself, who've been gifted with . . .," he paused and looked back down, ". . . abilities."

Jeremiah stared in awe as Angelina's father's eyes began to glow a deep red. "It can't be," he whispered in disbelief.

"I'm afraid so." Her father winked and climbed out over the edge.

"Don't touch me," Jeremiah yelled out, his fingers slipping. "You're one of them!"

Her father effortlessly climbed down the rocky wall. "We can't all choose who or what we'll be."

"I mean it, stay away."

"Or what? I won't save you?" He laughed.

Jeremiah's hand slid off the branch. He stared, wide-eyed in horror, as he began his treefall toward the ground.

"No dying today, son," her father called out. He slid down the rocky wall, his fingers leaving long gashes on his way down.

Jeremiah felt the cool breeze rush through his hair and closed his eyes. He never thought he would go out this way. He felt a strong grip on his arm and his eyes flew open in surprise.

"I got ya," her father said with a smile.

"How did you?" Jeremiah stuttered.

"Ask questions later," he said with a wink. "Let's worry about getting back up there first."

Jeremiah nodded.

"I need you to wrap your good arm around my neck."

"Won't that hurt you?"

Her father laughed. "It's hard to hurt someone like me."

"But your injuries . . ."

Her father smiled mischievously.

"They were fake?" Jeremiah asked in disbelief.

"There are certain things that must be hidden from human eyes. Your minds are too fragile to understand what you don't know."

Jeremiah knew that, in some sense, he was right. Humans feared the unknown and, in most cases, would try to destroy whatever they didn't understand. Jeremiah did as he was told and wrapped his muscular arm around the man's neck. Her father, using amazing speed and strength, climbed up the rocky wall with ease. He grabbed Jeremiah by the shirt and flung him up over the ledge, following close behind him.

"Stand up, and let's have a look at that arm."

Jeremiah crawled to his feet, holding his injured arm protectively.

"Now, this is going to hurt a bit." Her father gripped his shoulder tightly. He heard another loud snap and cried out in pain. He fell to his knees, a single tear falling down his face.

"You'll live, kid." Her father smiled and patted him on the back. "You'll live." He walked over and picked his daughter up with ease. "We must be on our way. I'm sure they're onto us."

Jeremiah looked at him in disbelief. All this time, her father had been one of them. He sighed and swallowed his pride. Crawling back up to his feet, he began the long hike back toward the rock shelf behind the waterfall.

He breathed a sigh of relief as he crawled in behind the loud rush of water and slid down the smooth wall. Angelina's father set her down carefully next to him.

"You should get some rest. We have a long hike tomorrow," her father said looking down at him.

Jeremiah nodded in agreement, closing his eyes. The sound of the rushing water was soothing to his worried mind. He smiled, picturing Nicolai's angry face once he realized they had escaped from the cottage. He was sure he was out searching for them. He just hoped he had found a good enough spot to hide for the night.

Exhaustion had begun to take its toll, and his head rolled to the side. He opened his eyes again and smiled wearily at Angelina's father.

"Don't worry, son. I'll keep an eye out."

"You know, everyone thought you were dead," Jeremiah whispered groggily.

"For a brief time, I thought I was too," he answered sadly.

"I heard them talk about you. Laurana said she had taken care of you."

"Yes," he replied. "But she doesn't know I'm like her and have extremely fast healing skills. I simply played dead."

"Clever, old man, very clever." Jeremiah laughed, closing his eyes again.

Sleep welcomed him with pleasant dreams of Angelina in her beautiful black gown, his arms around her lovingly as she placed her hand on his face and smiled up at him. It felt so real. In fact, it felt too real, and he awoke with a jolt, feeling a smooth hand against his scruffy cheek. His eyes fluttered open, and he wondered if he was still asleep as Angelina looked at him with the same amazing smile on her face.

23

Revelation

"Angelina." A sweet familiar voice whispered through the darkness.

"Hello?" I called out helplessly. "Where are you?"

"Angelina, remember who you are," she whispered. "Remember who you are."

I tried to take a step forward, and an invisible wall stopped me. I ran my hands over the smooth surface in front of me. My heart beat faster as I realized the invisible wall surrounded me completely.

"Help!" I cried out. I was scared and alone. I was trapped in an invisible box of darkness with no way out. "Please, someone help me," I cried out again as the tears began to make their way down my cheeks.

"I'm here," the voice whispered calmly.

I sniffled and pushed against the wall of darkness. "Where? I can't see you."

"You don't have to see me to know that I am here."

"How did I get in here?" I sobbed.

"Your mind is healing your body in the outside world. Therefore, your subconscious is here in the darkness."

Had I just heard her right? Did she just say my mind was healing my body in the outside world?

"Yes," she replied quietly, "you heard me

right."

"That's just creepy," I replied, staring into the darkness, "How do I get out of here?"

"All you have to do is wake up."

"But I am awake," I commented, confused by her words.

"Your subconscious is awake. Your mind, however, is not."

My head began to hurt. Her words were nothing but riddles. "Who are you?"

"I'm simply someone to help you find your way out of the darkness."

"But you just said . . ."

"Exactly. All you have to do is WAKE UP." She screamed, and my eyes flew open. A loud noise filled my ears, and I sat in awe once I realized I was sitting behind a waterfall. How had I gotten here? Where was Nicolai? I felt relieved when I heard my father's voice.

He smiled. "Hey you."

"Oh, Dad," I croaked, finding my voice. "I thought you were dead."

"That's the rumor, so they tell me." He winked.

I rubbed my eyes. "What happened?"

He sat down next to me and nodded toward Jeremiah, who was peacefully sleeping against the rock wall. "That guy over there, he saved you."

My mouth dropped open. "Jeremiah is here?" A tear of happiness ran down my cheek. He had come for me. "Where's Nicolai?"

My father stared into the falls. "He's looking for us."

"What do you mean he's looking for us? How did we lose him?"

"Well, we didn't lose him. We escaped from him."

My eyes widened in surprise. "Why on earth would we want to escape from him? He's not evil —is he?"

He shook his head. "No, honey, he's not, but the people he's with are very deadly indeed."

"Who is with him?" I asked, anger filling my veins.

"Laurana . . ."

I clenched my teeth together. "And?"

"Ctephanyi."

"Are you kidding me? How did she get . . ." Then, I remembered. I touched my forehead and the memory of being hit flashed before my eyes. "Someone else was with them."

He nodded. "Yes."

"How did we get away?"

He glanced over at Jeremiah again. "He took a risk, and it was worth it."

I smiled and sat back. "Yeah, he was always the risk taker, wasn't he?"

"Well, if I recall, it was you who was the risk taker." He laughed. "Remember when your mom made you that red cape, and you thought you could fly?"

I joined in his laughter. "How could I forget? I wore that cape every day for a week."

"Your mother was so proud of that cape. It was the first thing she had ever sewn."

"Well, she did a great job."

We sat in silence for a moment, reminiscing of past memories.

He finally broke the silence. "He loves you, you know?" The tone of his voice had grown serious.

I sighed. "I think it's too late for me to love him back."

"You love Nicolai."

"Yes, very much."

"You hardly know him."

I turned to look into his hazel eyes. "I can't explain it. I've just always known that there was someone special out there for me."

He finished my sentence, "And he's the one."

I nodded. I felt so lost without him. He had captured my heart and given me something I had never felt before—true love.

My father wrapped his arm around me and pulled me close. "Things will work out as they should. They always do."

I sighed. "I sure hope so."

He squeezed my arm. "You gave me quite the scare back there, ya know."

"Why's that?" I asked, looking up at him.

Sadness filled his eyes. "I thought I was going to lose you."

"Oh, Dad." I hugged him.

"I couldn't bare losing you, Angelina. You're my world." He shared in my hug, holding me tight. "My life would end if you weren't in it."

I smiled at him lovingly. "Well I'm here and I don't plan on going anywhere anytime soon."

"I sure hope not," he said, kissing the top of my head.

Jeremiah's eyes opened groggily. "Angelina?"

I moved from my father's arms and went to him, running my hand down his scruffy cheek. "You're awake," I whispered, swallowing the lump in my throat.

"So are you." He smiled.

I felt a tear fall down my chilled cheek. "My father told me everything."

Jeremiah wiped the tear away gently before pulling me close to him. I fit so perfectly in his arms. His body was so warm next to mine, and he smelled so earthy, it reminded me of the times we had gone camping together as children.

I leaned back and kissed him on the cheek. I could tell by his body language that he wanted to surrender himself to me, to be the only man I could ever want or need. I ran my hand through his blond hair and laughed.

"What's so funny?" he asked, raising an eyebrow.

"Yeah, what's so funny?" a familiar voice called out behind us. I watched the blood drain from Jeremiah's face once he saw Nicolai's fiery orange eyes staring back at us through the opening of the rock shelter. They were cold and menacing.

Jeremiah wrapped his arms around me protectively. "It's going to be okay," he reassured me. I glanced past Nicolai, looking for signs of Ctephanyi or Laurana. I knew we were in serious trouble, and I had no idea how we would get out of it.

24

Angry Tension

I pulled myself free from Jeremiah's arms and pulled my knees up to my chest. The tension sat heavy in the air and I figured it was only a matter of time before these two decided to kill each other. My father, sensing my anxiety, moved closer to me and wrapped his arms around me protectively. I snuggled closer to him and enjoyed how good it felt to have him near me again. I wasn't sure how he made it out of the forest alive, but he had done it safely, and I was happy to have him back.

Feeling Nicolai's gaze upon me, I looked up. The anger in his eyes was unmistakable. However, there was something else visible in them that sent a chill up my spine. I wasn't quite sure what it was. Jealousy perhaps? He came in a few feet and bent down in front of me. He ran his cool hand down my cheek and studied my face as though I were some sort of alien. I raised an eyebrow as he picked up my arm and began bending it back and forth. I knew what he was doing as the memory of Laurana breaking my arm was still fresh in my mind, and I was sure someone had hit me on the head. A look of amazement crossed his face.

"How do you feel, my love?"

"I feel pretty good, I guess," I answered honestly. "In fact, I feel better than I have in days," I replied with a slight smile on my face.

"Your arm and all your other wounds are healed," he stated matter-of-factly.

"Yes, I saw that," I answered quietly.

"Amazing. You're truly amazing, did you know that?" he complimented, his beautiful dimple showing as he smiled.

My heart leapt into my throat momentarily as his lips brushed mine. He stood up and walked back to the opening of the falls.

"Well, are you all coming?" he questioned loudly, his strong voice commanding us to stand up and follow him.

Without hesitation, Jeremiah stood up and dusted off his dirty pants. My father stood up right behind him. Sighing, I stood up and frowned. Off into the woods again. I had become quite tired of looking at trees.

We made our way out of the falls and carefully down the steep path. Nicolai led us through the dense forest, and I grew curious as a small cottage appeared in the distance. I stopped, suddenly feeling dizzy as a memory of eating dinner with Nicolai at a beautifully carved wooden table hit me with nauseating speed. Confusion weakened me as I attempted to absorb the new memory that had filled some void in my mind.

Sensing the disturbance, Nicolai turned around and rushed to my side. "Angelina, are you okay?"

I tried to regain my composure and smiled weakly. "Um, yeah?"

I glanced over at Jeremiah and saw the unmistakable look of worry on his handsome face. I was so happy when I woke from my mysterious slumber and found him by my side. Deep down, I knew he would come for me, but a new dilemma had now presented itself. I loved Nicolai, but held a special love for Jeremiah too. Why couldn't life just be simple like it seemed to be in the movies?

Nicolai put his hand on the small of my back and led me out of the forest and toward the cottage. He opened the door and eyed me curiously as we walked inside. The first thing to catch my attention was the carved table. For a moment, I held my breath. Impossible, I thought to myself. I walked over to it and ran my hand across its smooth surface. I was sure it had something to do with my past.

"Angelina, would you kindly grab a glass of water for Jeremiah? I do believe he's a bit thirsty from his long walk," Nicolai asked out of the blue.

Jeremiah opened his mouth to protest, but Nicolai raised his hand to hush him. Raising an eyebrow, I did as he asked. I went to the open cupboard and picked out a beautiful white china glass. Without so much as a thought, I walked out the front door and headed straight for the well. I pulled the bucket up using the sturdy rope that was attached to it, sat it on the ledge, and carefully filled the glass. Walking back inside, I handed the glass of water to Jeremiah who looked at me in awe. I glanced at Nicolai who was copying the same look.

"What's with you two?" I questioned.

"How did you know where to go?" Jeremiah asked, the look of surprise still on his face.

I opened my mouth to answer, but nothing

came out. Confused once again, I looked at Nicolai, and a smile spread across his face. I suddenly felt faint and knew it was time to sit down.

My father, noticing my confusion, walked over and placed his hand on my shoulder. He nodded at Nicolai. "I think it's time we told her."

The smile faded from Nicolai's face as he nodded in agreement. He walked to one of the closed doors and disappeared inside briefly. Moments later he reemerged with an arm full of interesting items. He quietly placed the items on the table one-by-one before sitting down beside me.

"Angelina, are you sure you're ready for this?" he asked taking my hand into his.

"Yes, I'm ready," I answered, eyeing the table curiously.

"Alright, do you see these items I've placed on the table?"

"Yes, I see them."

"I want you to take each item, hold it, and tell me the first thing that comes to your mind."

I nodded to let him know I understood, though I was mighty curious what was behind his little game. My eyes scanned the items on the table, counting five in all. Shrugging, I grabbed the red rose-embroidered handkerchief. Amazingly enough, a memory presented itself. It was an image of me in a beautiful white gown and Nicolai in a pair of black slacks with a simple white cotton shirt. The handkerchief fell from my trembling hands.

Jeremiah frowned, "Are you okay?"

Stuttering, I replied, "I—I think so."

I pushed the handkerchief toward Nicolai. "This was given to me on my wedding day."

I was amazed by the words that had just come out of my mouth. My wedding day? What was I saying? Nicolai must've seen the wonder on my face because he put his hand on mine.

"It's okay. Keep going," he urged calmly.

Feeling a bit more reassured, I picked up a knife with an old wooden handle. A memory of me kneeling down in front of my father as he lay dying presented itself. This was a lifetime ago, and yet the father in my vision reminded me so much of the father I knew and loved. A warm tear fell down my cheek as I handed the knife back to Nicolai. "This is the knife that was used to kill a bear when it attacked my father and me in the woods."

Nicolai wiped the tear away and smiled. "Yes, but your father saved you."

Smiling weakly, I eyed the last few items on the table, opting for the silver picture frame. I ran my finger down its smooth edges, admiring the happy couple in the picture. I could tell they were in love by the way she smiled at him as he embraced her.

"This is a picture of me and my husband," I uttered, looking up at Nicolai in disbelief.

"Yes, your husband," he repeated.

The guilt I felt was instant as Jeremiah's face went sullen. My head began to hurt from all the unknown memories, and the confusion I felt was overwhelming. Sighing, I pushed away from the table and walked over to the window. I heard another chair slide across the hardwood floor, and felt Nicolai's familiar embrace around my shoulders.

"Angelina, life is so much bigger than any one of us knows. So many spectacular things are given to us, and we take them for granted. When we take those things for granted, life takes them from us to make us realize how important they were in the first place."

I turned around to face him. "Nicolai, what are you saying?"

"Please, let's sit down, and we . . ."

"No, tell me. I'm tired of sitting down. I'm tired of everyone hiding things from me. My whole life has been a mystery to me and for the longest time I thought I was going crazy. Do you know how hard it is to walk into a room and have everyone look at you and wonder what's wrong with you? I deserve to know."

He nodded and went back to the table. "You're right," he whispered, picking up the picture frame that held the picture of the once loving couple. He ran his pale finger down the photo and looked at me, sadness filling his ember eyes. "A very long time ago, there was a young man who happened to come across a beautiful young woman in the woods. He was saddened by the sight he'd come across, as the young woman seemed to be saying her final words to her dying father. The young man was amazed by her strength and beauty. It was truly love at first sight."

Jeremiah coughed and looked down as if he were trying to hide the expression on his face.

Nicolai gave him a dirty look and continued, "They were soon married. The young man's mother was against their union, so she banished him. But he loved the young woman with all his heart and vowed to protect her and stay by her side always. One day, the young woman's friend fell very ill, and she begged her new husband to let her go into town to get some much-needed medicine. The husband finally agreed to let her go. Hours went by, and he grew very worried, so he went looking for her. He found his beloved lying in a pool of her own blood." His eyes grew dark with hatred. "Three human men had taken her life."

Jeremiah cocked his head to the side. "And what did the young man do to them?" he asked smugly.

"He made them pay dearly for what they had done to her. The man was devastated, and even though his mother had banished him, he summoned her, begging her to save the woman he loved. His plea fell upon deaf ears, which angered the man so much, he killed many of his own kind until his mother made him a deal."

I tried to swallow the lump that had formed in my throat. "What kind of deal?"

"If he could find a soulless baby whose parents were grief stricken and would agree to take part in the deal, she would save the young woman's life."

I knew where he was going with this, but I asked anyway. "Did he find them?"

"Yes. The man was smart. He acquired a job as a doctor in a maternity ward and, after many years, he came across a young couple who were expecting their first child. Unfortunately, there were complications and the baby didn't make it. While the mother of the infant was still asleep, he offered the deal to the grief-stricken father, who eagerly agreed, as they had wanted this child badly."

Warm tears began to fill my eyes. "So what happened?"

"The young man's mother kept to her side of the bargain and raised his young wife's soul, putting it into the baby. However, to punish her son, she put stipulations on their deal. He had to watch her grow up all over again but could never tell her his true name for fear of her memory returning. Once she hit the age of twelve, he had to bring her back to his mother so she could turn the girl into one of their kind."

The tears spilled down my cheeks. I knew who he was referring to. I glanced at my father and saw the tears in his eyes. I was that girl. I was born a soulless baby and was brought back to life. It all made sense now. The red-eyed intruder, Laurana, and the man I had only known as Ialocin. I began to feel sick to my stomach.

Nicolai reached for me. "Angelina," he murmured.

I backed away and looked at him with disgust. "Don't touch me."

"Why are you so angry?" he asked.

"How dare you! Why didn't you just let me go? I don't even know who I am anymore."

Jeremiah, coming to me in my time of need, put his arms around me, and I buried my head in his chest.

"I just want to go home," I muttered quietly, sniffling.

He caressed my hair. "Then, let's go."

"No," Nicolai protested loudly.

"Why not?" Jeremiah replied. "Can't you see she doesn't want to be here with you anymore? She just wants to be normal. If you truly love her, then let her go. She isn't the same person she used to be. Can't you see that?"

"And you are? Why don't you tell her Jeremiah? Why don't you tell her about the little deal you made? Perhaps she'd like to hear about that."

I stepped back and looked up at Jeremiah's face. It was now full of anger and regret. "What deal, Jeremiah? What's he talking about?"

"Angelina, I only did it because I wanted to find you and take you home."

"What did you do?" I demanded angrily.

"Yeah, why don't you tell her Jeremiah? She deserves to know." Nicolai retorted.

Jeremiah sighed and sat back down. "I came across Nicolai's mother, Ctephanyi, in the woods. She made me a deal. If I brought Nicolai to her, she would help me find you. She gave me a special ability." His eyes brightened. "Soon after, I ran into Laurana."

I could feel my anger building. "And . . .?"

"Laurana and I also made an agreement. She was also looking for Nicolai, and we agreed to help each other."

"Wait, the stranger in the woods who attacked us—that was you?"

"Yes, but . . ."

I put my hand up to my head with sudden realization. "You were the one who knocked me out!"

"I was afraid that Laurana would kill you," he answered quickly.

"You helped her capture the both of us. You didn't rescue me. You were in this with her!" I reached up and slapped him across the face. He raised his hand to his cheek and stared at me in silence as my anger continued to build. "How could you? How could you after all these years?"

As I went to slap him again, my father grabbed my hand. "No, Angelina, please don't do anything you're going to regret."

"Regret? How could I regret anything?" I pointed toward Nicolai and Jeremiah. They've both made choices that affected our lives."

"Honey, listen . . ." my father continued.

"No, Dad. I'm done listening. How could you both do this to me?" I glared at them. "I will never forgive either one of you." I walked out of the cottage, slamming the door shut behind me. The warm tears fell down my cheeks as I walked angrily down the cobblestone path. The edge of the woods was in sight, and, even though I'd had enough of the forest, it now looked more welcoming than the room I was just in with two men who had betrayed me.

"Going somewhere?" a female voice questioned behind me.

The tears began to stream down even harder when I realized whose voice it was. Turning around slowly, I came face-to-face with the red-haired lady I had seen as a child, only this time her voice wasn't so soothing. This time, she wanted to do more than talk. She had promised that one day we would be together, and it looked like today was that day.

25

New Home

I threw my hands up in frustration. "Great, can this day get any worse?" That's when I saw three more people walking close behind her. "I guess so," I grumbled to myself once I realized one of them just happened to be my newfound enemy Laurana.

"Hello, Angelina." The red-haired lady smiled, wiping away the tears that had fallen down my pale cheeks. "Don't cry, my dear. All will be okay very soon."

"I remember you," I whispered. "You came to me in the cave."

"Yes. You were so young and fragile back then. Now, look at you. You've grown into a strong, beautiful woman. It's no wonder my son loves you."

"Your son?" I asked in surprise. She couldn't mean . . .

She nodded. "Yes, your thoughts are correct. Nicolai is my son."

Without uttering another word, she walked past me and went inside the cottage, followed by what I assumed were her guards.

Then it hit me. Of course! The puzzle pieces were finally starting to come together. They had come to collect on their promise. They were going to turn me into one of them.

A nauseating feeling washed over me. "No," I whispered.

"Aw, Angelina, you're not looking so well. Why don't you come with me, and we'll get you a nice cozy seat inside." Laurana smirked, grabbing my arm firmly.

I unwillingly followed her back into the cottage and stumbled forward as she pushed me inside. Nicolai, quick to come to my aid, stopped once I gave him the death look. Ctephanyi walked over and put her hand on his shoulder, which he shrugged off. He looked at her, his eyes full of hatred. "She knows," he said.

"Ah, so she knows what's in store for her, then." Ctephanyi smiled wickedly.

"Mother, please, you don't have to do this. Can't you just let us live in peace? Don't you want me to be happy?"

"Of course I do, my son, but you know we can't have a human living amongst us."

"Then let us live amongst the humans."

"After much thought about the situation, I can't let that happen. I lost my love because of humans, and even though her own race killed her past spirit, it just shows how evil and selfish they are. Do you really think I would let you live amongst a race that murders its own kind for sport?" Her eerie white eyes began to glow.

"Please don't do this. I beg you. Not all humans are the same."

"Now, Nicolai. We're wasting time with this silly argument. A deal is a deal." She motioned for her guards to grab my father and me. "You'll thank me one day."

Laurana stood behind Nicolai, watching his every movement. The guard tugged at my arm and ordered me out the door. I instinctively attempted to wrestle myself free from of his tight grasp.

"Let go of me," I growled.

Ctephanyi laid her petite hand on my arm. "Angelina, there's no reason to fight what's going to happen. You will become one of us, and who wouldn't want that?"

"I don't want it. Your race sickens me."

She raised her brow. "Then my son also sickens you?"

"No . . .," I stammered, "that's not what I said."

"It's not?"

"You've taken everything I love away from me," I protested.

"Everything, my dear? Look around you. You have your father, and, of course, you have my son, who loves you more than his own kind. How can you say I've taken everything away from you?"

"What about my mother? What did she do to deserve your wrath? She was an innocent bystander, and you killed her," I replied angrily, fighting back the tears.

A look of confusion crossed her face. "Your mother?"

A fresh tear ran down my cheek. "Yes, my mother," I said through clenched teeth.

She glanced at Laurana. "Would you happen to have anything to do with killing this young girl's mother?"

Laurana stood back, insulted by the accusation. "Of course not. This is the first I've heard of this."

I knew she was lying. "Then who was the red-eyed monster that broke into my house and tried to kill me after killing my mother?"

Ctephanyi motioned to one of her guards. In a flash, he was next to her and they were speaking to each other quietly. The guard nodded his head and left the cottage.

She turned her attention back to me. "My sympathies for the loss of your mother, my dear, but I fear you've accused the wrong people. However, I'm quite curious who was trying to get to you before us."

"Great, so someone else is after me too?" I sighed, I had always wanted to be popular, but this was not the popularity I had in mind.

"It appears so, and the question at hand is why? I've sent my guard to see if he can get any information on this red-eyed creature you speak of."

"What about him?" Nicolai asked nodding toward Jeremiah.

"Ah, yes, the other human. We've no need for him anymore." She waved her hand carelessly. "Get rid of him."

"No!" I screamed, jumping in front of him. "If you kill him, I will refuse Nicolai."

"My dear, there is no refusing Nicolai. Your hearts are entwined together through the past and into the future. This human will bring you nothing but heartache and trouble."

"I don't care. Please, I beg you! I will do whatever you want—just don't harm him. I—I love him."

I gulped as I realized all eyes were on me. The look on Nicolai's face told me I had hurt him with my words. Jeremiah's, on the other hand, was one of utter surprise and triumph.

"It's true. I love him. I always have."

He put his hand against my face and pulled me close to him. My lips met his. His kiss was so different than Nicolai's, and I suddenly knew what Ctephanyi meant. Even though his kiss was warm and welcoming, it lacked the passion and love that Nicolai's held. No butterflies, only a dull ache for my longtime childhood friend.

I pulled away and looked into his eyes. He had felt it too. "Please, I beg you. I will become whatever you ask of me, but let my friend go. He's innocent and only wants what's best for me."

She contemplated Jeremiah's fate. "I do love a good deal."

"Anything. I just want him to be happy."

"How interesting that you would give up anything for another human. Your race always surprises me." She paced back and forth for a few minutes and finally stopped. "Here is your deal. I will release him under one condition. Your human is a great hunter as I've come across him in the forest. I admire his speed and strength, and his spirit is full of great determination. I would have him join us as a protector of my land."

"No, please," I begged. "Let him go."

"My dear, I am afraid you misunderstand me. I will not turn him into one of us. Perhaps Nicolai is right about the human race. We may need an emissary in the future for our species. I will let him go, but he will swear to protect the forest and all creatures within it. If he fails, then his blood will be on your hands, and I will have you

189

kill him," she warned, her white eyes aglow.

Jeremiah nodded toward me.

I gave in. "It's a deal."

"Splendid." She motioned for Jeremiah to come to her. She took his hand into hers and it began to glow a translucent blue. He fell to his knees, his face full of pain, and I lunged toward him, but Nicolai was faster than I. He wrapped his strong arms around me to keep me from disturbing the transformation that was taking place right before my eyes. Ctephanyi smiled wickedly as Jeremiah cried out in pain.

I looked up into Nicolai's fiery orange eyes. "Please stop her," I begged.

He looked down and shook his head.

Anger coursed through my body. "Perhaps the crimson moss can stop her."

That caught his attention, and he grabbed my hands firmly. "No, you will not hurt my mother."

I stared at him in despair. "I thought you loved me."

"I do," he whispered, "but this is the only way we can be together."

"I hate you," I hissed.

My words hit their mark, and he released me, his eyes full of undeniable hurt. I rushed to Jeremiah's side, and Ctephanyi let him go.

"Wow," I muttered, breathlessly falling to my knees beside him. I couldn't believe the transformation. He was even more handsome than he'd originally been. His beautiful blue eyes were electrifying with their white hue. His hair had turned completely platinum, and his shirt was snug over his refined muscles.

"You can stop your drooling," he laughed,

hugging me.

I let out a strangled gurgle. "I—can't—breathe . . ."

He cringed. "Sorry, that's going to take some getting used to," he commented, flexing his arm. I smiled at how completely impressed he was by himself.

"You look amazing," I whispered.

"Thank you for everything." He reached in for another hug and I eyed him cautiously.

"I won't break you." He laughed.

"Oh, alright." I reached in for another hug. This one was far more tender and loving.

He kissed my forehead and looked directly in my eyes. "I came here to save you, and you saved me instead."

I kissed him on the cheek and sat back. I was amazed by his transformation. The twinkle in his eye had returned, and he almost looked happy. I went to thank Ctephanyi, but grew quiet with surprise as I realized I wasn't the only fan of Jeremiah's new look. The expression on Laurana's face reminded me of the look a child gets when they get a shiny, new toy.

She stared at him with admiration and lust. Jeremiah, confused by the look on my face, followed my gaze. I laughed to myself as his boyish grin returned. He flexed his muscles to impress her, and she looked away embarrassed.

I turned toward Ctephanyi. "What did you do to him?"

"He's now what we call Nwyfre."

"Nwy-what?"

She smiled. "My dear, Nwyfre simply means life-force."

I looked at her, confused. "Life-force?"

She nodded. "I have taken the very life from his soul and infused it with the forces of nature." She admired her work. "He will most certainly make a formidable foe."

"You've infused him with the forces of nature," I repeated slowly.

"Yes. He can now control all forces of nature such as lightning, wind, rain, and so forth."

Jeremiah's eyes lit up. "So, in some sense, I'm kind of like one of the X-Men!"

Ctephanyi looked at him, confused. "A what?"

I shook my head and smirked at him. He was such a dork.

She brushed off her confusion and nodded toward the door. "Shall we be on our way then?"

Her guard motioned for us to go outside. My father, who had been watching from the corner, refused.

"I will not go with her," he stated sternly.

Ctephanyi whipped her head around. "Oh yes, you most certainly will."

My father grabbed the wooden knife off the table. "Try me."

She nodded at the guard. "Please take care of this. I do not have the patience or time to deal with another stubborn human."

"No!" I called out as Nicolai picked me up and carried me outside. "You put me down right now!" I ordered.

"Angelina, he will be okay," he whispered. "You have to trust me."

"How can I? You are the biggest traitor of them all."

He held a finger to my lips to hush me. "He

can take care of himself."

I shook my head helplessly and stared at the cottage. "I will never forgive you."

He ignored my statement and kept walking. I stared at the cottage as a flood of old feelings crowded my emotions. I hated Nicolai for betraying me, and Jeremiah for standing by helplessly. I hated Ctephanyi for her cruel intentions, and Laurana—well, I just hated her. I had lost everything that ever mattered to me and I really couldn't care less what they turned me into. If anything, once I was one of them, I knew I would lose the ability to care about anyone or anything, and I was okay with that.

26

Unforgiven

Jeremiah glanced at my unhappy face as we followed Ctephanyi through the forest. Nicolai caught his eye and glared. Being the cocky person he was, Jeremiah winked at him and turned around.

Nicolai sighed. "You have to trust me, Angelina. Things will turn out as they should," he murmured softly.

I ignored him and focused on my surroundings. I found it odd that the birds had stopped singing their sweet songs and the trees now seemed almost barren without their beautiful crimson leaves. The crimson moss that could usually be seen snaking itself around the trees and running across the ground was black and shriveled. Rock formations stood tall in the distance and, for a moment, I felt like I had walked into a *Travel Channel* documentary on Stonehenge. I was curious if there had always been signs of this strange species. Had we humans always just assumed the world's oddities came from aliens?

Ctephanyi placed her hand upon one of the mystifying structures and, one by one, small, intricate runic symbols began to appear on them. The ground trembled angrily under our feet. Suddenly, a portion of the ground gave away, revealing a set of stairs that led into pure darkness. Ctephanyi nodded to Laurana. "We need to get them inside. Something or someone is nearby."

Laurana smiled. "Shall I take care of it?"

Ctephanyi shook her head. "No. I sense this creature is very strong and isn't human," she warned before disappearing into the darkness.

Curious fear could be seen in Laurana's arctic eyes. "You heard the lady. Let's get moving."

Nicolai held onto me tightly as he carried me down into the darkness. I knew immediately human eyes weren't meant for this place, because no matter how hard I tried, I just couldn't get my eyes to focus. I wondered if perhaps someone had cast a magic spell to keep others out.

"Don't worry, I won't drop you," Nicolai whispered.

The stairs seemed to go on forever, and I was relieved when we arrived at the bottom of them. He finally set me down, and my eyes adjusted to the welcome sight of lit torches along the walls of a dim tunnel. I was pretty sure their secret hiding place was safe from all mankind. Nobody was going to find this place.

Nicolai grabbed my hand and led me down the tunnel. We arrived in front of a large wooden door with the same beautiful runic carvings engraved into it. Ctephanyi placed her hand upon it and muttered something incomprehensible. The carvings began to glow softly and the door opened slowly. A bright light appeared, and my hand instantly rose to shield my eyes.

Ctephanyi walked through the opening, stopping momentarily to offer me her hand. "Don't be afraid. Our world does not hold dangers like the one above us."

Hesitating, I turned around and looked at Jeremiah who nodded in approval. I sighed knowing there was no turning back and took a step forward, immediately feeling a powerful sensation run throughout my body.

"Well, here goes nothing," I grumbled, taking another step toward the opening. I knew that once I crossed into their world, my time as a human would be short. I envisioned them whisking me away immediately and doing weird, magical things to me. I was curious what I would be like. Would I be evil like Laurana and Ctephanyi or loving like Nicolai? I guess I didn't really care anymore. My mother and father—the two people I loved most—had been taken from me, leaving me bitter and alone in a big world. I had become a part of something so much bigger than the small world I knew growing up. I took one last look at Jeremiah and held my breath.

Jeremiah smiled at me and held out his hand. "Let's do it together."

Nicolai glared at him as my hand slipped away from his and joined Jeremiah's. I nodded and, together, hand-in-hand we walked through the door. It closed behind us, and at that moment, another chapter of my life came to an end.

27

Hidden Beauty

The ceiling was covered in a million tiny stars; each one twinkled with perfection, begging me to make a wish. Looking closer, I noticed that they were actually small, intricate, illuminated diamonds.

"Oh, how beautiful," I said.

"These diamonds," Ctephanyi said, "are illuminated with the souls of the ones that have passed on before us. They are the light in our darkness."

Jeremiah stared at the diamond sky. "So their souls become trapped in them?"

Ctephanyi turned to look at him. "No, dear boy. When our kind die, we take them to a very sacred place where their blood is fed to the earth, and their soul willingly goes inside a diamond to shine as a constant reminder of their love and dedication."

"Their blood is fed to the earth?" I asked, wrinkling my nose.

Nicolai laughed. "It's not what you think, Angelina. You see, once the blood is fed to the earth, it thanks us by growing the beautiful crimson moss. That is a constant reminder that our people are at peace with the earth and all that inhabit it."

I stared at him in disbelief. "The crimson moss is actually fused with the blood of your species? That's just gross."

Laurana glared at me. "Tell me, Angelina, what is it that your species does to honor one another? Bury them in the cold shallow ground so they can rot? Oh wait, you wouldn't know yet, but I'm sure you will soon, with your mother dying and all."

I lunged toward her, "You bi . . ."

Jeremiah grabbed me around the waist, pulling me back toward him. "She's not worth it," he mumbled, giving her a nasty look.

I sighed. He was right. He squeezed my hand, reminding me to calm down, and I exhaled slowly. I reminded myself that I was in one of the most beautiful places anyone could have ever imagined, and I wasn't going to allow her to ruin my view of it.

I took a step forward and, to my surprise, the ground illuminated underneath me. Smiling, I took another step. "The ground lights up!"

Ctephanyi laughed. "Yes, my dear. Because we live underground, we are under constant darkness. However," she pointed at the white illumination under my feet, "that helps us find our way around."

"Amazing," I whispered.

My surroundings were definitely different from what I was used to. Beautiful carved-wood homes stood side-by-side, a different colored symbol engraved on each one. Curious glowing eyes watched us from behind window openings and glass doors.

Ctephanyi stepped in front of me and smiled. "My dear, what did you expect? Pure darkness?" She chuckled. "Come. There is much to see."

We followed her through the city, our

footsteps lighting up with each step. I passed a few curious bystanders, each beautiful face staring at us with their odd-colored eyes. I wondered what color my eyes would be, and felt Nicolai's warm breath in my ear.

"They'll be the most beautiful amber color and will glow like the sun setting on a warm fall day."

I smiled, enjoying the cool crisp air on my newly flushed cheeks. I closed my eyes and took a deep breath in. This was not at all what I had expected. If anyone were to find out about this place—I shook my head again and tried to push away the gruesome images that had begun to creep inside my head. If humans were ever to go up against this species, I feared the worst—for the humans.

Ctephanyi motioned for us to follow her into the most exquisite of all the buildings, which turned out to be her home. It fit her personality perfectly with its smooth marble pillars and wooden double doors that had a picture of a beautiful goddess carved into them. I had never seen such grandeur in my life.

"Who's that?" I questioned, pointing toward the picture.

Nicolai smiled. "That's Hecate, goddess of the underworld."

"Oh, she sounds kind of scary," I whispered, temporarily forgetting my anger toward him.

He laughed. "Yeah, she's one of those goddesses you don't mess with."

I nodded and heard Jeremiah's breath catch as we walked through the double doors. I couldn't help but let out a small gasp, myself. The inside was completely normal. After all the beauty we had just witnessed, this seemed so—boring.

"I like comfort. What can I say?" Ctephanyi said with a smirk.

I couldn't argue. She had good taste. She led us over to a worn leather couch and motioned for us to sit down. I couldn't help but notice the giant bear rug that lay in front of it. I carefully tiptoed around its furry head and sat down. She laughed and walked into an adjoining room, returning a moment later with a tray containing five crystal glasses and a pitcher of what looked to be lemonade. She set the pitcher on a small table next to her, carefully poured the yellow liquid into each glass, and offered one to each of us. I smiled politely and took a sip. The tangy sweetness was quite refreshing. I quickly gulped down the rest of the glass and looked up. All eyes were on me, and I blushed. "I guess I was thirstier than I thought."

Jeremiah shook his head smiling. "Don't let her give you that line. She loves lemonade and will drink that whole pitcher if you let her."

I punched him in the arm softly, and he laughed. Nicolai smiled and put his hand on mine. For a moment, I debated pushing it off, reminding myself I was still angry with him, but he flashed me his devilishly handsome smile, and I decided to let it stay put.

Ctephanyi crossed her long slender legs and tapped her fingers on the arm of the chair. The awkward silence became almost unbearable. Finally, a guard walked in from the other room and whispered something in her ear. Her face remained motionless. She nodded, and he, in turn, motioned for the other guards in the room to follow him. Once they all left, she turned toward us and smiled, her perfect white teeth sparkling under the soft glow of the lamplight.

"Angelina, I do apologize that we've had to meet under these—circumstances." Her smile faded. "I do regret that tonight will not be the night you become one of us. We have some information on your red-eyed intruder."

"What? Really? Do you know who it is?"

"Yes, dear, I'm afraid so."

"Mother, what monstrous being has done such horrible things to Angelina's mother?" Nicolai asked, squeezing my hand.

I looked at him, and for the first time, I could feel hope rise within me. If there was one thing I could do before being turned into some new species, it was finding the evil creature and repaying him for the injustice he had brought to my mother.

Ctephanyi sat for a moment in deep thought, shaking her head and occasionally opening her mouth to say something. Nicolai's eyes showed a bit of worry. Apparently it was unlike his mother to have nothing to say.

"Mother?" He tried to hide the anxiety in his voice.

Ctephanyi looked at him and smiled reassuringly. "There seems to be some mistake, I'm sure of it."

"Mother, please, what is it? Let us ease your mind and create a plan to rid ourselves of this evil creature that plagues the world above us."

She stood up and walked over to the fireplace where she retrieved an antique photo album. She clutched it close to her chest and walked toward us, motioning for Nicolai to scoot over. He gave her a look of disappointment but did as he was told. She sat down next to me and placed the book on her knees. She ran her delicate fingers over the intricate letter "H" inscribed upon it. I could only imagine the look on my face once I saw the letter on the book. I slowly reached for the silver chain that hung around my neck, pulled it out, and held the locket in the palm of my hand. Inscribed on the front was the same letter. They matched perfectly. Ctephanyi looked at me and, for once, I saw surprise on her face.

"Where did you get that?" she asked, watching the locket intently.

"It was given to me a very long time ago," I replied, closing my hand around the locket. I was afraid she'd snatch it from me. Reading my thoughts once again, she placed her hand over mine and smiled.

"Dear, I'm not going to take anything away from you. I believe enough of that has been done already."

I looked back down at my hand and opened it, allowing her to examine it a bit closer.

"May I?" Her voice almost pleaded for me to say yes.

I obliged, and she picked the locket up, running her delicate fingers over the small keyhole. Smiling, she closed my hand back around it and opened the book. I wondered what she was about to show me and watched as she turned to the first page. A black and white photo appeared of a young Nicolai standing beside a tree. He appeared unhappy in the photograph, with his arms crossed and a frown upon his youthful face.

"This was a happy day." She laughed, running her fingers across the picture.

"Really? That's what he looked like happy?" The words slipped right out of my mouth. "I'm sorry. I didn't mean that to sound . . ."

"No, dear, it's fine. He always had that look about him. We could never really tell what kind of mood he was in. However, this particular day was a good one." She ran her hand over the picture again. "You see, on this particular day, he'd gotten to see the world above for the first time. I'll never forget the way his eyes widened at the sight of the trees, the wonder upon his face as he placed his bare foot on the green grass, or the way he basked in the warmth of the sun above. After that, I couldn't seem to keep him home. He was always so curious about the things that were unknown to him. He would spend hours on the surface trying to become familiar with the things he didn't understand."

She turned the page revealing a picture of Nicolai sitting on a large rock by the river. He had a slight smirk on his face, but he was somewhat older. I looked at him with a grin, and he quickly reached over to turn the page.

"Mother, must we really do this? I'm sure Angelina is getting bored looking at these old pictures." He looked quite embarrassed.

"Oh no, I think this is great," I said, enjoying the torment I knew he was feeling from my seeing his past. It was only fair since he'd gotten to actually watch me grow up. Each picture taught me more about him: how he'd carved his first bow or what he thought about the cities that began to grow on the edges of the forest. I felt as if I were watching him grow up right before my eyes. I listened intently and, for a moment, I forgot that there was anyone else in the room.

"Now, my dear, these next few photographs you may recognize. I only ask that you don't say anything until we're finished going through them," Ctephanyi politely requested, looking over at Nicolai.

He looked just as puzzled as I felt. I nodded in agreement, and she picked up the corner of the next page. She held it for a moment, hesitating to turn it over. The suspense was overwhelming. Finally, she flipped it to the next photograph, and my breath caught. It was a picture of me as a baby. I recognized the curly brown hair, the pale skin, and the chestnut colored eyes. She turned the next page and, once again, I found myself looking at a younger version of me.

I admired the photo and remembered the day well. It had been a scorching day, and everyone in the neighborhood had decided to have a barbeque. All the children had their bathing suits on for the annual water balloon war. I sat quietly, staring at the picture in front of me. I looked up at Nicolai and could see he was just as engrossed as I was. Apparently, he had no clue that his mother kept pictures of me. It shocked both of us to see that she actually cared enough for him and me to make sure she kept memories of both of us. Turning the page, I laughed at the picture of me in my prom dress. I smiled at the image of Nicolai standing near me in the background. He was leaning against a tree, arms crossed, eyes watching ever so intently.

"You were there?" I whispered quietly.

"Yes, he was," Jeremiah interrupted suddenly.

"You knew?" I asked, turning my head toward him.

"I realized it one night in the woods. I remembered that night, how you'd come down the stairs looking absolutely gorgeous."

I blushed and made a face at him.

Nicolai wrinkled up his nose in disgust. "You know, you almost kissed him that night."

I had kind of figured the jealousy between the two of them would've faded when Jeremiah went through his transformation. However, I was sadly mistaken. Perhaps Laurana could change that, I thought to myself, noticing her watchful eye on Jeremiah's every move. It was becoming quite obvious that she had feelings for him.

Looking back down at the picture, I smiled and turned the page. There I was in my graduation gown with a big cheesy smile on my face. My mother was next to me smiling proudly. I could feel the warm tears begin to form in my eyes. Ctephanyi carefully peeled back the paper that held the picture in place and handed it to me.

"I can have this?" I asked, astonished by her gift.

"Yes, my dear. You've given my son something I could never give him. You've given him true love. Though I do so wish you weren't human, I've always known he would never give up on having you in his life. I knew one day things would fall into place, and we would have this very conversation." She patted my hand.

I began to rethink my thoughts of her. Perhaps she wasn't the evil monster I'd envisioned. In fact, she seemed to be a caring mother who just wanted the best for her only son. After all, he was all she had left.

I held the picture close to my heart and thought of how badly I wanted to find the red-eyed monster that had taken my mother away from me. I wanted to make him pay for what he'd done. Sensing my frustration, Nicolai reached behind his mother and caressed my hair. I smiled, shaking off the evil thoughts, and waited for her to turn the page.

Ctephanyi glanced up, the smile fading from her face as she slowly flipped to the next page, revealing a photo of herself leaning against a dashing man with dark features.

"No," I whispered in disbelief.

The man had the same frown Nicolai had carried in many of the previous pictures I'd seen. He stood proudly, his stern eyes staring straight ahead and his muscular build standing firm. There was only one problem with this photograph: the man in the picture was the red-eyed intruder who'd pushed his way into my home, killed my mother, and tried to kill me. The chills ran through me. I remembered that look—the glare of those eyes.

"Angelina, what is it?" Nicolai questioned, a worried tone in his voice.

"It can't be."

"What? What is it?" he asked, standing up.

Ctephanyi closed the book and stood up. She walked over to the mantle and carefully set the book back down. She looked at me at nodded.

"So it's true, then."

Nicolai looked at his mother with confusion. "What's true?"

She turned her back toward him and tapped her slender fingers lightly on the old photo album. "Angelina, would you kindly tell him who the man in the photograph is?"

"Why would she need to tell me who's in the photograph? I know he's been gone a long time and I've never met him, but I've seen my father's face before."

I slid closer to him and took his hands into mine. He looked at me curiously as I tried to muster up the courage to tell him something I knew he wouldn't want to believe.

"Please, my love," he pleaded. "What is it? What are we all in so much shock about?"

"Nicolai, do you remember the night I was attacked in my house and my mother was murdered?"

"Yes, of course I do."

"Well . . ." I let go of his hands and slowly stood up. Glancing over at Jeremiah, I knew he'd understood immediately what I'd been hinting at. His jaw was tightly clenched, and his muscular hands were now balled-up fists. He watched the scene in front of him intently, waiting for any opportunity to jump in and let out his pent up frustration.

"Please, just tell me," Nicolai begged.

Sighing I turned back around to face him. "Nicolai, the man in the photograph—he's the man who killed my mother. He's the man who tried to kill me."

"Impossible! He's dead!" he cried out, an

astonished look on his face.

"No, it's true. I would recognize that man's face anywhere," I replied solemnly.

Nicolai turned to his mother. "He's alive?"

"Yes. I fear what she says is true, my dear son. I don't know how it's possible, to be quite honest."

Nicolai stood up and began pacing back and forth. "Where would he have hidden all these years without us noticing him? And why would he want Angelina?"

"That my son I don't have an answer for, but I assure you we're going to find out." She called for her guards, and they came in instantly.

"It seems the rumors are true. Spread out, and find him. When he's found, bring him to me, but be wary, for he'll be a formidable foe." She nodded and they left as quickly as they'd come.

Silence filled the room. Jeremiah was deep in thought, and I was sure he was thinking of a clever way to get us out of yet another mess. Laurana sat quietly picking at her fingernails while Nicolai stared at the wall in disbelief. Ctephanyi appeared calm and collected as she sat back down next to me on the old couch. She grabbed my hand and held it next to her cheek. It was so smooth and cool.

"Soon you'll be like this: beautiful, never aging. I know it's not what you'd hoped your life would be, but it will grow on you, and you'll see things you've only ever dreamt about. You'll be in a family that will protect you to the ends of the earth."

My eyes met hers. "Are you not afraid?" I asked.

"Afraid of what, my child? My husband who has mysteriously come back to life after years of being presumed dead? No, I'm not afraid. In fact, he is the one who should be afraid." Her eyes began to glow as the anger rose within her. "It's been a long day. Why don't you all retire for the night? You'll need your strength for our journey tomorrow."

"Journey?" I questioned.

"Nicolai, please show the humans to their rooms. Laurana come with me. We've much to discuss."

Without saying another word, she stood up and walked out of the room with Laurana following right behind. Nicolai held his hand out to me, and I accepted it with a smile. He pulled me up off the couch and drew me into his arms, kissing my forehead lovingly. Jeremiah stretched his muscular arms and yawned loudly to let us know he was still in the room. My cheeks flushed, and I stared at him. I couldn't get over how different he looked.

Nicolai led us through the large house and down a dimly lit hallway. Stopping in front of one of the doors, he opened it and peered inside. "Jeremiah, this is your room."

He gave Nicolai a dirty look. "Angelina, are you sure you want to sleep alone tonight? I can be your teddy bear while you sleep to keep away the monsters."

I playfully punched him in the arm, and he chuckled, closing the door behind him. Nicolai frowned, and we continued down the hallway. Stopping in front of another door, he opened it, only this time he walked inside. I followed him and smiled at the room that had been chosen for me. It was charming with its hand-carved canopy bed, an antique armoire, and beautiful rose wallpaper. It reminded me of home.

I sat down on the bed and ran my hand over the soft quilt that covered it. I knew I'd be asleep as soon as my head hit the pillow. I looked over at Nicolai, and I could tell by the look on his face that he wanted to ask me a question but just wasn't sure how. Reading his body language, I already knew what he was about to ask. I smiled at him shyly and nodded. His eyes lit up and a boyish grin spread across his handsome face.

He opened the armoire doors and took out a long silk gown. "Here, put this on. I'm sure you're tired of wearing those dirty clothes."

I took it from him gratefully and admired its soft, smooth silkiness. I looked around the room for a place to get dressed, and a thought hit me. If Nicolai had watched me my whole life, how many times had he seen me get dressed?

Laughing, he put his hand on my shoulder. "I may be a man, but I've always respected your privacy."

"Well, thank you." I replied, feeling my face grow hot.

"I'll turn around while you get dressed. I promise not to peek."

"No peeking?"

He laughed and turned around. "No peeking. I promise."

I quickly undressed and slipped the silk gown over my head. It slid down my body, hugging my curves in all the right places. It was an awkward feeling to be in something so extravagant even though it felt absolutely amazing on my skin.

"Okay, you can turn around."

Nicolai turned around with an impressed look upon his handsome face. He wrapped his arms around my silky waist. "You look ravishing."

I lay my head against his chest and smiled.

He leaned back and kissed my forehead. "You must be exhausted."

I nodded sleepily.

He pulled the quilt back and guided me into the bed where he gently tucked me in. "Are you sure you want me to stay?"

"Yes, please stay. I feel safe when you're with me," I urged, my eyes getting heavy with sleep.

Satisfied with my answer, he pulled his cotton shirt up over his head. Suddenly my eyes weren't so heavy anymore. I admired his beautifully chiseled chest and muscular arms. He crawled under the quilt next to me, and I breathed in his intoxicating scent. He reached over me to turn the lamp off, and I had to restrain myself from taking advantage of him. The room grew dark, and I cuddled next to his cool body while he caressed my hair gently.

"Angelina?"

"Yes?" I replied sleepily.

"Are you still angry with me?"

I closed my eyes. "No, I'm not angry anymore."

"I want you to know that you're my world," he whispered softly in my ear, "and I will do whatever is necessary to protect you, even if that means giving up my life."

I nodded in agreement. I knew exactly what he meant. When I was with him, everything felt right. He was the only person I'd ever felt this strongly about. I drifted off to sleep knowing I had finally found my fairy tale prince who made me feel like a princess. I only hoped this story had a happy ending.

28

Companionship

I awoke the next morning only to find myself alone. Disappointed, I stretched and buried myself in the soft quilt. Though my sleep was one of the most peaceful I'd had in days, I had hoped to wake up next to Nicolai. I surveyed the room and noticed a wicker basket on the floor by the armoire full of neatly folded clothes. A small white card stood on top of them next to a beautiful white rose. I rolled off the bed and shivered as my bare feet came down on the cold marble floor. Wrapping the quilt around me, I went to the basket, picked up the rose, and held it to my nose, enjoying its sweet scent. Laying it back down carefully, I picked up the small card. It read:

> *Even the most beautiful of roses will never compare to the beauty that is within you. I will see you soon. Enjoy the new clothes.*
>
> *Your dearest,*
> *Nicolai*

I smiled holding the card against my chest. I couldn't wait to see him. Bending down, I rummaged through the basket taking delight in my new wardrobe. I quickly changed, deciding on a fitted sweater that matched my eyes, a pair of flattering jeans, and a wool jacket. I put the quilt back on the bed and went to the door, startled by Jeremiah's presence as I opened it.

"Hey there, sleepy head," he said. "They're all waiting for you."

"Who're they?" I asked puzzled.

He smiled, giving me a wink. "You'll see."

I followed him down the hallway and through a door that led to a winding staircase. We walked down the steps toward a set of large double doors with the letter "H" carved into them. Gasping, I looked at Jeremiah, and he nodded, pulling them open. Inside, there was a long wooden table surrounded by people, each with unusually colored eyes staring back at me. Noticing Nicolai's beautiful orange eyes, I walked slowly toward him, apprehensive as the other eyes followed me. I sat in the empty chair next to him and smiled weakly as he placed his hand over mine.

"Who are all these people?" I whispered.

"My mother has called them all here to help us figure out how my father has come back from the dead, and why he would want you."

"Are they all like you?" I asked looking around, noticing that some of the faces were noticeably different from the others. One in particular caught my eye—a man who looked to be human. He was handsome with short, messy, blond hair, dark brown eyes, and a wicked smile. I shivered as he watched me more intensely than the others.

"No, not all of them are of our kind. The one watching you, he's a vampire."

"A vampire? He looks completely normal." I took another look at the man across the table from me. I would never have guessed him to be a vampire. He didn't have pointy fangs or pale skin. In fact, he looked just as human as I was.

Nicolai glanced over at the vampire. "Kind of scary, isn't it, knowing that something so deadly can look so normal?"

"Why is he looking at me like he wants to eat me?"

Nicolai laughed. "Well, probably because he does."

Shuddering at the thought, I took one more look at the man across from me, realizing that all the stories I'd heard as a child had truth to them. Shuddering again, I decided to focus my attention elsewhere, so I counted the faces at the table. There were thirteen including myself. One chair remained empty, which I assumed was for Ctephanyi. Out of the thirteen, three immediately caught my attention. The vampire, of course, was one of them, but there was also a pretty female who sat at the end of the table. She had short, curly, brown hair, lavender eyes, and olive-colored skin. She smiled at me and, for some reason, I knew I was going to like her. I had the feeling I had met her somewhere before. A mysterious man with jet-black hair, powder-white skin, and red eyes sat quietly at the other end of the table. He kept to himself, except for the occasional glance in my direction. Our eyes met, and I watched as one of his eyes went from blood red to bright white. Shocked, I opened my mouth to say something, but the man held his finger to his mouth to hush me. I smiled politely and looked down. I felt out of place with all the odd creatures around me. They made me feel so small and vulnerable.

The room grew quiet as the double doors opened and Ctephanyi walked in followed by a slew of guards. They placed themselves behind each person seated at the table. I didn't blame her for the extra protection.

Everyone continued to watch her in silence as she stood proudly at the head of the table, looking around. She seemed pleased by the turnout and smiled.

"You all know why you were brought here. We have a matter at hand that needs to be resolved immediately." She looked in my direction, and I could feel my face turning red as all eyes focused on me.

"Why should we help this human?" a voice called out from the end of the table. "Let him have her, that's what I say." I looked down to see where the voice had come from and saw that it was the man with the red eyes. I glared at him and raised my brow. How dare he.

"Mathias, that's enough. This human is not what you think," Nicolai interrupted with warning in his voice.

"No, Mathias is right. Why should we help this human?" another voice objected, this time coming from a bright-blue-eyed girl.

"She'll save us all," I heard a sweet voice say.

I looked to see where it was coming from. It was the girl with the lavender eyes, smiling. Surprised looks were on many of the faces around the table.

"Why do you say that?" the vampire asked.

"She is the only one who can stop what is going to happen," she said simply.

Mathias rolled his eyes. "What's that supposed to mean? Why do you always speak in riddles that none of us can understand?"

She smiled at him as he glared at her and shook his head. Ctephanyi tapped her slender fingers on the table, and it began to tremble. Everyone immediately focused on her.

"Bethani, what do you know of this?" she asked, looking at the pretty lavender-eyed girl.

"My goodness, you don't know?" She smiled up at her sweetly.

Ctephanyi frowned. "This is not a time for games, my child."

"Oh, but this is no game. She will save us, all of us. You'll see."

A sudden look of realization washed over Nicolai's face. His expression changed from worry to anger to knowing, and I wondered what had just crossed his mind.

"This is getting us nowhere," Ctephanyi continued. "As you're all aware, my husband who died hundreds of years ago has come back. He's taken his wrath out on the humans and has tried to abduct Angelina. For what reason, we do not know. It's imperative that we find him before he puts us all in danger. If the humans knew of our existence . . . " Her voice trailed off.

"She's right. If the humans knew of our existence, it would create a bloodbath," another voice exclaimed.

"That's a bad thing?" A devilish grin crossed the vampire's face.

Nicolai tried to hide the smirk on his face. "Stephen, that's not funny."

"Enough! That's quite enough." Ctephanyi

raised her voice. "It's time we make a choice. We need to find him and bring him to justice, or let him continue on his destructive path, which, in turn, will put us all in great danger. What do you all say? Are we in agreement?"

Each person at the table looked at each other, each one pondering what had been said and wondering if I did indeed hold the key to their futures. Sensing their hesitation, Nicolai stood up and cleared his throat. They all turned their attention toward him.

"As you all know, I would give my life for this human. It's rare that one can say such a thing especially since human interaction has been forbidden within our lands. I have defied my mother, my species, and have even killed my own kind for her."

I watched as surprise ran through the many faces around the table. Apparently, they were unaware of everything Nicolai had done to be with me.

He looked down at me. "Now that I've experienced a love such as this, I can never let it go." I blushed yet again and tried to not think of all the eyes that were on me.

"Love is a powerful weapon. Though some of you may disagree, it's the one key that can unlock many doors in the world. I've seen this with my very own eyes. You see, there's a secret that I've kept for a very long time now." He hesitated.

I glanced over at Ctephanyi and watched her gaze shift toward him. Curiosity had hit its mark, and if anyone were paying close attention, it was her. She generally knew everything that was going on, and it was rare for secrets to be kept from her.

"A very long time ago, I ran across this human in the forest. I watched as she knelt in front of her dying father who'd been wounded protecting her from a large bear."

"So, you're saying this human watched her father die? That happens every day in the human world, my friend," Mathias pointed out without emotion.

"Yes, Mathias, you're correct in that assumption. However, on this day, I watched something truly amazing happen." Nicolai smiled at me again, that charming dimple taunting me. "You see, after her father passed, she went to the wounded bear. Instead of taking her anger and sorrow out on the animal that had just murdered her father, she did something miraculous. She laid her hands on the bear—and healed it. With my own eyes I watched the bear stand up, its wounds completely gone. It stood for a moment watching her, as if to say thank you before running off into the woods."

I scanned the many faces around the table and could see looks of disbelief in their eyes, including Ctephanyi's. Jeremiah, who happened to be standing in the corner next to Laurana, caught my eye and winked. Laurana stared at me, as if she'd already known this secret. I turned back to Nicolai, who was giving everyone a moment to digest what they'd just heard.

"So you're saying Angelina has the same ability to heal the dying?" the vampire asked, intrigued.

"Yes, that is exactly what I'm saying."

"Please correct me if I'm mistaken," the

vampire continued, "but isn't this human a reborn soul? Isn't it impossible to pass that power from one life to the next?"

"In all of our history, we've never encountered a species with the ability to heal the dying—until now," Nicolai declared.

"Impossible," Ctephanyi whispered in disbelief.

"Maybe not," Jeremiah said, stepping forward. "After Angelina was severely injured in the woods, Nicolai took us to his cabin. I saw her body heal itself. Broken bones, open wounds, bruises—it was as if she'd never been injured at all."

"If what you're saying is true, then what a powerful ally she could be to all of us," Mathias announced, looking at the others around the table. A few of them nodded in agreement.

"Bethani, is what Nicolai speaks of true?" Stephen inquired, looking at her. She smiled her sweet, childlike smile and stood up.

"Oh yes, it's very true. Nicolai does not have the ability to lie. This human is indeed gifted. She has the capability to do much more than heal." She walked toward me.

"What do you mean? What else can she do?" Stephen blurted out, intrigued by the new development.

I wanted to disappear. Fear began to grow within my heart, as I knew what they were all thinking. If any one of them had me, I could potentially become their own personal weapon. Too bad, I didn't know what special abilities I apparently had.

"She can do many things, as you will all see

very soon." Bethani stopped behind my chair. I was afraid to turn around.

"How is this even possible?" Ctephanyi asked. She was just as intrigued as everyone else.

"We've all heard the stories of a race that was here long before any of us," Bethani said. "The humans vanquished their entire species in a matter of years. During that treacherous time, many of them were sold into slavery or were used as weapons in war. This species just happened to be the most powerful of all species ever known, however, their greatest weakness was their peaceful nature. The humans took advantage of that fact."

"Are you saying this girl is a relative of this ancient species?" Ctephanyi suggested, her gaze shifting toward me.

"Oh yes. You see, each one of their species possessed a certain power that would disappear when they died. But Angelina is different." She looked around the room. "Right now, she is the most powerful person here."

"How can that be?" Mathais asked. "Ctephanyi, when you raised this soul did you notice anything different?"

"No." She shook her head. "In fact, of all the souls that have been reborn, hers was the easiest."

"Of course it was. Her soul knew it would come back eventually, and you gave it the perfect opportunity," Bethani answered curtly.

"And this girl has no idea of the powers she possesses?" Mathias questioned again.

"Of course not. Her full powers have yet to be awakened."

"Perhaps this is why the abduction was attempted," Stephen interjected. "Maybe he knew what she was."

"And if he had her, he could use her as a powerful weapon to destroy all of us," Mathias stated matter-of-factly.

"But why would my father want to destroy all of us?" Nicolai looked at his mother.

"Perhaps we are not the ones he wants to destroy." Ctephanyi replied, a look of understanding on her pale face. "Perhaps he wants to destroy the humans."

Everyone at the table grew quiet. They all knew she was right. He wanted to wage war against the humans and use me as his weapon. I felt sick to my stomach.

"Don't worry, Angelina. I'm here to protect you." Bethani placed her warm hand on my shoulder. A memory flashed before my eyes. It was Bethani walking next to me in a field of flowers. Blinking the image away, I realized that I felt oddly comforted by her presence, and I knew there had to be some underlying story behind this memory.

"We've met before?"

She winked. "Oh yes."

Surprise crossed Nicolai's face. He was obviously unaware of this fact. "You've met her?"

Smiling, she looked at him and simply replied, "Yes."

"How is that possible? I've watched her grow from the time she was an infant. I would've felt your presence."

"Well, Nicolai, I'm afraid that's my secret, and

I'm not quite ready to share it yet." She patted my arm and walked back to her seat.

Ctephanyi looked overwhelmed. "Well, this is definitely an interesting turn of events."

I glanced over at Jeremiah who was watching her intently, ready to come to my side if needed. I knew even though she'd gifted him with special abilities and an oath had been made, he would forever be loyal to me.

Nicolai looked to his mother for guidance. "What do you suggest we do?"

Ctephanyi sat back down and closed her eyes. Opening them again, she smiled and looked directly at me. "Why don't we ask Angelina what we she suggests we do? After all, she is the key to our future."

I was speechless. I looked around the room as they all awaited my answer. Jeremiah left Laurana's side and walked over to stand behind me. Placing his hand on my shoulder, he proudly nodded. "I will speak for her."

"Another human has been amongst us?" Stephen said, surprised by the fact he hadn't noticed Jeremiah earlier.

"Yes, I am, in fact, human. I am Angelina's guardian," he answered proudly.

A girlish giggle came from the end of the table.

Jeremiah set his sights on Bethani and frowned. "What's so funny? I would challenge any of you to try and hurt her. I can promise you that I won't make it easy."

"Oh, Jeremiah, your heart is so pure. Your love for her is so overwhelming it makes my head dizzy." She giggled again.

"How do you know my name?" he asked surprised.

"I know a lot of things. I know that as a boy, you took it upon yourself to be the man in her life when all in her life were lost. You gave her a glimmer of hope, and that was all she needed to be able to smile again. You did what many could not and, in turn, it created an unbreakable bond between the two of you." She sat quietly for a moment then very softly said, "I believe you would die for her." Her smile faded.

Jeremiah had tears in his eyes. She'd spoken the truth, and it hit home for both of us. He'd always been there. He was the reason I'd never given up hope that my father was still alive.

Jeremiah, trying to regain his composure, replied, "You're right. I would die for her."

"Well, if you're willing to die for her and speak for her, then what do you suggest we do?" Mathias asked, his gaze still on me.

"I suggest we find him and fight. We can't let him wage war against the humans. If that happens, it won't be good for either side." I knew the people that sat around the table intimidated him, but he would never let them know that.

"So, you're suggesting we seek him out. Then what?" Mathias questioned.

"Kill him again." Jeremiah's bright blue eyes were full of anger.

They all turned to Ctephanyi. It was in her hands now. The options had been laid out in front of them. She looked around the table and stood up.

"As many of you know, I am not very fond of the human race. However, I will not let them die by the hands of our species nor any other. For thousands of years, we've walked this earth in peace with them, and a war is not in the best interest of either party. It'll only create suffering and tragedy on both sides. We can't allow this to happen. Our only option is to find him and kill him." Her white eyes began to glow.

Nicolai slammed his fist on the table and stood up. "He may be my father, but his actions are unacceptable. It is time we stepped in and put a stop to this."

"If this is agreed upon, I'll need volunteers to help find him and also to make sure he doesn't get his hands on our most precious weapon." Ctephanyi looked at me.

Everyone at the table began to talk amongst themselves, each one weighing the options and deciding what the best course of action would be.

Suddenly, Mathias stood up, "I will go. After all, I would rather be on the winning team than the losing one."

Bethani followed suit. "I will also go."

"Oh, why not," Stephen said, also standing up. "This should be fun." His wicked smile spread across his handsome face.

"Laurana, you will also join them." Ctephanyi pointed at her.

Laurana went to protest but quickly decided against it. "Yes, I'll go," she replied unhappily.

"Then, it's settled. You'll all leave tomorrow morning. As for the rest of you, be prepared, in case our plan fails."

Everyone nodded in agreement. The decision had been made. They'd find him and kill him, only this time they'd make sure he'd never come back.

I just hoped we'd find him before he found us. I looked to Nicolai for assurance. He kissed my forehead and smiled. "Don't worry, my love. Everything will be alright."

I laid my head on his shoulder and sighed. I hoped with all my heart he was right. The fate of many relied on our success. I had to do whatever I could to help. Failure was not an option. Even if it meant dying so everyone else could live.

29

New Purpose

I stared out over the balcony at the ceiling full of diamonds, each one twinkling and more wondrous than the next. They were beautiful, like much of the other odd things that existed in this strange place. It was hard to believe that their species' departed souls were actually illuminating the way through the darkness. In some sense, it was an endearing thought, but in another, it was completely morbid.

It was a nice change of pace, being able to consult my thoughts alone on the balcony. I was definitely feeling overwhelmed by all the new information that had been brought to the surface. I had always felt different in some way, and now I knew why. All those years of wanting to feel like a normal person now seemed like a silly dream. That was not the deck of cards that I'd been dealt, and I was okay with that. The fate of many rested upon my shoulders, and I had to find a way to succeed.

Sighing, I tried to calm my nerves. Our journey would begin in the morning, and I needed to make sure I was ready. Sensing a presence behind me, I turned around. It was Ctephanyi. She looked radiant in her long white gown, her red hair hanging loosely across her shoulders. I turned back around and returned my gaze to the ceiling of diamonds. She stood next to me for a moment in quiet silence, and then surprised me by turning and putting her hand on my cheek. Trying to fight back the tears I'd been holding for some time, I turned and looked at her.

"My dear, sometimes life makes little sense to us. At any time it can change, giving us the opportunity to ask why." She smiled and wiped away a fallen tear.

"All my life I knew I was different, but to be this?" Another tear fell down my cheek. "Why would God do this to me?"

With a smile still upon her face, she caressed my damp cheek. "Sometimes God does things that we don't understand in the moment, but will make sense in the future. He knows what he's doing, just as he did when he made you into the beautiful woman that stands here before me. There will always be tests and tribulations my dear. It's how we handle them that make us the people we become in the future."

It was nice to be comforted by her words. Perhaps she was right—one day I would understand, but for now, my path would remain a mystery. Ctephanyi placed her hands on my shoulders and pulled me in for a hug. Surprised by her motherly action, I hugged her back.

"You know, I've never had a daughter until now."

"I hope I don't disappoint you."

"You won't," she assured me. She walked to the far side of the balcony and looked up at the impressive ceiling.

"It's breathtaking, isn't it?"

I nodded in agreement and for a moment we both stared in silence.

"May I ask you a question?" I kept my gaze on the ceiling.

"Of course, my dear. Ask away."

"Why is it that you hate humans so much?"

"Ah, why do I hate humans? That does seem to be the age-old question." She sighed and stood, trying to gather her words carefully. "To be quite honest with you, it started before Nicolai was even born. You see, our kind has been around for thousands of years. We're a quiet race, mostly keeping to ourselves, which I grew bored of. Once the humans began to settle on the edge of the forest, I grew curious. Eventually, it overwhelmed me, and I began secretly sneaking to the surface where I would watch them from afar, admiring their ability to love and live in harmony amongst each other. One day, as I was walking through the woods, I came upon a half-human man named Josiah. Apparently his father, one of my species, had fallen in love with a human woman, and Josiah was the product of their union, or so I thought. He taught me many things of the human world: the love they wished for, the hate they carried, and the need to always have more. I admired him, and the more time we spent together, the more I wanted to live in his world of mysteries. Growing suspicious of the time I was spending above ground, my parents had me followed. Once they heard of my adventures, they grew angry and forbade me to see him or return to the surface. I defied them. I packed my things and left for the life I thought I wanted. Josiah took me to the small town he lived in with his charming young daughter. His wife had passed on during labor, leaving him to raise his little girl alone. Feeling sympathy for them, I suggested an arrangement in which he would let me live there as long as I wished, and in return, I would look after his daughter while he worked in the mill. A short time later, I learned the girl was gifted and possessed immense power. I begged him to let me take her to my people, to help him understand the power she possessed. He refused, calling me a traitor. He accused me of wanting to use her powers for my own selfish reasons."

For the first time, I was able to see true emotion on Ctephanyi's pretty face. Looking back at me, she continued. "One evening, as we ventured into the forests to collect firewood, I caught a glimpse of red eyes watching us nearby. Josiah also noticed them and called out to the owner. The man stepped forward, and Josiah recognized him immediately. It was his father's brother, Elias, who happened to be a pureblood of my race.

Josiah watched as his uncle studied his daughter, and he too noticed something mysterious about the young girl's demeanor. Elias read my thoughts and was able to see exactly what power the girl possessed. He attempted to coax his nephew into bringing her underground, where she could develop her powers properly. Once again, Josiah refused, feeling angry and betrayed by the both of us. He grabbed his daughter and fled from the forest. He was fearful we would take her from him. We went in search of him later that evening, but it was already too late. He'd packed up the few things they owned and disappeared."

"You were only trying to help him."

"Yes, I just wish he would've seen it as you do. Elias and I began to spend time together, eventually falling in love. He took me home, below ground, and catered to my every need. I soon realized that what I thought I wanted was a mistake. If I had just looked to my own species, I would've seen that they possessed the same abilities the humans possessed and more.

"So, I assume you eventually married him?" I questioned, smiling at her story. It reminded me of a fairy tale I'd once been told as a child.

"Yes, and it was quite lovely," she cooed, replaying the past memories in her head.

I watched as she ran her fingers over the banister. "What happened after you married?" I asked.

A frown suddenly crossed her pale face. "Soon after, I became pregnant with Nicolai. It was a joyous time for having a child, as it was the one thing we both wanted. At the same time, trouble began brewing above in the human world. The humans had discovered magical powers within a rare species, and began taking them into slavery."

"Why would they do such a thing?"

"Humans are cruel, and they wanted to use the power for their own selfish reasons."

"Did they take Josiah's daughter?" I questioned.

Ctephanyi looked at me and smiled. "You're a smart girl. You see, Josiah heard what the humans were doing and went into hiding with his daughter. But it was too late. The humans had already caught wind of the immense power the little girl possessed."

"What did he do?"

"Well, he knew the humans would come for them so he did the only thing he could do. He gave his daughter to a woman who lived deep in the forest. They had been friends for hundreds of years."

"Hundreds?"

She laughed. "Yes, our species have quite the lifespan."

"I bet it was hard for him to just leave her like that," I said, sad for the man in the story.

"It's hard for any parent to lose a child. However, before he left her, he gave her a small, black wolf puppy. He hoped they would grow up together and one day the wolf pup would be able to protect her. Plus, it was something to remember him by."

"So, what happened?"

"Well, one evening, we received news that Josiah had been captured by the humans. This angered my husband greatly. Josiah was still his family, and he felt it was his duty to rescue him. He vowed to free him and left a few days later."

"Did he find him?"

Her face went dark, and tears began to form in her ivory eyes. "No, they found Elias instead."

My eyes widened. "The humans found him?"

"They did, and after they tortured him, they left him to die by the side of the road."

I gasped. "What about his nephew, Josiah?"

"It was all a lie. They never had him. They thought they could get information from Elias about where Josiah's daughter was."

I shook my head. "That's terrible."

"What's terrible, my dear, is that I went into labor, and Nicolai was born fatherless."

I knew somewhat how she felt. I had lost my own father and had watched my mother try to hide her tears.

"Poor Nicolai." My heart ached for her. No wonder she hated us as much as she did. I could only imagine giving birth alone. I looked up at her curiously. "Did they ever find the little girl?"

She shook her head. "No, but there is rumor that Josiah's mother knew where she was hidden."

"Josiah's mother?" I asked surprised.

"Yes, his mother was human, so she blended in well with the other humans and was never a suspect."

"What happened to her?"

"She disappeared, fearful for her life. She knew they would eventually find some sort of connection between her and her son, and would come for her next."

"What about Josiah? Did they ever find him?"

Hatred filled Ctephanyi's eyes, and I quickly regretted my question.

"He was never found," she replied fiercely.

"So he's still out there?"

"Yes. However, if I ever come across him, I will make him pay dearly for acting so cowardly." A wicked smile spread across her face.

"But why? What did he do that was so wrong?"

"My husband, Elias, went to rescue him, however he didn't return the same decency. Our species are connected directly through our bloodlines, so when one feels pain it sends a ripple effect throughout the family. It's a call for help in some sense. I'm sure my husband called for help, and that coward ignored his pleas."

I trembled at the image of Ctephanyi finding Josiah. Her wrath was one nightmare I would not want any part of.

"Well, dear, it's all in the past now." Her voice lowered as she calmed herself down. "However, Nicolai only knows that his father was killed by humans. I've never told him the rest of the story."

"He doesn't know about the girl?" I asked, surprised.

She put her arm around me and gave me a small squeeze. "No, if Nicolai knew of the blood that was on Josiah's hands because of his thoughtless actions, he would've grown up with vengeance in his heart. So this will be our little secret."

I nodded.

"Angelina . . .?"

"Yes?"

"Thank you."

"For what?" I asked with a confused look on my face.

"For showing me that not all humans are the same." Smiling once more, she walked out of the room.

I stood for a moment shocked by everything I had just heard. My head began to hurt as I tried to take everything in, so I stumbled back into the room and shut the balcony doors. I felt dizzy and decided it was time to crawl into bed. I pulled back the antique quilt and curled up on the bed, enjoying the coolness the sheets offered me. I lay thinking of Nicolai and how we'd both grown up fatherless. I knew how devastated I had been and could only imagine how he had felt.

30

Dark Comfort

I heard a soft knock on my door and peered toward it. I wondered who it could possibly be and debated whether or not I wanted to move out of my comfortable position. The door cracked open, and I stared into the darkness, barely able to see anything.

"May I come in?" Nicolai whispered.

I laughed. "Of course."

He crawled in bed next to me and nuzzled my neck. I surrendered my comfortable position for something much more pleasurable, and that was being curled up right next to him.

He kissed me tenderly on the lips. "I didn't want you to be alone."

Returning his gentle kiss I smiled. "Thanks for thinking of me."

Running his hands through my hair, he kissed me once again, more passionately this time, not giving me an opportunity to object, which I was secretly thankful for. Putting aside my inhibitions, I pulled his shirt over his head and ran my hands over his muscular shoulders and down his chest. He caressed my face with his strong hands, kissing my neck softly, each kiss promising more would follow. My body tingled with excitement. I kissed his forehead and ran my hands through his messy hair. He began to slowly unbutton my shirt, kissing me softly with each button he undid. Closing my eyes, I breathed him in, not wanting the moment to end. The time had come for us to show each other just how much love we truly felt. Knowing this night would be one of my most memorable experiences, I allowed myself to enjoy every single moment of it-every kiss, every touch, every new sensation.

I awoke the next morning delighted to see the man I was destined to be with lying next to me. I enjoyed knowing I would never again have to wake up alone. Rolling over, I kissed his shoulder, amazed by how cool his skin felt against mine. Opening his eyes, he smiled. His little dimple taunted me as he ran his fingers through my tangled hair.

Suddenly, there was knock at the door that startled us both. We laughed at the thought of getting caught, and I urged him to get dressed quickly. As he buttoned up his pants, I dug through the covers, looking for his shirt. He laughed, as I was momentarily unable to find my way out of the barragè of blankets. Finally managing to find his shirt, and my way out, I threw it at him. Laughing once again, he threw it back at me, and, so it wouldn't get lost again, I decided to put it on.

I admired his muscular chest as he walked barefoot toward the door. I hid myself under the soft quilt, pulling it as close to my body as possible. He opened the door a few inches and poked his head out to see who the mystery visitor was. Hearing Jeremiah's voice from the hallway, I cringed, imagining the look of disapproval upon his face. I couldn't quite make out what they were saying, but I had a feeling it was important. A few moments later, I heard Nicolai close the

door, and deciding the coast was clear, I poked
my head out of my safe haven just in time to see
him take a flying leap onto the bed. I laughed as
I flew a few inches up off the mattress, feeling a
cool breeze against my bare skin. Jumping on top
of me, he began to growl like a wild animal.
Laughing, I tried to push him off of me. In
return, he playfully held my arms down and
kissed my face.

"They're waiting on us." He continued to kiss
every inch of my face.

I laughed blissfully and struggled to free
myself from his grasp.

"I think"—kiss—"we should"—kiss—"go." He
smiled mischievously at me.

"Then perhaps you should get off me and let
me wipe this slobber from my face."

"Slobber?" He licked my nose. "Now, you have
slobber on your face."

"You're so gross." I finally pushed him off
me. Wiping my face with the corner of the quilt,
I rolled off the bed modeling the newest addition
to my wardrobe. He lay on the bed propped up
on one arm and smiling a boyish grin.

"What are you smiling at?" I asked, as I
quickly got dressed.

"Well, perhaps it's the fact that you still have
a little slobber on your face. Or perhaps it's the
fact that I just can't get enough of you."

"I think I like the second answer better."

He rolled off the bed and walked over to me,
wrapping his strong arms around me, pulling me
close to him.

"I know this whole thing has been very
confusing for you." He caressed my hair as I

rested my head against his chest. Another gentler knock came at the door and Bethani poked her head inside.

"Well, apparently, we need to start locking our door." Nicolai winked, a playful look on his face.

"I'm sorry to disturb you, but we must leave now," she demanded in her sweet voice. "He's onto us."

"What do you mean he's onto us?" I asked, stepping away from Nicolai.

"A traitor is amongst us. All will be revealed in due time." She left without saying another word.

"Must she always speak in riddles?" Nicolai muttered under his breath.

"Who do you think it is?" I questioned, my mind running through the few it could be.

"I'm not sure, but we'll find out. I promise." He pulled me close to him. Gently kissing my head, he turned me around to face him. "I will never let anything happen to you, not ever again."

"I know." I smiled, looking up at him. "Guess what?"

He bent down to kiss me again. "What?"

Gently licking the tip of his nose, I laughed. "Now, you have slobber on your face!"

He pulled me closer to him and, once again, growled like some sort of wild animal, playfully biting down on the side of my neck. Giggling, I pushed him away and walked over to the antique chair so I could put my shoes on. He watched me quietly for a moment, a thoughtful look on his face.

"What's wrong?" I asked.

"Nothing. In fact, everything is right." As he stood in front of me smiling, he said, "You've come back to me—in heart, in mind, and in body. I couldn't ask for anything else. Except this . . ."

He got down on one knee, and my breath caught as I stared at him, wondering if maybe I was still in bed dreaming. Pinching myself, I wondered how I'd gotten so lucky.

"Angelina, life gives us so few opportunities to find true love. If you're lucky enough to find it, you need to hold onto it with every ounce of your existence, because it's the one thing everyone wants but so few have. The first time I laid my eyes on you, I knew. I knew you were the one God made for me."

My chin quivered as he reached into his pocket and pulled out an exquisite white gold engagement ring. It was breathtaking, with beautiful diamonds positioned perfectly around a larger diamond, each one complementing the other. It was unlike anything I'd ever seen.

"This ring has been passed down through my family for generations. When my mother gave it to me, she told me to give it to the one person I knew I couldn't live without. That person is you. You've worn it once before. I'm asking that you wear it once again."

Without hesitation, I shook my head yes, letting the tears of happiness fall. He slid the ring onto my finger, where it fit perfectly. Leaning over, I kissed him. "I've waited for you my entire life," I told him.

We stood and smiled at each other, knowing in our hearts that we would soon be joined together forever. Kissing him again, I looked down and admired the ring that was meant to be mine.

"Though I don't want to ruin the moment, we really should go," I said, turning my love-struck gaze toward the door.

"Yes, we should. My mother will be thrilled to know you said yes." He winked at me on his way over to the armoire to pick out an outfit.

A surprised look crossed my face. "She knew you were going to ask?"

"Yes. Last night, you made her see things much differently. She now understands why I love you and is excited to have you join our family," he confessed, choosing an outfit to change into.

"Well, then we should go tell her the news."

Once he was finally ready, I wondered how someone could look so stylish in less than five minutes. I knew I would eventually have to pry that secret out of him.

I opened the door, and we walked down the hallway in happy silence. He led me down a different path, this time crossing another hallway into a large room decorated with priceless paintings and odd artifacts. Looking around, I noticed everyone was accounted for.

Another set of doors opened, and Ctephanyi walked in followed by two of her guards. Standing in the middle of the room, she glanced at each one of us.

"Welcome, everyone. I do hope you all had a restful night's sleep, as your journey begins today. This will not be an easy task. Each of you will be tested. Your weaknesses will be played upon, and you will know the truth and loyalty of your fellow companions. It's imperative that we find Elias. He is very powerful and will do what he can to make you doubt yourselves. Protect Angelina. She may be our only hope."

Each one nodded showing they were in agreement.

She walked over to me, smiling as she noticed the large diamond on my ring finger. "I see you said yes."

Glancing over at Jeremiah, I nodded.

"Congratulations are in order. Once you return, we shall have a grand celebration." She leaned in and whispered. "This time around, I only ask to help plan the wedding."

Nicolai smiled proudly, happy that his mother finally wanted to be a part of our lives. She stepped back and stared at the both of us. For a moment, I thought I saw a tear of happiness begin to form in her eyes. Noticing my stare, she quickly turned around to face the others. She nodded to her guards, and they quickly left the room, returning moments later with a small wooden box. She took it from them and motioned for Jeremiah to stand before her.

"You will protect my family, even if you disagree with certain unions." She slowly opened the unusual box to reveal a jewel-tipped golden dagger. She motioned for him to take it. He picked it up carefully and studied it closely. Runic symbols were etched into the blade, and the tip glowed a dull green.

"What am I supposed to do with this?" he questioned curiously.

Looking him straight in the eye, Ctephanyi replied, "When the time comes, you'll know what to do." She then walked back to the middle of the room and took one last look at the six of us.

Pleased, she clapped her hands and the guards returned to her side. "Now go, be safe, and look out for each other's well-being, because all you will have is each other."

She motioned for her guards to open the doors.

Each one of us looked at the other, hopeful that we would succeed in our task of stopping Elias before he could do any damage. We filed out of the double doors in a single line and walked quietly down the path through the wondrous city. The guards led us back to the mystical door that opened to the world above. They placed their hands upon it and it began to glow, slowly revealing the darkness behind it. I watched in amazement as each person walked through the opening and disappeared into the darkness that would eventually lead to the sunlight above.

With fear in my heart and hope in my mind, I took one last look at the beautiful diamond-encrusted ceiling that sparkled above me. I hoped with all my heart that I could soon return with news that our task was completed successfully. Nicolai gently nudged me and looked toward the door. It was time to go. Taking his hand, I let him lead me into the darkness, knowing that we would soon be back in the world I knew—the world where fairy tale creatures are real, nightmares become reality, and some secrets are better left alone.

31

Beastly Encounters

"Stay close together," Mathias ordered. "Elias is at least a two-day journey ahead of us, but the animals in the forest can be just as deadly if you cross them."

"You know where he is?" I asked, my eyes trying to adjust to the bright surface light.

"We've received word as to where his location is, yes," he answered simply.

I looked up at Nicolai, and he nodded at me in reassurance. "Everything is going to be okay. I promise."

I smiled as the crisp, cool air brushed against my flushed cheeks. The sounds and smells of autumn tingled my senses. The hidden city may have been amazing, but I believed I loved this place much more. I admired the life it held and the beauty that surrounded me—well, with the exception of the crimson moss. I was still grossed out by it now that I knew why it had its crimson color.

I touched different things as we walked and listened to the life the forest possessed. I had taken it all for granted before, and I promised myself to never take them for granted again. I looked up ahead and made eye contact with Jeremiah. He looked away in disdain. The guilt I felt was nauseating. How I wished I could ease his heartache. Perhaps if I took his mind away from me and made it focus on someone else . . .

That was it! As much as it sickened me, I had noticed Laurana's interest in him. Though I hated her and wanted to physically harm her, perhaps I could make something happen between the two of them.

I slowed my pace and Nicolai looked at me, confused. "Are you okay?"

"Go ahead. I need to take care of something." I smiled and let go of his hand.

Still looking confused, he continued on without me. Pretending to be tired, I stopped and held my side. Laurana soon caught up, looking down at me with an annoyed look on her face.

"You humans are so weak."

"Not all of us are weak," I stated, glancing over at Jeremiah.

"Well, perhaps there are exceptions every now and again . . ." she said with desire in her voice.

"Why don't you go talk to him?"

"What? Why would I do such a silly thing?"

"Why not? After all, I've seen how you two look at each other." Her pretty blue eyes lit up with hope that he might feel for her as she felt for him.

"Do you really think so?"

I forced myself to give her a big, fake smile. "Of course, I think so." I wanted to throw up in my mouth. The thought of them together made my stomach hurt, but if it took Jeremiah's pain away, then it would be worth it. "You should make the first move. After all, he's kind of a wimp when it comes to talking to girls."

"I don't know . . ."

"Come on, I'll go with you."

"I don't need your help," she snapped, walking

a bit faster to catch up to him.

I smiled, watching my plan unfold before my eyes. I hoped one day Jeremiah could let go of the love he held for me and give it to her. Barf, I thought to myself. Noticing the group was getting far ahead of me, I tried to pick up the pace. Each one seemed to be deep in thought and failed to notice the distance that they'd put between us.

Breathing heavy, I cursed at myself for all those years of unhealthy eating, though I'd have given my right arm for a cupcake right about then. I stopped to catch my breath and listened to the forest around me. The birds were singing their sweet songs. The wind whistled through the crimson colored leaves, and the . . .

I suddenly noticed an odd sound coming from my left and spun around to see what it was. I froze in place as my eyes met that of a large cougar standing only a few feet from me. If my bladder had been full, I might've made a mess of myself right then and there. It crouched down and glared at me with its midnight-colored eyes. I nervously glanced toward my companions and cursed under my breath when I saw they were too far away to help me.

"Nice kitty. Good kitty," I cooed as I slowly backed up, my eyes scanning the ground for something I could use to defend myself. It growled back at me and bared its deadly teeth.

"Nice kitty. Man, what I wouldn't give for a big dog right about now," I grumbled under my breath, recalling a childhood memory of my favorite cartoon. In it, the dog always chased the cat away, leaving the mouse safe and unharmed.

Today, I was that mouse, and I looked around for my dog. As if on cue, a low growling could be heard on my right. I turned my head slowly and came face-to-face with a large, jet-black wolf baring its teeth, drool dripping from its snarling face.

"You've got to be kidding me," I muttered.

Apparently, today was not my lucky day. The cougar inched forward in its crouched position, and the wolf watched us both intently. Suddenly, as if in slow motion, the cougar leapt toward me. I closed my eyes and awaited my fate. The wolf growled, and I felt a cool breeze pass by my face. My eyes flew open. The wolf had pinned the large cat to the ground, its mighty jaws clamped around its neck. The angry cat wrestled the wolf, smacking it in the face with its large razor-like claws. In return, the wolf pummeled the cougar, knocking it up against a tree. Hearing a grotesque sound, I watched in horror as the mighty wolf clamped down on the cougar's leg, breaking it. The cougar screamed out in agony, continuing to fight for its life.

An odd helpless feeling washed over me, and I ran toward the dangerous animals.

"Angelina, no!" I heard Nicolai yell in the distance.

It was too late. I bent down in front of them and lay my trembling hand on the wolf's back. The cougar continued to kick the wolf with the strength it had left. The wolf, its mighty jaws around the cougar's neck, began to loosen his grip.

"Let him go," I commanded, my voice shaking.

"Angelina, move," Jeremiah ordered, aiming

his bow at the wolf's head.

"Let him go," I repeated, slowly running my hand through the wolf's coarse fur.

"Angelina, get out of the way," Jeremiah ordered again.

Bethani placed her dainty hand on the bow, lowering it. "No, she will be fine," she said.

Jeremiah watched cautiously, ready to release his arrow into the animal if he needed to.

"Come on, now, let that cougar go." My voice was steadier. Turning my head slightly, I began to feel a calming sensation run through my body. The wolf finally let go and turned to look at me. It was as if, for a moment, we understood each other. He licked my hand and whimpered softly as he came to sit by my side. I moved closer to the cougar as it lay bleeding and panting. I placed my hand upon it and was immediately able to feel its fast heartbeat. The rumbles of its growl created soft vibrations underneath my fingertips.

"Shh, it's going to be okay," I cooed, running my hand across its soft fur. Fear disappeared and love took over instead. Feeling a warm sensation begin to course through my hand, I let it flow into the fallen animal and, in return, it began to purr.

"What's happening?" Stephen asked, disbelief in his voice.

"She's realizing what she can do," Bethani answered.

"What exactly is she doing?" Mathias questioned, watching intently.

"She's healing it," Nicolai answered with a surprised look upon his face.

All of them were speechless, as the cougar's

wounds seemed to magically heal themselves. Still shaky, the animal stood up and stared at the crowd of strangers that had surrounded it. Smiling, I kissed its leathery nose, and it licked my hand with its sandpaper tongue. We all watched as it ran off into the forest, stopping for a moment to let out a loud roar.

I stood up and dusted the dirt and brush from my pants. I burst into laughter when I noticed all the surprised faces staring at me.

"What?" I asked, still chuckling as I walked over to Nicolai with the wolf following behind.

"You just . . .," Mathias stuttered.

Nicolai smiled proudly. "Pretty amazing, isn't she?"

Jeremiah pointed toward the wolf that sat by my side. "Looks like you have a new friend."

"Yeah, looks like it," I replied, looking down into the coal-colored eyes staring back up at me.

"Angelina has a new pet. It's great until it rips out our throats while we're asleep," Stephen muttered, rolling his eyes. "Well, perhaps you should give your mongrel a name."

"Perhaps you're right," I replied giving him a dirty look. It was a shame the sun didn't burst him into flames, like it did to fictional vampires.

"Well, what's it going to be?" Jeremiah asked.

Thinking for a moment, I smiled and bent down to scratch my new friend behind the ears. "I think I'll call him Cole," I murmured, looking into his eyes again.

"I think that's very fitting," Nicolai commented.

"Gee, I thought you'd name him something like fluffy or some other cutesy name," Stephen remarked, once again showing off his cocky nature.

I stared at him wondering if any of the vampire stories were true. Staking him seemed mighty tempting at that moment. He stared back at me, a devilish grin forming on his face. I really didn't like him.

Turning my head, I patted my leg for Cole to follow me. I'd never had a pet before. My parents had always said there was too much time involved in raising them. Now, I had one, and a wolf no less. After all the things I'd found out over the past few days, having him in my life seemed as predestined as everything else had been. With my mind wandering, I managed to trip over a hidden log.

Mathias caught me by the arm and laughed. "You have the ability to heal, but the inability to walk without falling. Interesting."

Smiling weakly, I thanked him and kept walking.

"Where are we going, anyways?" I asked, suddenly realizing nobody had mentioned this important issue.

"You mean you don't know?" Stephen's eyebrow rose.

"I wouldn't have asked if I knew." I wanted to rip his eyebrows off.

"Oh, Angelina, don't be angry with Stephen. It's his curse to be arrogant," Bethani said, winking at me.

"Arrogance is a virtue, isn't it?" he replied, laughing.

"Silence is a virtue, so how about you practice that instead?" I hissed sharply.

"Oh, I think I like her feistiness."

Ignoring him, I turned to Mathias. Though his outside appearance seemed intimidating, his actual demeanor was welcoming. He was intelligent and seemed to always be watching. His red eyes studied the things around him, trying to decipher the riddles of the world.

"If you're going to ask me, go ahead," Mathias asserted, a smile on his face.

"You know where we're going?"

"Yes, I do. Ctephanyi pulled me aside and gave me the information. However, none of you are to know the details that were given to me."

"Well, that doesn't make any sense," I replied.

"Does anything make sense? Maybe it doesn't at this very moment, but eventually all dark comes to light," he said, his eyes changing to a beautiful emerald green.

Taken aback, I stared into them and saw a reflection of myself sitting by the river with Cole by my side.

"What the . . .?" I blinked the image away. "How did you do that?"

"Everyone is born with a gift. Some realize it right away, but others take years of trial and tribulation before their true gift becomes apparent to them."

"What's your gift, if I may ask?"

"Of course, you may. I have the ability to see the past, the present, and sometimes short pieces of the future."

"So, you're like the ghosts in that Christmas story, only all wrapped into one."

Laughing, he stopped and took my hand into his. I watched as his eyes changed to an icy white color, and a vision of Nicolai, covered in blood and kneeling in front of me, flashed in his eyes. The smile fell from his face.

"I'm sorry. Your past is such a sad one," he said, letting go of my hand.

Smiling at him, I put my hand on his arm. "It's okay. That's why I plan on making my future a bright one."

He smiled back at me, and we began walking again. The others were a short distance ahead of us. Nicolai turned around every so often to check on me, an almost jealous look on his face.

"He loves you very much, you know," Mathias pointed out, also noticing his facial expressions.

"Yes, I know."

"He would do anything for you." Mathias glanced at me, his eyes turning green again. This time, he showed me Nicolai's limp body lying on the ground, his bloody head in my hands.

"No," I whispered. "Are you saying he's going to . . .?"

"I'm not saying anything, but choices lead to consequences."

"It can be changed right? It can't be written in stone."

"Yes, it can change. Remember this: sometimes, one must think with one's head and not with one's heart." His eyes changed back to their blood-red color.

We continued walking in silence. My mind wandered, a million different possibilities running through it. I questioned myself, debating how I could change the glimpse of future that I'd been shown. I was grateful to Mathias for giving me the opportunity to try and alter the path that had been written, but I had no idea when or where it would take place. I would remember what he told me, and could only hope that when the opportunity presented itself, I would get the chance to change it.

32

The Key

The group continued walking for what seemed like hours. Cole, my silent partner, had wandered into the woods but continued to watch me ever so carefully. Nicolai had slowed down so he could walk next to me, and Mathias had joined Stephen in the front. It made sense for Mathias to be the leader, as he was the only one who knew where we were going. Bethani stayed a short distance behind me, every so often laughing out loud at nothing. I occasionally turned around to fulfill my curiosity, disappointed when I couldn't figure out what had caused her to laugh. Looking a short distance ahead of me, Laurana could be seen courting Jeremiah. She would point out different things in the forest, and his blue-eyed gaze would follow. He was beginning to show interest in her. I smiled to myself and hooked arms with Nicolai.

"What are you doing?" he laughed.

"Oh, nothing. One can't enjoy a walk through the woods with one's fiancé?" I nudged him playfully.

"Fiancé? That word does have a nice ring to it." He twirled me around in front of him.

Bethani laughed her little laugh again, and this time I couldn't help but laugh back. Glancing at her, I came to the realization that I was beginning to adore each one of my companions—with the exception of Stephen. Each one was so different but all had a similar purpose: to protect the human race.

With dusk on the horizon, we decided in unison that it was time to set up camp. Jeremiah, choosing a somewhat comfortable location, began gathering firewood with the help of Laurana. Mathias disappeared into the forest, while Stephen sat down, falling asleep against a tree. Apparently, everything I knew about vampires was incorrect. They didn't burst into flames in the sun, they actually slept, and they didn't have fangs. Nicolai went in search of food with Cole following behind him, hoping to join in on the hunt.

Sitting down next to a tree, I took my shoes and socks off. The cool leaves felt good against my achy, sweaty feet. Shoving my toes under them, I gathered more leaves around me, burying my feet up to my ankles. Bethani noticed what I was doing and cocked her head to the side, a curious expression on her face. I motioned for her to sit next to me. Smiling, she obliged, her pretty lavender eyes full of curiosity. I took off her shoes noticing she had no socks, and instructed her to put her feet into the leaves. Gathering more of the fallen leaves that surrounded me, I threw them on top of her feet, burying hers similarly to mine. She laughed, enjoying every moment.

"Have you never done this before?" I questioned.

"No I've never done such a thing. Is this what humans do for enjoyment?" she asked, her lavender eyes sparkling.

"Well, sort of . . ."

"I like it." She tossed a small pile of leaves at me.

"Good, then you'll like this." I stood up, grabbed a pile of leaves, and crept quietly over to where Stephen was sleeping. Bethani watched with childlike wonder on her pretty face. I tiptoed quietly, aiming for his head. Just as I was about to throw my secret leaf bomb at him, he jumped up and pummeled me to the ground. Surprise overtook my body, and I lay there staring up at him.

"I have excellent senses, my dear." He winked, grabbing a pile of leaves and throwing them in my face.

"Get off me," I muttered.

"Can't take the heat?" he challenged as he continued throwing leaves at me.

I tried to move my arms from his grip.

"Next time, try something a little more surprising." He stood up and walked back to the tree he'd been sleeping against. Sitting down, he laid his head back, a single leaf hanging from his shirt.

I wiped the leaves from my face, stood up, and frowned. Bethani was laughing as she pointed to the leaves that had become tangled in my hair. Trying my best to pull them out, I shrugged and returned to my spot beside her.

"Didn't go as planned, huh?" She scanned my hair, pulling out another leaf.

"No, not exactly." I replied, taking the leaf from her and throwing it on the ground.

Hearing rustling behind us, we both turned around. Mathias appeared, smiling at my hair full of leaves.

"Get into a fight with a tree?"

"Very funny."

He walked over and sat down next to us. I watched as he pulled a small folded piece of paper from his pocket and offered it to me with a smile, quietly saying, "You mustn't open this until the time is right."

Taking it from him, I held it close. "How will I know when the time is right?"

"You will know."

I put it in my jeans pocket and thanked him. Smiling, he lay down, resting his head on his arms. Bethani smiled as she watched him.

"He likes you," she whispered.

"What?" I asked, wondering if I'd heard her correctly.

She continued smiling, throwing a leaf at me. I threw one back and, before I knew it, we were in a leaf war. Laughing like children, we temporarily forgot the task at hand and enjoyed the moment. Jeremiah emerged from the forest with Laurana following on his heels, both carrying large armfuls of firewood. Taking one look at me, he laughed.

"Having fun are we?" Dropping the pile of wood on the ground, he smiled.

"Must be nice to sit around and not have to help set up camp," Laurana mumbled.

"Don't be jealous of their fun, Laurana," he joked, grabbing a fist full of leaves and throwing them at her. Surprise crossed her face, as she'd probably never been hit in the face by leaves before. She stood there for a moment, debating what to do. Finally, she shrugged her shoulders and went to sit down. Disappointment played across Jeremiah's face. Feeling bad, I stood up, hiding a fistful of leaves behind me. I ran up and shoved them in his face. He picked me up, throwing me over his shoulder and began running around our makeshift camp. Laughing, I began to playfully punch him in the back, begging him to let me go. Laurana watched with jealousy in her eyes.

Nicolai emerged from the forest with Cole and stopped momentarily, debating whether to get angry or to laugh. Jeremiah, noticing the look on his face, stopped, and put me down. I fell to the ground, taking a moment to let the dizzy feeling go away. I heard soft rustling by my head and began laughing again as Cole frantically licked my face.

"You sure you want to kiss her now?" Jeremiah asked Nicolai as he began to start a fire.

Nicolai walked over to me and gently pushed Cole out of the way. Cole let out a low growl. He trotted back into the woods, howling once to let Nicolai know he didn't approve.

"Someone's a tad bit jealous," Jeremiah said as he continued working on the fire.

"Which one? The dog or the boy?" Stephen asked without opening his eyes.

Mathias chuckled, his head still resting on his arms. "Apparently both."

Jeremiah finally got the fire lit and sat down next to Laurana. "Are you cold?" he murmured.

Sitting up, I looked at her as she studied his face, debating what to say. When she glanced over at me, I slowly nodded my head and mouthed "yes."

She shook her head slowly in agreement.

Scooting closer to her, he took off his jacket and wrapped it around her slender shoulders. With his arm around her, he rubbed her arm gently, trying to warm her cool skin. With a surprised look on her face, she glanced over at me again and mouthed, "thank you."

Smiling, I leaned my head against Nicolai's chest. This was nice. Everyone seemed to be in high spirits and, for once, I felt as if everything was going to be alright.

Bethani excused herself politely and disappeared into the forest. I was beginning to get used to her odd behavior. Laughing to myself, I envisioned her dancing with imaginary fairies in the dark. In an odd sort of way, she reminded me of my best friend Marie, but much more fun. Feeling a stab of regret, I realized I actually missed the simple everyday things I'd had in my life. I missed the sounds and scents I'd taken for granted for so long. Even more so, I missed my best friend Marie.

Closing my eyes, I thought of the time Marie and I had gone shopping for prom dresses, each of us trying on a million different gowns until we found the perfect one. I thought of the many visits we'd made to the small movie theater, watching the newest releases, and enjoying the welcoming aroma of popcorn, which always tempted our taste buds. Feeling my stomach growl, I opened my eyes.

Nicolai kissed my forehead. "Someone's hungry."

Embarrassed, I wrapped my arms around my belly and smiled sheepishly. My thoughts had comforted me in such a way that I hadn't even realized I'd fallen asleep for a short time. Looking around, I noticed Mathias was no longer lying down, but was instead sitting in front of the fire watching the flames dance in the night air. Stephen, sitting beside him, was carving something out of a piece of wood. A wicked image crossed my mind as I imagined him carving a stake for me to use on him. Shaking off the thought, I noticed Bethani had returned and was leaning up against a tree with her bow carefully perched next to her. Cole lay by my side sleeping, his ears twitching every so often, catching unheard sounds within the forest. Jeremiah was cooking some strange animal Nicolai had caught. Laurana was at his side, her pretty blue eyes focused on his handsome face.

Yawning, I stood up and stretched, the sudden movement waking Cole. He jumped to his feet and looked around, ready to pounce on anything that moved near me. Bending down, I patted his furry head, and he licked my face in return. I motioned for him to lie back down. He stared up at me with pleading eyes, huffing as he let his legs fall out from under him. He placed his head on top his paws and watched me intently, curious what I was going to do next.

"You know, it's like that mutt thinks he owes you something," Stephen noticed, glancing at Cole.

"I don't know what you're talking about," I snapped back.

"You don't find it odd that a black wolf mysteriously appears, saves your life, and seems to care more for you than lover boy there." Stephen pointed his knife at Nicolai.

A flash of orange lit up Nicolai's eyes, and I immediately knew Stephen had hit a nerve. If he had been smart, he would have used caution with what came out of his mouth next. Otherwise, he would learn the hard way that his witty comments weren't always wanted.

"What? You know I'm right," he stated with a smug look on his face.

Though I didn't want to admit it out loud and give him some sort of satisfaction, I knew he was right. It was strange that Cole had rescued me from the hungry cougar. It wasn't in a wolf's normal nature to save a human from anything. In fact, they were usually the ones doing the attacking.

Bethani laughed, and everyone turned to look at her.

Stephen shook his head and redirected his knife toward her. "You're always laughing at things that I don't find funny. Why is that?"

"There are so many hidden things that are beginning to come to light. Memories can't stay hidden forever," she answered vaguely.

"Then why don't you make it easy on everyone and remind us of what we have forgotten." He returned his knife to the wood he'd been carving.

"That would be too simple and potentially dangerous. When the mind is ready to remember, it will," she answered, a sly smile on her pretty face.

Stephen shook his head, annoyed by her answer. Mathias shifted his gaze from the fire and glanced over at me, giving me a kind smile. Smiling back at him, I noticed his eyes had turned their emerald green color. I was curious what he'd seen. I was sure Bethani had triggered a vision within him. Hoping he would tell me later, I sat back down and encouraged Jeremiah to hurry with dinner. He hushed me, reminding me that he was the chef, and that it would be done when it was done. Grumbling, I lazily picked up a twig and threw it in his direction. The smell of whatever he was cooking made my stomach growl anxiously. Nicolai laughed and began to caress my arm, causing Cole to lower his ears and growl fiercely.

"Perhaps they're right. I may have a competitor for your affections," he said as he stood and walked away.

I patted Cole on the head, and his ears instantly perked back up. His tail beat softly against the ground. It was amazing how much love I felt for this wonderful animal. Not only had he saved my life, he'd shown me a tremendous amount of love and loyalty. I couldn't imagine my life without him.

"Angelina?"

Looking up, I noticed Bethani looking at me strangely.

"Yes?" I replied, my hungry stomach now feeling a bit unsettled.

"What is that you have around your neck?" she asked, standing up.

"What?" Surprised, I looked down to see my locket had come out from underneath my shirt. Realizing it must've happened when I'd been wrestling around in the leaves, I shrugged my shoulders, not wanting to delve into the entire history of how I'd been given the locket by Nicolai. "Oh, this thing? I found it lying on my floor the night Elias came for me."

"Do you have the key?" Her lavender eyes fixated upon the dainty locket.

"No, I don't know where it is."

Jeremiah looked up, an odd expression on his face. "Did you say key?"

"Yes, the key for the locket," Bethani replied.

He grew quiet for a moment. Then, he stood up, reached into the pocket of his pants and pulled out a small golden key.

"Where did you find that?" I asked surprised.

"The night you disappeared, I went into your house looking for clues as to what had happened. This small key here just happened to be on your bedroom floor."

"That's—impossible," I said, looking over to Nicolai, who was watching from a distance with a concerned look on his face. "It was lost."

Jeremiah winked. "Maybe you didn't look hard enough."

"Or maybe," Bethani speculated, a thoughtful look on her face, "someone dropped it when they were in your bedroom after you'd already left."

We all sat in silence, wondering who'd dropped it after I fell out of the tree.

"Wait a minute," I exclaimed, suddenly coming to a realization. "When I was climbing out onto the tree, someone else was in the room besides Elias."

"What do you mean someone else was in the room with him?" Nicolai asked, quickly returning to my side.

"Well, when I saw the red eyes in the window, something else knocked him out of the way. Then something flew up against the window and shattered it."

"She's right," Jeremiah said, his eyes lighting up. "When I was looking around, I saw some sort of strange animal hair stuck on a shard of glass in the window."

"Why are you just mentioning this now?" Nicolai demanded. "This information should've been brought to light the night we were all discussing these matters."

Getting defensive, I moved closer to Cole. "I didn't think of it until just now."

"So now, we have another mystery person in the picture," he muttered.

I couldn't believe he was irritated by this new information. Noticing the disgruntled look on my face, Bethani motioned for me to come to her. Standing up, I walked over to her, slowly turning my head to give Nicolai a disgusted look. I hoped I'd gotten my point across. Cole trotted behind me, wagging his tail happily, pleased that Nicolai was in the doghouse.

"Jeremiah, may I have the key please?" Bethani asked, motioning for him to bring it to her.

"Sure." He carefully dropped the small golden key into the palm of her hand.

"Angelina, do you remember our earlier conversation when I said that the mind will remember when it's ready?"

Shaking my head yes, I watched as she carefully took my hand and opened it, placing the key inside. She closed my hand around the key and smiled.

"Sometimes things follow us from our past to our future. This locket was yours a very long time ago. What lies inside will trigger your past memories and help you realize who you really are. It's up to you to decide when to open it."

"This will help me remember my past?" I tightened my grip on the tiny key.

"Yes. However, be prepared, for some of your memories may not be so pleasant. You must be sure that this is what you want, because once it's opened, it can't be undone."

"I understand. Thank you," I whispered softly, putting the key in my pocket. I would sleep on deciding whether or not I really wanted to know what had been hidden from me for so long. Sitting down against a tree, I sighed. I'd been given so many paths recently, and deciding which one to follow weighed heavy on my shoulders. Glancing up at Nicolai, I could see he still had an irritated look on his face. Frowning, I patted my leg for Cole to come to me. He laid his head on my leg and looked up at me with his dark eyes. I petted him and whispered, "You won't ever judge me, will you." He answered by licking my hand.

Jeremiah announced that the food was finally ready and offered me a nice-sized portion of the mystery meat. I took it from him mindlessly and picked at it, occasionally giving Cole small meaty chunks. Everyone ate in silence, each one keeping to his own thoughts. I threw Cole the rest of my food and lay my head against the tree. I had a lot on my mind and decided maybe it was best for me to just call it a night.

I attempted to get comfortable and Bethani, once again being as wonderful as she was, took a blanket out of her backpack and covered me with it. I was grateful to have her with me and thanked her as I curled up next to Cole's furry body. I was exhausted and angry, hurt by Nicolai's words yet grateful for the friend Bethani had become. This mixture of emotions was overwhelming.

I felt myself begin to fall asleep, and I prayed that I'd be able to answer some of the questions swirling around in my mind. After all, tomorrow would be a new day, and with a new day, came new opportunities for a fresh start. Answers might become more apparent. Things that were in the dark might come into the light. Patting the key that was tucked safely away in my pocket, I let myself fall into a dreamless sleep.

33

Past Revealed

I awoke when Bethani nudged me. She held her slender finger to her lips to hush me and motioned for me to follow her. The rest of my companions were spread out around the makeshift camp, still asleep with the exception of one—Nicolai. I surveyed the area for him, but he was nowhere in sight. I figured he probably wandered off to think about the argument we'd had earlier.

I stood up quietly and Cole rose to his feet, a curious look in his warm brown eyes. I ordered him to stay and he let out a soft whine. I bent down and rubbed him between his ears. "I'll be right back, I promise."

I tiptoed softly through the camp and followed Bethani into the dark forest. We walked for a few moments in silence, the crisp air blowing slightly against my warm cheeks. I shivered, wrapping my arms around myself in an attempt to keep warm.

We stumbled into a clearing that was lit up by what seemed like a million tiny fireflies. Bethani continued on until she reached the center and motioned for me to join her. I hesitated momentarily, but my curiosity got the best of me, and I hurried to her side. She raised her hand and laid it upon my cheek. I gave her a confused look and wondered what she could possibly be doing. When she reached for the locket, I immediately tried to stop her, and she looked at me, her lavender eyes sparkling underneath the moonlight.

Placing her other hand on mine, she smiled, whispering, "It's okay. Trust me, it's time you knew."

My heart began to beat a little faster as she once again reached for the locket. This time I allowed her to pull it out from underneath my shirt.

"Where's the key?"

Reaching into my pocket, I pulled out the small golden key and offered it to her.

She shook her head slowly. "This is something you must do. A very long time ago, I made a vow to you, and after seeing the strain of the world on your shoulders as I did last night, I knew it was time to tell you." She closed my hand around the small key. "You know what to do."

She let go of the locket, and it dangled loosely, begging me to open it. Bethani walked quietly out of the clearing, leaving me alone to do the one thing I knew it was time to do. I opened my hand and stared at the key, laughing to myself as I realized it was in fact a new day, which meant the possibility for new opportunities. I'd fallen asleep hoping the answers to the many questions I had would reveal themselves, that I would be able to make the decisions that needed to be made and, amazingly, this tiny key could unlock all of it. It held all the answers to my past and could potentially change who I was to become in the future. I wondered if I was ready for this next step in my life. What was the worst that could happen? After all, it was every girl's dream to find out that the fairy tale creatures we'd been told about as children truly existed, to be loved by an extremely handsome mythical man, to potentially be one of the most powerful beings on the face of the earth. Who wouldn't want that?

I held my breath and used my free hand to hold the locket still. I felt a tingling sensation run through my fingers as the key met the tiny dark hole. This was it. This was the moment I'd waited for.

"Angelina, wait!" Nicolai cried out from the edge of the clearing.

Turning my head, I could see Bethani grab him and try to hold him back. He struggled to free himself from her strong grasp. My hand began to lower away from the locket as I watched a look of despair cross his handsome face.

"Angelina, open it," Bethany commanded. "It's time you found out who you truly are."

"No, please, don't do it," Nicolai begged.

Lowering my hand completely, I looked at Nicolai's face. Why didn't he want me to open it? Walking toward him slowly, I urged her to let him go. A look of disappointment crossed her pretty face, though she did as I asked. Nicolai gave her a dirty look and ran to me.

He wrapped his strong arms around my waist and pulled me close to him. "I'm sorry, Angelina. Please forgive how I acted last night. I promise there are good reasons behind my behavior."

Though his arms were quite welcoming, I took a step back and looked at him again, trying to decipher the reason he didn't want me to open the locket. Perhaps he was hiding something. I thought back to the previous night's altercation and remembered the irritated look on his face when he found out that someone else had tried to stop the red-eyed intruder from capturing me. He'd also seemed upset when Bethani told me the key was the answer to unlocking my past. He was hiding something from me, and I was about to find out what it was.

I felt a lump forming in my throat and took another step back. This was the man I was supposed to marry, the man that had promised to always love and protect me. But now he was hiding something, and that hurt more than any other action ever could. Angry tears began to form in my eyes, and I turned around. I didn't want to show him the weakness I'd begun to feel. A million doubts crossed my mind, and I tried desperately to push them away. Maybe he was just like every other man I'd ever come across. Maybe I was wrong about how he'd felt about me. Maybe it was all an act.

I stood in silence for a moment, trying to regain my composure. I took a deep breath and spun around to face him. It was hard to look him in the eye. He was so incredibly handsome, and the look on his face was that of utter hurt and confusion. I suddenly realized he'd read my mind, and the anger and betrayal began to grow within me even more.

"Can't I keep my thoughts to myself just this once?" I managed to croak, pushing down the lump in my throat.

"Angelina, please let me explain," he urged.

Bethani watched in awkward silence behind us, her lavender eyes darting back and forth between the two of us.

"Why don't you want me to open the locket? Is there something you don't want me to see?"

He lowered his eyes in shame. "There are some things that are better left in the past."

"Like what, Nicolai? What are you hiding? I mean all this time you've wanted me to find out who I was, who I am, and now you want to be a hypocrite and hide it from me?"

"No, that's not it . . ."

"Then what is it? Explain it to me, because I'm pretty confused on what your problem is." I put my hands on my hips and tried to swallow the animosity that continued to amplify throughout my body.

He looked back up, and his beautiful orange eyes were full of sadness. "Angelina, you have to trust me. I've only ever given you my loyalty and love. I would never do anything to hurt you," he confessed walking toward me slowly.

"Then what are you hiding? Why do you want to keep my past life a mystery?"

A warm tear fell down my cheek, and he wiped it away. "Life holds many mysteries, and sometimes the answers to those mysteries are more than any one person can handle."

"How do you know I can't handle who I used to be? I'm a lot stronger than you think," I snapped back.

He looked at me thoughtfully. "Very well, then. Are you sure you're ready to know everything about the person you used to be?"

I nodded my head yes, and he sighed, pulling me close to him once again.

"Then who am I to keep the truth from you?"

He placed his hand under my chin, gently tilting my head upwards to make me look at him. "I only ask one thing of you."

Guilt formed a ball in the pit of my stomach as I looked into his eyes. I could see the sincerity in them, and knew all the doubts that had crossed my mind about him were false.

"Nicolai, I'm . . .," I began to say.

He held his finger to my lips and I pursed them together. He bent down and kissed me delicately and, in return, I hugged him.

"Thank you," I whispered.

He pulled away and put his strong hands on my shoulders. "I only ask that we do this together."

Bethani watched from afar, a quaint smile upon her face. I nodded a silent thank you toward her and took Nicolai by the hand, leading him back to the middle of the clearing. Looking up, I could see the early morning sun's bright light peeking through the tree limbs, and I knew I needed to hurry before the rest of my companions woke up. I didn't need any more distractions. I motioned for Nicolai to open his hand. I looked at the tiny key and smiled. He was right; we needed to do this together. I gave him the key, and he patiently waited for me to turn the locket over, so we could unlock the secrets it had held for hundreds of years.

"Are you ready?" I whispered, glancing at Bethani, whose gaze hadn't shifted from either one of us. It was like she already knew what was going to happen.

Nicolai placed his free hand around my hand, and together we held the locket firmly in place.

He inched the key toward the small keyhole slowly and, for a moment, the world around us seemed to stop. I held my breath as he put the key into the keyhole. He grabbed my free hand and together we turned it. A small click could be heard, and the locket popped open.

Nicolai smiled and kissed me once again. "I'll be right here when you get back."

The ground began to tremble beneath us and loud claps of thunder could be heard in the sky above. I watched in awe and held onto Nicolai as tightly as I could, not knowing what to expect. The wind picked up, and the tree branches swayed back and forth violently. My hair whipped around my head wildly in the howling wind, and I struggled to shield my eyes from the debris that flew around us. My grip on Nicolai loosened, and in a flash, he was gone, along with everything else around me. I closed my eyes and prayed for it to be over. As if my prayer had been heard, the ferocious wind suddenly halted, the ground stood still, and an eerie silence fell upon my ears. I was afraid to open my eyes, fearful of what I was going to see, knowing deep down I was terrified of coming face-to-face with the person I'd been. What if I'd been an absolute nightmare? Maybe Nicolai was right. Maybe I wasn't ready. Oh well, it was too late now.

34

Pity

I opened my eyes and found myself looking at two teenage girls lying on the ground in front of me, laughing with each other, not a care in the world. A black wolf puppy wagged its tail frantically as one of the girls threw something across the ground. The puppy ran and retrieved the foreign object, returning it back to his owner. One of the girls looked oddly familiar with her short, blonde, curly hair and lavender eyes.

I looked around and noticed the clearing was now quite a bit larger and full of hundreds of different types of flowers, each one filling the air with their fragrant scent. A charming cottage could be seen just inside the tree line. I walked toward the young girls and noticed they could neither see nor hear me.

A tall man with sandy blonde hair emerged from the forest and called out a name that I didn't quite catch through the girls' sweet laughter. The girl with the blonde hair stopped laughing and ran toward him, while the other girl continued to play with the puppy in the field of flowers. I followed the blonde girl and guessed the man to be her father as their facial similarities were very distinct. She stopped in front of him and he whispered something in her ear. Tears sprung into her pretty eyes immediately and she nodded as he handed her a large burlap bag. She slung it over her shoulder and he pulled her close, hugging her as a single tear fell down his face. He put his finger on her forehead and I watched in astonishment as the very tip of it began to glow. Her eyes instantly filled with understanding.

Hearing a loud commotion in the distance, I turned to see a large group of burly men on horses coming toward us. I could tell they were human and each one was armed with some sort of weapon. The girl's father urged her to run into the forest and hide. She did as she was told and ran as fast as her little legs would carry her. The other girl stood up, expressionless, with the wolf puppy by her side. Understanding crossed her young face and she too fled into the forest. The wolf pup followed, letting out a long howl.

The men drew near and I heard their boisterous laughter. A few of them went into the cottage and a woman's scream rang out. The girl's father, hearing the shrill scream, ran toward the cottage but was instantly stopped by one of the larger men. I watched in disgust as the man threw him to the ground and kicked him repeatedly in the stomach. Forgetting they couldn't see me, I ran up to the man and attempted to push him. A strange look crossed his face, and he turned his head. I came eye-to-eye with him, and he stood with a confused look on his face, saying nothing.

Another man rode up and commanded the girl's father to get up. The larger man broke eye contact with me, shook off the eerie feeling, and made his way over to his horse. He opened his saddlebag and pulled out a long coil of rope. He strutted back over to the girl's father, who was now covered in blood, and threw him up against a nearby tree.

The other man on the horse let out a hearty laugh. "Tie him up along with the female we found inside the cottage," he commanded. "They'll both fetch a pretty penny at the slave auction."

"Could you imagine if they actually fought back?" the man holding the rope commented as he began to bind the injured man's wrists.

"It's not in their nature, which is probably best, especially knowing how powerful these creatures can be."

"Have they found the girl yet?"

The man on the horse frowned. "Not yet, but we'll find her soon enough."

With that, he rode off into the distance with the others following behind him.

The large man pulled the rope, forcing the girl's father to follow him.

I felt helpless as I watched the large man get on his horse. He began to ride away slowly, the injured man struggling to keep up.

The ground began to tremble again, and this time a thick mist formed around me. I felt as if I were in the dream sequence of movie, only this movie was my own. The mist only lasted for a few moments before fading away, and I realized I was in the middle of the forest with the two girls from earlier, but they were a few years older. I immediately recognized the blonde girl to be Bethani and felt foolish for not realizing it earlier. Her lavender eyes and childlike smile were unmistakable.

Hearing a playful growl, I turned to see that the wolf pup was now fully grown. A sudden realization washed over me, as I concluded the girl and the wolf were actually Cole and me.

"Every one of them have been captured and put into slavery," my younger self exclaimed.

"The humans know no better. They think by doing this, it will raise them to an insurmountable amount of power," Bethani replied as she sat cross-legged on the hard ground.

"It's only a matter of time before they find me. You know that."

"Angelina, they won't find you. The future has been written, and they don't win."

I almost choked when I heard my name, as disbelief ran rampant throughout my mind. My name really was the same then as it was now? How was that even possible?

"How do you know, Bethani? The future can change. Perhaps I should show them what power I really possess." My younger self giggled, touching the tree beside her. My mouth dropped open as the tree bark began to turn black. Death crept its way up the tree, killing it slowly. The leaves began to wilt and fall from the now blackened branches.

Bethani crossed her arms. "You know that isn't the way to handle this."

Sighing, my younger self took her hand off the tree. "You're right—as usual."

"They'll arrive soon, you know."

"Then my time grows short."

"Do you know when you'll return?" Bethani asked, picking at a plant next to her.

"Yes, when the humans overrun the earth, and all other species hide their true selves from them.

That is when I will return."

"Your wolf will miss you. He loves you very much." She threw a stick for the wolf to retrieve.

"He was the last gift given to me by my parents," my younger self answered, sadness filling her chestnut-colored eyes.

"Have you given him your essence?" she asked quietly.

"Yes, and he will live for many years to come after I am gone, the same as you."

Realizing my mouth was still open, I closed it, swallowing hard to stomach the fact that I could not only give life, but also take it away. No wonder Elias wanted me so badly. I was the perfect weapon.

"Will I know who you are when you come back?" Bethani asked.

"Of course, you will. We are of the same blood. However, I must warn you that when the time comes to address me, I won't know who *you* are. You must take great care in telling me of my past, for a human mind is a fragile instrument."

"A human? That is what you've chosen to return as?"

"By then, our kind will be no more, except for you. I advise you to stay well hidden, for they will search the ends of the earth for more of us."

Bethani grew quiet. I could tell her mind was full of questions, and she was trying to find the best way to ask them. Not being able to hold it in anymore, she blurted out, "Why must you leave? Can't we just stay hidden and let the time pass by?"

"If it were only that simple, my dear friend. You see, in order for this world to survive, I must leave temporarily. If the humans were to find me, they would use my power to destroy each other. I can't allow that to happen." My younger self smiled kindly, adding, "We've both known this day would come."

"I know—it's just . . .," Bethani's voice quivered, "I'll miss you."

Sadness filled her eyes, and as I watched the scene in front of me, my heart began to ache for them. I now understood what I'd felt when I'd first met Bethani. She had been my guardian watching over me, loving me as her best friend for thousands of years, waiting patiently for the day I would return.

The ground began to tremble once again. For a split second, I thought I caught my younger self with a smile on her face, particularly intended for me. The mist rose up around me, and I closed my eyes, awaiting my next vision.

Hearing loud noises around me, my eyes fluttered open. My heart stopped as I realized I was in the middle of town. I stared at the people that walked past me and immediately knew I had been taken back to the time our town was settled. I admired the women in their tight corsets and button-up boots. The men were quite classy in their two-piece tweed suits and top hats.

A loud scream redirected my attention to the crowd of people that had gathered at the building that was now Tom's Tavern. I made my way toward them, and a very familiar man walked past me. I took another look, realizing the man resembled my father.

I followed him through the crowd of people and watched as he pushed past them to help a woman who'd fallen on the ground. Whispers ran through the crowd, and I tried to stand on my tiptoes to see what was going on. For a moment, I thought my eyes were playing tricks on me. The woman he was helping up was old Mrs. Bailey from the little country store. It couldn't be. I rubbed my eyes in disbelief and opened them again to the same image. I looked around and tried to place the exact date. There were no paved sidewalks or streets, only dirt paths. Horses pulled carriages, and men in tailored suits chauffeured busty, well-dressed women carrying lacy umbrellas. Though I'd hated history, I had paid enough attention to figure out this was sometime in the early 1900's. If that were true, that would make both of them well over a hundred-years old. How was that even possible?

I continued watching as he led her into one of the old buildings. I decided it was in my best interest to follow them and made my way in behind them, noticing the building was an inn. It reminded me of my mother's bed and breakfast with its worn tables and chairs. A long counter stood in the middle of the room with a registration book lying open on top of it. I followed them up a set of stairs to what looked like a guest room. He set her down on the bed, and walked into the bathroom. He grabbed a towel, ran it under some warm water, brought it out to her, and carefully wiped the dirt away from her face.

"Mother, you know you can't go out in public like that," he scolded as he continued to gently wash the debris from her face.

"I am so lost—so lost without him," she

stuttered.

"I know, but if the people were to find out what I am . . ."

She ran her finger down his cheek. "You're perfect."

"I have a surprise for you." He smiled, setting the towel on the bed.

Her eyes lit up. "I love surprises!"

He stood up and walked to the window. "I found her."

She gasped and held her fragile hand over her mouth. "Where? Where is my granddaughter?"

He stared out the dusty window. "She was hidden from us. The fools wondered why she was so powerful."

"What did they expect by crossing one of our kind with yours?"

"Exactly. Now, everyone in the world wants her."

"What are you going to do?"

"I'm going to get her back. I have devised a very wise plan, but I cannot tell you about it."

A look of disappointment crossed the old woman's face. "And why not?"

"They will come to you first, especially when they realize I'm your son."

She smacked her leg in anger. "I wouldn't dare tell them a thing!"

"Mother, don't you think I know that? They'll make you talk. They have ways of doing things . . ."

They were both silent for a moment. Finally, the old woman stood up and walked toward him. Laying her wrinkled hand on his shoulder, she uttered, "I miss them both so very much. I know

I can't bring your father back, and she is the only thing we have left."

Nodding, he turned to give his mother a brief hug. She pulled away and smiled. "Josiah, please bring her home."

I wanted to throw up in my mouth. Josiah? It couldn't be. He was my . . .? No, impossible, because that would mean Mrs. Bailey was my grandmother? Perhaps this is what Nicolai hadn't wanted me to find out. How was it even possible that he was my father? If I were the oldest species known to man, then somewhere along the line, I'd been lied to.

The tremble of the ground beneath me was a tremendous relief, as I wanted this disturbing vision to end. The mist wrapped its thick arms around me and, soon, the inn disappeared along with Mrs. Bailey and my father. I tried to push the repulsive images out of my head and noticed I was once again in the forest. I felt dizzy and dragged myself to a nearby fallen log to sit down. Putting my head in my hands, I tried to accept what I'd just witnessed. Josiah was my father, and there was absolutely nothing I could do to change it.

The sound of twigs breaking around me caught my attention, and I looked up to see a massive black bear emerge in front of me. It clawed the ground with its ferocious paws. I heard laughter in the distance, and the bear and I waited patiently to see whom it belonged to. My father and my younger self soon graced us with their presence. The monstrous bear shuffled toward them lazily. My father didn't pay it any attention but continued walking, whistling a familiar tune. The bear let out a fierce growl and swiped at his leg. Fearing the worst, I closed my eyes, not wanting to see the bloody aftermath of the bear attack. I heard laughter again and opened my eyes to see my father scratching the now submissive bear behind the ears. My younger self stood nearby, holding a basket of berries and smiling thoughtfully. I could tell she was admiring her father and the beast, perhaps creating a memory she hoped to remember one day in the future. As she studied them, a look of revelation crossed her face.

"He's close." There was slight nervousness in her voice.

"Good. Now, we must make it look real," he replied, turning to look at her.

"It will be perfect."

"You need him to fall in love with you. His mother is the only person who can bring you back."

"Father, everything will work as it should."

"Have you dismissed Bethani?" he inquired.

"Yes, she and Cole have taken refuge with the vampires."

"The vampires? Of all people she picked them?"

"You know how she is—such a free spirit. She claims they are the closest to our kind, although, unlike us, they fight and kill for fun." She shrugged her shoulders. "It's time. We must get into position."

He pulled a large knife from his belt holster. "Angelina?"

"Yes, father?"

"Come to me for a moment."

She did as he asked, and he wrapped his arms around her and held her close. "I love you so very much."

She pulled away. "Father, this is silly."

His voice grew weak. "No. It will seem like an eternity until we see each other again."

"We're bound by blood father. We've found each other once; we will find each other again."

"Take this." He handed her the knife along with a small white box. Studying it for a moment, she opened it, her eyes lighting up once she saw what was inside. Reaching inside the box, she pulled out a beautiful golden locket.

The same locket I was now wearing. My eyes were glued to her as she turned the locket over, running her fingers over the etching on the front.

"H?" she questioned.

"Hecate," he whispered lovingly, kissing her gently upon her forehead. "This was given to me by your mother who used to be the most powerful being ever known to walk this earth. Once she fell in love with me, she was forbidden to stay here any longer."

"So, she didn't die when I was born?"

"No, my love. If anyone found out who your true mother was, they'd take you from me for sure."

"So, you're saying the Goddess Hecate is my mother?" I asked, stunned.

He nodded. "She gave me this locket to help you remember who you are when the time comes."

"She knew this would happen?"

"She knew many things, my dear. She was quite intriguing. She used to tell me that in order for one to be happy in life one must find something worth living for, and she was right. My dear, you're that one thing."

My younger self sniffled. "Father, you're making this harder than it needs to be."

"Once this is over, I will need you to find the woman I introduced you to earlier, she will help you finish your task."

"She's aware of what must happen?"

"Yes, she knows. She knows more than you may think. She's been helping me watch over you since you were a child."

A surprised look crossed the girl's face. "And I never knew her before this?"

He smiled and kissed her cheek. "We're running out of time."

"You're right. We should get this over with."

He took her hand and placed it upon his heart, in turn placing his hand on hers. "I am taking a piece of your heart and am giving you a piece of mine, so that once we're reunited, we will become whole."

My chin began to quiver right along with hers. Placing my hand on my own heart, I thought back to days when he would do that very same gesture with me.

Taking the locket from her, he opened its delicate clasp and placed it carefully around her slender neck. "A father's love knows no bounds. I will be there for you when you return. This, I promise you."

He took a step back, clearing the lump that had begun to form in his throat. Bracing himself, he motioned for her to order the bear to attack him. With tears in her eyes, she raised her hand toward the beast and whispered her father's wishes for it to attack him. The bear let out a powerful growl and did as it was told, unleashing the large, razor-sharp claws that had been hidden in its mighty paws. With one ferocious hit, it knocked her father to the ground. Lowering her hand, she nodded for it to come to her. The bear looked at the body it'd just broken, swiped the ground a few times with its monstrous paw, and trotted up next to her.

She apologized to the bear and pushed the blade of the knife her father had given her into its soft furry body. The bear groaned and fell to the ground, a look of confusion in its warm brown eyes.

"I'm so sorry." Tears ran down her flushed cheeks.

It lay slowly dying, panting the last few breaths left within its lungs. She walked over to her father and knelt down, placing the knife back into his bloody hands. She threw the basket she'd been carrying to the ground and watched as the freshly picked berries scattered. Laying her hand on her father's chest, she began to cry, begging him to return to her.

Whether they were real or fake tears, I couldn't tell. All I knew was that my former self was one heck of an actress.

Thoroughly entertained, I continued watching as she pretended to be unaware of the fiery orange eyes that were now observing her every action. Sniffling, she went to the dying bear and laid her hands upon its head letting her hands run freely down its body, coaxing it to be still. It was no surprise to me what happened next. I looked up to see Nicolai's face, full of wonder as to what she was. I remembered that look. Heck, I'd seen it for myself a few days earlier. The mist began to form once again and the ground trembled beneath me. I closed my eyes and prayed my next vision would be decent. Nicolai had been right. Some things were better left in the past. Knowing it was too late, I waited patiently, wondering what heart-wrenching thing I was going to be shown next.

35

Regrettable Actions

Nicolai dropped to his knees, feeling utterly defeated by the thought that he'd lost her. Knowing many of the scandalous secrets that had been hidden from her, he cringed, wondering if she'd come back jaded and overwhelmed. He hadn't meant to be so hard on her, but he knew, in time, she would regret opening the locket, and she was too pure of heart to have such negative feelings swimming within her mind. Feeling a hand on his shoulder, he looked up, trying to hide the sorrow from his eyes.

"There is nothing you can do now but wait for her return," Bethani stated quietly.

"I shouldn't have let her do it," he answered. "This will change her."

"We both knew of the consequences beforehand. It was time for her to see who she really is."

"What if . . ." His despair wouldn't allow him to finish his sentence.

"She doesn't love you when she returns?" Bethani finished for him.

Nodding, he looked down, nauseated by the potential truth behind her words.

"It is said that true love can follow you from one life to the next. It's so powerful it buries itself deep inside the soul, transferring to each new life, carrying with it fragments of memories and feelings, each time renewing hope that one day you'll be lucky enough to find the person you are meant to be with." Bethany turned to leave. "I believe that regardless of what she discovers, neither of you can live without the other. Your hearts will not allow it."

Looking back up at her, Nicolai watched her walk through the clearing and back into the forest. He was grateful for her wise words, as they somehow managed to ease his anxious mind. Hearing a howl behind him, he knew Cole was nearby and had come to the upsetting realization that his master was gone. Nicolai knew the rest of his companions would soon be joining him, wondering how he could let such precious cargo disappear. He contemplated leaving, dreading the accusations that would soon be directed toward him. However, leaving would be the most selfish act he could perform, for she would need him once she returned—or at least he hoped she would.

He felt as though someone was watching him, and he glanced over his shoulder to see Jeremiah emerge from the forest with an enraged expression on his face.

"And so it begins," Nicolai muttered as he stood up to brace himself for what was about to happen.

"Where is she?" Jeremiah called out, small sparks of electricity shooting from his fingertips.

Nicolai looked down and shook his head. "She's gone."

"No! You did this! You let her go!" Jeremiah rushed toward him and pulled his arm back, ready to unleash the new hatred he felt for the man that had betrayed Angelina's trust.

Letting his powerful fist do the talking, Jeremiah punched him square in the jaw. Nicolai faltered and dropped to his knees. He caught himself with one hand and used the other to pull Jeremiah down with him.

"Stop this," Nicolai commanded as the copper taste of blood filled his mouth.

"How could you? You let her go! What have you done?" Jeremiah replied, punching him in the gut. Nicolai doubled over in pain, knowing he could inflict immense pain upon Jeremiah if he truly wished to do so. Instead, he continued to let Jeremiah take his aggressions out on him, partly because he knew he deserved it. He felt another blow to his face and raised his arm to try and shield himself. By the time Angelina returned, he'd probably be disfigured, and she wouldn't recognize him.

"Jeremiah, stop," Mathias yelled as he ran toward them. "There is no point in beating him to death. It's not his fault. He only did as she wished."

"No! He could have stopped her!" Jeremiah turned toward Nicolai and threw another punch. "Why didn't you stop her?"

"I—I couldn't," Nicolai answered breathlessly. He wiped the blood that oozed from his face.

Jeremiah pushed Nicolai away from him. "Yes, you could've! She was so pure and innocent. Do you realize what you've just done?"

"Don't you think I know what I've done? How do you think it feels to know that I've potentially lost the only thing that keeps me alive?" Nicolai stood to face his attacker.

Cole jumped out of the edge of the forest and

ran toward Nicolai at full speed. Drool dripped from his snarling lips. Nicolai sighed and once again braced for the impact, reminding himself that it would all be worth it in the end. Cole plowed into him, knocking him to the ground. Throwing his arms up in front of his face, Nicolai used every bit of strength he had to keep Cole from ripping him apart. The wolf snapped at him with his razor-sharp teeth, infuriated that his master was gone and that it was all Nicolai's fault.

"Enough," Bethani commanded as she gracefully reentered the clearing. Cole snapped at Nicolai once more and then retreated back into the forest with a long howl and his tail between his legs. Nicolai, wiping the blood and drool from his face, stood up and assessed the damage that had been done to him.

Stephen stumbled out of the forest with a disappointed look on his face. What'd I miss?" he asked as he surveyed the area. "Oh, wow. Looks like someone got the best of you," he pointed out to Nicolai.

"It looks to me as if they've watched too many reruns of *Fight Club*," Laurana joked, appearing behind Stephen. "What happens in fight club stays in fight club," she mimicked in a deep voice.

Mathias let out a hearty laugh, followed by Bethani's sweet girlish giggles.

"Yeah, well, it was deserved," Jeremiah chimed in.

Mathias's laughter stopped abruptly.

"What is it? What's wrong?" Jeremiah asked as he watched the strange man's eyes go through a multitude of colors.

Alarmed, Bethani pulled an arrow from her quiver and set it carefully into her bow.

"He's coming for her," Mathias answered bluntly.

Jeremiah threw him a cautious look. "Elias?"

"Yes."

"How much time do we have?" Jeremiah asked.

Looking past Jeremiah, Mathias watched a dark figure emerge from the other side of the clearing. "None."

They all stood fast, prepared to defend themselves. The figure continued walking toward them, casually whistling a strange tune none of them recognized.

Nicolai's face paled. "Father, you're alive?" he asked, his voice quivering.

"Well, it seems that way," Elias replied, putting his hands in his pockets. "Your dear, sweet Angelina isn't the only one that your mother has risen."

Confusion filled Nicolai's eyes as he studied his father, deciding whether or not to believe him.

"I see you didn't know. Well, that's a woman for you."

"Are you telling me that she brought you back and has known about you this entire time?" Nicolai's fiery orange eyes began to glow.

"Of course. You see, son, a woman's love surpasses all the powers bestowed upon the creatures of the earth. It's selfish and unforgiving, showing loyalties to the person she chooses to give her love to."

"I don't understand. Why would she send us out here to stop you?"

Glancing back, Elias said, "Why don't you ask her yourself?"

Ctephanyi made her way toward them, a devious smile upon her beautiful face. Taking her place next to Elias, she motioned for Laurana to join them. Jeremiah's face was instantly plagued with hurt and betrayal. Laurana lowered her eyes and took a step forward.

"You don't have to do this," Jeremiah pleaded.

"Do you remember our very first conversation?" she whispered.

"The one where you tried to kill me?"

"No, the conversation where you said it sounded as if I were scared of her."

He nodded slowly. "I do."

"Well, you were right. I am downright terrified. Don't you understand? She's more powerful than all of us put together."

"Laurana, listen to me. There is fear in all of our hearts. How we choose to display that fear makes us who we are. Betrayal is not the answer."

"Why does my choice matter to you anyway?" she snapped as she watched him pull something out of his jeans pocket.

Looking at her with flushed cheeks, he grabbed her hand and gave her the item he had taken from his pocket. Observing it closely, she could see it was a heart shaped rock.

"I found that when I was very young—skipping rocks was kind of a hobby—and I promised myself that one day I'd give it to the woman I'd marry."

Startled by his admission, she ran her fingers

over the rock's smooth surface. "What about Angelina?"

"What about her? Our paths were meant to go in very different directions. I know this now. Do I love her? Of course, I do—as my best friend, nothing more, nothing less."

"Are you saying you love me?"

She closed her hand around the heart-shaped rock as he kissed her gently. "That's exactly what I'm saying."

Laurana looked directly at Ctephanyi. "A man once told me that a woman's love shows its loyalties to the person she chooses to give it to." Jeremiah put his arm around her protectively. "My loyalty lies with him."

"That's your choice?" Ctephanyi frowned, offering her one last opportunity to join them.

"Yes, that's my choice."

"Fine, then you shall die right along with the rest of them."

"You'd kill me too? Your only son?" Nicolai interrupted.

"Of course not. Once we have Angelina, she'll be more accepting of her situation if you're with her."

"Mother, she's come to love you. How could you lie to her?" he questioned angrily, clenching his fists. "Using her as a weapon will solve nothing."

"My dear boy, we have no intention of using her as a weapon."

"Then what's the point of all this? Why send us on a journey that leads to nothing."

"The plan we devised was quite simple really. If you give a creature, regardless of its species, bits and pieces of information, it will always make its own assumptions about why something is happening. Your beliefs led you all to think Elias had come back, seeking revenge against the human population. I simply went along with it. The best part was fooling Josiah into thinking you were all going to kill Elias."

"Josiah? Are you referring to my cousin?" Nicolai questioned.

"He is your step cousin," she corrected. "You see, for the longest time we thought the woman your uncle married was human. However, she actually turned out to be of the same species as Angelina. She had been given the ability to change her physical characteristics at will, which Josiah also inherited. They were able to walk amongst humans because they could transform into them. Fascinated by this fact, your uncle took it upon himself to care for them, eventually falling in love with the idea of having a family. Since she was eager to have a father figure for her son, she agreed, and they were married shortly after.

"Everyone keeps referring to these people as a species. What exactly are they?" Jeremiah asked.

"Nobody really knows," Ctephanyi replied. "Some say they're angels from the heavens above sent here to protect us all from destroying ourselves. Others argue that they're actually children of the ancient gods that once ruled over the earth. They're the only ones who know the truth. Isn't that right, Bethani?"

All eyes turned toward her.

Still holding her arrow in place, Bethani replied with a wink, "Yes ma'am."

"So, this Josiah. What does he have to do with all this?" Stephen asked, changing the subject.

Elias put his arm around Ctephanyi. "Good question, Josiah is the reason my brother was murdered. He is the reason my only son never had a father growing up."

Nodding in agreement, Ctephanyi's milky white eyes stared off into the distance. "Josiah is Angelina's father."

Elias laughed loudly at the shock on Nicolai's face. "Surprise, surprise."

"How is that possible?" Nicolai croaked.

"When Angelina was born into this world, she had many gifts, the ultimate one being the ability to give life or to take it away. The humans, hearing of her special talents, tried to find her to use her power for selfish reasons. Once they found out who her family was, Josiah abandoned her, leaving her with friends while he hid. He let his own blood take the punishment for his cowardly acts."

"Why take her? Why kill her mother?"

"He needed to see how it felt to lose his family, the only thing that ever mattered to him. He needed to feel the anguish and pain that we felt. Do you know how many humans I've had to sacrifice to raise your father's spirit?" Ctephanyi asked looking at him once again. "And how I felt when you fell in love with that traitor's daughter?"

It was all beginning to make sense. Looking down, Nicolai shook his head in disbelief, sickened by the numerous lies he'd been told. "All those humans that were sacrificed . . . my own father killed the mother of the one person I was meant to be with and for revenge of all things." He looked up at his parents, hatred in his eyes. "You are both monsters."

"No, my son, Josiah is the monster," Elias argued, leaving his wife's side. He strode toward Nicolai slowly, continuing, "Once we have Angelina, he'll see how it feels to be alone."

Mathias stepped forward, his eyes changing, images of the past and present running through his mind. "It's almost time."

"Time for what?" Elias asked stopping momentarily to look at him. Mathias ignored the question and, instead, gave Nicolai a quick nod, a silent communication that he understood.

Nicolai's eyes lit up, and he smiled at his father. "I'm surprised you haven't noticed that the one thing you came for isn't here."

Elias's blood-red eyes burned brightly as he surveyed the area, realizing Nicolai was right. "Where is she?" he demanded.

"She's somewhere safe."

Nicolai's answer seemed to anger him even more as he slowly raised his arm toward Bethani. "I'm going to ask once more. Where is she?"

Stephen looked to Bethani for an answer. Smiling at him sweetly, she tightened her finger on the bow string, her sights set on the heart of Elias. "I know that look," Stephen said. Things were about to get bloody.

"Nicolai, do you think this is a game?" Elias asked, his red eyes ablaze.

"No, father. I think your plan has failed."

Elias raised his hand in the air. "We'll see about that."

Bethani let the arrow fly, and they all watched

it hit its mark. Ctephanyi fell to the ground, the arrow embedding itself into her chest.

"Wasn't she aiming for *his* heart?" Jeremiah whispered pointing toward Elias.

"Now you know what her gift is," Stephen whispered in return. "She can manipulate the things around her to make us see what she wants us to see. Really sucks when you try hitting on her. She makes you think you're kissing her when you're actually making out with a tree."

Jeremiah snickered. "I'm guessing you've some experience with that."

Elias lowered his arm, surprised by his fallen wife. Running to her side, he bent down assessing the damage that'd been done to her. He sat her up, and she smiled weakly at him, a tear running down her pale cheek.

"Well, I didn't see that coming." She smirked, trying to find humor in the situation. "She missed my heart—barely."

"I'm going to make them suffer," Elias promised bitterly as he pulled the arrow from her chest. He laid his hand over the gaping wound, and blood pouring out around it.

"Go. I can put pressure on it," she urged, taking his hand off her and replacing it with her own. "She is the only one that can heal it."

Standing up, he twisted his neck slightly, letting the joints loosen. His eyes matched the crimson leaves, burning brightly as he lifted his arms over his head and brought them back down to the ground with an immense force. The ground began to shake violently and slowly opened, creating a deep crevice in the earth behind him. They all watched in horror as a dark creature crawled out of it.

Bethani pulled another arrow from her quiver and set it into her bow, firing automatically. A loud shriek came out of the creature as it fell back into the darkness it had come from. Another figure emerged, followed by numerous others.

"What are they?" Jeremiah asked.

Nicolai knew exactly what they were. He'd seen them occasionally during a soul rising or when his mother was sacrificing a human. "You humans call them the shadow people. They live within the darkest depths of the earth, only coming out when they are summoned or the possibility to overtake a human body arises. They thrive on fear and hatred. It's where they get their power from." His eyes focused on the dark creatures that awaited their next command.

"How are we supposed to kill them?" Stephen questioned, his features beginning to change.

Nicolai stuttered for a moment, trying not to make it obvious that he was watching Stephen's transformation. "They—um . . ."

"It's cool, man. I didn't want you to have to see this, but it looks like we're going to need every bit of help we can get." His once perfect teeth were now razor sharp.

"I just—I've never seen a vampire change," Nicolai admitted, embarrassed by his reaction.

"Yeah, well, we're not the prettiest things to ever walk the earth. But hey, at least we don't go poof when we see the sun."

Nicolai grinned at the cadaverous-looking vampire. "These creatures may look like shadows, but they die like everything else. Heed my warning. Whatever you do, don't let them get near you at the point of death. That's when they can possess your body."

Stephen looked over at Bethani. "The only thing I want possessing my body is that blonde over there."

Bethani rolled her eyes at him and pulled out another arrow.

"Well, that wasn't the response I was hoping for," he teased. "Nicolai, your girl is going to be ecstatic when she returns right smack dab in the middle of all this."

Nicolai glanced over at Mathias. "Hopefully we'll have it taken care of by then."

"No promises," Mathias retorted bluntly, avoiding his eyes.

Elias, looking quite pleased, turned to face his son. "Why not avoid all of this?" He motioned toward the dark shadows behind him. "I tell you what. I'm going to give you one more opportunity to tell me where Angelina is."

"Please, just tell him," Ctephanyi begged, her dying voice weak.

Nicolai turned to look at his companions. Each one nodded, prepared to fight side-by-side with him in order to save Angelina. Looking toward his mother, he felt a stab of pity. He wished she hadn't let vengeance invade her heart. "Mother, I'm sorry. I can't allow this to happen. This is not the answer and will not bring either of you peace."

"Nicolai . . .," she gasped, trying to catch her breath.

Unmoved by Nicolai's speech, Elias lifted his arm toward the small army behind him. "Just remember, you chose this."

Elias ordered them to attack and watched with a wicked smile on his face as the dark army he'd summoned rushed toward their targets, each creature hoping for the chance to take possession of one of their bodies.

Jeremiah winked at Laurana, whose eyes had begun to glow their bright ice-blue color. "You ready for this?"

One of the dark shadows grabbed her by the arm. "It's about time something exciting happened," she exclaimed, using her other hand to grab it by the shoulder. She pulled it toward her and used her extraordinary strength to snap its dark neck.

"That's my girl," Jeremiah complimented as two of the creatures lunged for him. One managed to slice his arm with something sharp. He felt his own eyes begin to glow, and he clenched his fist, punching one in what he guessed was its face. It stumbled backwards and fell into Laurana who wrapped her hands around its head. Hearing another snap, he smiled. Clenching his other fist, he pulled his arm back and let it fly into the other creature. He used his new strength to grab it around the midsection and crush what he was sure had to be its ribcage. It fell to the ground, barely moving. Jeremiah had watched enough movies to know that even though it looked like it was dead, it probably wasn't. He put his own hands around its neck and gave it a quick twist, snapping its spine.

Mathias was enjoying the thrill of killing one after the other with his bare hands while Bethani concentrated on letting her arrows do all the work. Stephen sunk his devilish claws into each one, licking the blood from his lips, thirsting for more. Nicolai thanked his quick-healing body, as it was steady enough to kill the creatures easily.

Nicolai heard a low growl behind him and knew Cole had arrived, hungry for a fight. He hoped the ferocious animal used all his pent-up aggression toward him on the creatures instead. Cole leapt toward one of the creatures, ripping it to shreds with his powerful teeth.

More shadows emerged from the crevice, rushing toward them. Laurana attempted to keep her pace with killing each one, but they were beginning to overwhelm her. She felt a sharp stabbing pain in her leg and looked down to see one of the creatures sinking its teeth into her. She grabbed it by the shoulder, throwing it away from her. Blood began to seep through her pant leg. Hearing her screams, Jeremiah fought his way toward her. He flipped one of the creatures over his back, using his mighty strength to break its back. He called for help as he struggled to pull them all off her. There were just too many.

Nicolai heard Jeremiah's call for help and made his way over to them. Together, the two of them were able to free her from the creatures that had pinned her to the ground. Jeremiah took one look at her battered body and grew infuriated by the damage they'd done to her. He grabbed two of the creatures by the shoulders and smashed their heads together. Whipping around he grabbed one by the arm, twisting it until he heard a loud snap. He grabbed it by its other arm and pulled as hard as he could, spinning it around to snap its neck.

"Impressive," Laurana complimented wearily.

Cole yelped as three dark shadows pulled him to the ground, clawing at his furry body. Mathias attempted to help him but also disappeared beneath the swarm of creatures. He felt the darkness slowly creep into him, attempting to overtake his very soul.

Nicolai noticed the group succumbing to the evil creatures that plagued them and looked to the sky, praying for some sort of assistance.

Hearing faint words coming from somewhere behind him, Nicolai concentrated on deciphering what was being said. Relief washed over him as he finally realized it was Mathias.

"The time has come," Mathias said as he struggled to keep the darkness out. "She's returned to us."

The ground began trembling, and a thick mist formed around them, briefly shielding them from the dark creatures.

Elias surveyed the area for the person responsible for this dark magic. The mist continued to spread across the ground, wrapping its tentacle-like arms around them. Loud shrieking could be heard as the shadow people, fearful for their existence, attempted to flee back into the dark depths of the earth. Elias grew irritated and yelled into the unknown, begging the cowardly magician to show himself. The reply was a shrill cry from Ctephanyi. He stumbled through the thick white vapors, calling out his wife's name. Hearing no answer, he fell to his knees. He had to make the mist disappear so he could rush to her side. He heard a noise in front of him and scrambled to his feet, not knowing what to expect. Squinting, he could make out the figure of a woman walking toward him. His eyes widened as he realized he was staring at the one thing he'd come here for—Angelina.

She smiled, cruelty descended upon her face, her beautiful chestnut eyes ablaze with malevolence. "Just remember," she pointed a slender finger at him, "you asked for this."

36

Vengeance

My last few images were kinder to me. They showed me how I had come to truly love Nicolai, which relieved the guilt I felt from knowing the beginning of our relationship was created falsely. I had also come to the realization that my father, Josiah, was not the villain but had, in fact, done a very righteous thing. Blood may have been on his hands, but for a good reason. He had not only protected me but also protected the salvation of all the creatures of the earth, allowing them to continue living, giving them future opportunities to change their self-centered ways.

One thing I found unsurprising was that I had planned my own death, knowing Ctephanyi would eventually bring me back. Reliving that moment was incredibly painful as I was able to see the utter despair in Nicolai's eyes as he begged his mother to save my life.

I was truly surprised to learn that my father had explained his future intentions to my new mother. He had spent countless years looking for a woman who had had trouble giving birth to a living child. Luck finally turned its head, and he came across a heavily burdened woman trying to take her own life, believing she had been cursed for unknown sins. She had a devastating past, losing child after child. Her first husband left her for a woman who could give him an heir to his lineage. My father saved her, promising her he would be with her always, guaranteeing one day she would have a beautiful daughter—me. He knew Nicolai had also been looking for the perfect couple to bring back his true love, so when my mother got pregnant once again, he reassured her that this time would be different and devised a plan to be in the right place at the right time.

The night at the hospital when Nicolai approached him, he did everything he could to make Nicolai believe he didn't already know what was going to happen. He made the promise to return me once I reached the agreed-upon age, though he had absolutely no intention of following through. He knew they would come for him instead, which they did. Already figuring his wife and daughter would be devastated by his disappearance, he moved his mother back into town, buying the general store to keep her busy as she kept a close eye on both of us, eventually enabling her to win our trust. While in captivity, he endured many tortures, believing Nicolai would one day rescue him for the simple reason that he was the one thing I wished for most. And he was right.

Nicolai never knew that I wasn't the only one who could see him when I was a child. While my mother laughed at her young daughter's outrageous stories, my father just smiled, knowing the truth behind them.

Disappointment came when I was shown Ctephanyi's vengeful heart. Learning of her devious plan angered me and left me to wonder if her displays of affection toward me were false. She had been wise to give Jeremiah the golden dagger, knowing it was the only way to truly kill my father. I now understood the reasons behind her bestowing powerful gifts upon Jeremiah's body. They would give him the opportunity to overthrow my father, using the dagger to end his life. She put many lives at stake for an unjust cause. Elias shared in her hatred, as neither was able to see the bigger picture behind the sorrow and hatred that filled them.

My last vision saddened me as I watched Elias knock on the old worn door, my mother answering it only to be pushed inside. Knowing I was still home and would hear the commotion, she tried her best to give me enough time to escape, avoiding his questions about where I was. She had known he would eventually kill her. However, she had to try to protect her only child from being taken by the madman that had invaded their home.

Growing tired, he had punished her, taking her life and destroying everything else that lay in his path. While I watched the vision, I secretly thanked her for giving me that opportunity, the warm tears falling softly down my face. As he ransacked my room looking for clues to my whereabouts, he caught a glimpse of something hanging from the tree outside my bedroom window. He had opened the window, surprised to see me escaping right beneath his nose.

Preparing himself to come out after me, he was surprised to find himself being pulled back inside. He turned around and found himself face-to-face with a large black wolf. I smiled, knowing it was Cole who protected me from my perpetrator. The wolf pounced on Elias, snapping his enormous razor-sharp teeth at his face, aiming straight for the jugular. Turning his head turned to the side to avoid the massive teeth, Elias used his powerful arms to throw the wolf against the window, shattering it. The wolf shook off the pain and pounced once again, snarling, his black eyes full of hatred for the man who was trying to abduct his master. He used his large paws to bat at Elias's feet, knocking him to the ground. Elias dug his knife-like fingernails into the old wooden floor as the wolf sunk its teeth into his leg, attempting to drag him out of the room. Succeeding, the wolf growled in pleasure, knowing he'd given me just enough time to escape. He shook his head furiously so his teeth would shred the muscles in the red-eyed monster's leg. Finally, he let go and ran into the night in search of his master, knowing his job of protecting her had just begun.

Wicked thoughts ran through my mind at the many things I wanted to do to Ctephanyi and Elias. The majority of sorrows in my life had come from them, and I wanted to make them pay for all the years of happiness they'd taken away from me. My whole life, I had been worried about being normal, because normal meant I had a chance for some sort of happiness. If it hadn't been for the secrets that lay within the Crimson Forest, I would never have realized that being normal is for people who want to live in the comfort of their safe routines, who want to peer into the world with rose colored glasses and avoid the truth.

That wasn't the path chosen for me. I was meant to be so much more and do things normal, ordinary people secretly dreamt of.

Looking back through my history had changed me, turning me into the person I was meant to become. I was no longer afraid of the future. In fact, I looked forward to it, knowing I was the key to its survival. Smiling to myself, I picked the locket up and ran my fingertips over the smooth letter etched onto the front of it. The time had come for me to go back, to fight for the things I cherished most, and to show the world that good could overcome evil. I closed the locket and prepared myself, knowing of the battle that lay ahead of me. I had been shown a glimpse of the future, and I wasn't too pleased by Elias's summoning his demonic creatures upon my friends and making them suffer for protecting my secrets.

As the mist formed around me, I thought of how scared I was when Ctephanyi took me to her city to turn me into one of their species. She'd shown me photo albums, thanked me for making her see humans differently, and even welcomed me into her family. Anger pulsed through my veins, creating a tingling sensation through my body. The bitter truth had been laid out in front of me, unleashing my true potential, and I was ready to show the world that the fairy tales they had been told as children were true. In fact, there was more truth in them then any history book ever written.

Creating the mist around everything had been such a clever idea. After all, I had just spent an incredible amount of time in it. Why not share that pleasure with everyone else? The shrieks from the dark creatures were spine tingling, and I envisioned them attempting to run back to safety below ground. It was a shame I had already closed the crevice. I would deal with them after I took care of the two I had come back for.

Elias stared at me, debating what his best course of action should be—attempt to fight me or give up all together.

"Tell me, Elias, was it worth it?" I asked menacingly.

Looking at me, confused, he answered. "Was what worth it?"

Putting my arms in front of me, I parted them slowly causing the mist to dissipate in front of him and reveal Ctephanyi's frail body.

I pointed toward her. "This is what your vengeance has done."

"No," he whispered in disbelief, realizing his wife was no longer alive.

"She brought you back because she loved you," I said, "and just between you and me, I know you don't possess the power to return the favor."

I watched as he went to her, falling to his knees, his red eyes dimming at the realization that I was right. He picked up her lifeless body and pulled her close to his chest, shaking his head.

"Angelina?" a familiar voice rang out.

Turning around, my heart stopped as my father walked toward me.

"Father?" The mist continued to slowly dissipate around us.

"You've returned," he said.

"Yes, I have." I took his hands into mine. His features had changed, and he resembled Elias.

Noticing I was looking at him strangely, he winked. "It's a gift. I didn't want to go walking around and come up missing again. I figured if I looked like him I wouldn't get caught."

Nodding, I hugged him tightly.

He hugged me back. "You remember everything now."

"Yes, I remember." A tear fell down my cheek. "Thank you."

"For what?" he questioned.

"For loving me as much as you do."

It was as if everything began moving in slow motion. I heard a loud, manly yell and turned my head slowly to see him rushing at us, the golden dagger aimed at my father's heart.

"Jeremiah, no!" I yelled, raising my hand to stop him, but it was too late. A black flash whizzed in front of us as the knife embedded itself deep inside the warm body, blood soaking the ground.

"What have you done?" I sobbed, pushing Jeremiah to the ground.

"I—I thought he was Elias . . .," he stammered looking confused.

Falling to the ground, I picked up Cole's body and held it close, attempting to heal him. He used his last breath to lick my face gently before growing limp in my arms. He had watched me grow up twice, each time protecting me from all harm that had come my way. He knew I would be devastated by the loss of my father, so he did his final duty by ensuring I continued to have him in the future. He had given up his life for my happiness.

I knew the magic the golden dagger possessed

and knew bringing Cole back to life was impossible. I had always adored animal spirits because they were different than that of other spirits. They were made of pure love, held no regrets, and simply gave to the world around them, asking for nothing in return.

"Angelina," Jeremiah pleaded, begging me to listen to him.

I ignored him and walked away. Raising my arms over my head and snapping my fingers, fury coursed through my body. The remainder of the mist vanished completely and revealed the demonic figures who immediately scurried to find the crevice I had closed. I set my sights on them and snapped my fingers once again. Each one of the dark figures burst into flames, their bodies turning into ash. The wind gently blew their remains throughout the clearing. I continued walking, making the remaining creatures suffer. They would never again walk the earth. They would simply cease to exist.

I noticed Mathias lying on the ground, barely alive, and ran to him. I bent down and lay my hand on his chest, feeling something evil within him. He grabbed my arm and looked into my eyes, and I watched as they went through a multitude of colors. I caught a glimpse of a small piece of paper in the reflection of his eyes and nodded to let him know I understood his message. Reaching into my pocket, I pulled out the piece of paper I'd forgotten about. I unfolded it carefully and began reading it, my anger vanishing with each word I read:

Every person on this earth chooses whether

he will follow the path of darkness or the path of light. You've been given a tremendous opportunity. The path you choose will determine who you become in the future. Vengeance will never be the answer. Look around you. Remember the ones you love and those who love you. They are the people who are counting on you to do the right thing. Follow the right path, and you can achieve much greatness.

PS. Bethani was right. You saved us all.

I refolded the note carefully and tucked it back into my pocket. Smiling tenderly, I whispered, "This is going to hurt just a little bit."

I lay my hand upon his chest. Feeling the darkness inside him, I closed my eyes and concentrated on pulling it out. His body jerked violently as I reached inside him, grabbing hold of the dark shadow that had taken over his soul.

"You will not win, little guy. Just save yourself the hassle and come out." I struggled, placing my other hand on his chest to hold his body down. Mathias let out an ear-piercing shriek as the creature resisted letting go of him.

I clenched my teeth. "Well, you have two choices: either you come out now, or when I pull you out, you'll turn to ash just like the rest of your little buddies."

Mathias shrieked again, and using every bit of strength I had in me, I yanked, pulling the dark shadow right out of him. Mathias let out a loud gasp and rolled over, his arms hugging his chest. The creature squirmed in my hands, and I realized just how scary looking they actually were.

"If the humans knew about you, they would never leave their houses and would sleep with their lights on," I pointed out, a disgusted look on my face.

The ground began to tremble as I used my free hand to point toward it. It groaned angrily, opening up in front of me.

"Time for you to go home. If I were you, I would use my best judgment and stay down there. We don't want to meet again." I threw it into the darkness and snapped my fingers to close the gaping hole.

"Angelina?"

Turning around, I studied Nicolai's bloody face, curiosity in his fiery orange eyes and hope in his heart that I still loved him.

"Who are you?" I asked a serious tone in my voice.

Hurt replaced the curiosity, and despair replaced the hope as he hung his head and turned to walk away.

"Wait," I said.

He looked up solemnly, and I motioned for him to come. He obliged, stopping just in front of me. I put my hands on each side of his face and gazed into his beautiful eyes, letting him wonder what I was doing.

"Nope, I'm sorry, but I don't remember you," I stated bluntly.

Looking down once again, he shook his head. "My worst fear has come . . ."

I playfully licked the tip of his nose. His eyes widened in a look of sheer surprise.

"Oh man, looks like you've got slobber on your face," I joked.

He threw his muscular arms around me and pulled me close, kissing my face in a million different places.

"You didn't forget me?" he whispered in between kisses.

I kissed him tenderly on the lips. "Of course not. How could I forget the man I'm destined to be with?"

He pushed a piece of hair out of my face. "You know, a girl as special as you might find a guy like me kind of boring."

"Well, a guy like you might find a girl like me kind of intimidating." I laughed.

He hugged me again. "You're right. I am kind of intimidated."

Hearing a disgusted groan, I leaned back and peered over to see Stephen make a gagging face at us. "Please, get a room," he grumbled through his razor-sharp teeth.

I was surprised by his gruesome figure. "Wow, Stephen, you're really kind of scary looking."

"Yeah, well, this scary face saved the life of your best friend." He pointed at Bethani.

I let go of Nicolai and stepped back to look at her. I had never seen her in this kind of shape. She had bloody scratches on every inch of her pale body. I frowned, realizing she'd been the one who'd taken the greatest risk by shooting Ctephanyi with her bow. The consequences for her actions could've been deadly. She set her bow down and knelt on one knee in front of me as I made my way over to her.

"Why do you kneel before me?" I asked

confused by her gesture.

"When we were young, I made a promise to my father that I would be your guardian and that I would protect you at all costs. You have my fealty." She looked down, honoring my presence.

Kneeling down, I joined her. "Bethani, you may be my guardian, but I would rather you were my best friend." I smiled as she looked up at me, her lavender eyes sparkling. "We're equals. There's no need for kneeling." I stood up and urged her to do the same.

Laurana watched from a distance, wondering what my reaction toward her would be. I nodded at her to let her know that she and I were okay. She smiled, happy with that answer as she nursed the gash across her leg. Mathias had finally come to his feet and was looking around at the damage we had done to the clearing.

"What path are you going to choose?" he questioned.

"The right one," I replied as I headed back toward Elias. He was in the same position I had left him, holding his beloved wife. Nicolai followed close behind, tears filling his eyes once he realized his mother's life had come to an end. Elias looked up, sadness in his crimson eyes.

"This is what happens when you follow the path of darkness," I stated, looking at the woman he held in his arms.

"I would give anything to have her back." He choked back the tears.

"Would you?"

He pulled her closer to him. "Yes, anything."

Glancing back at Mathias, I smiled, knowing what needed to be done.

"You're sure? Anything?"

Elias nodded. "Anything."

"Then, close your eyes and just remember you said anything," I replied with a wink.

I turned around and looked at each one of my companions, each one bloody from a battle they had fought to protect me. My father nodded and put his arm around Jeremiah, who was still devastated by the fact that he had killed Cole.

I bent down and picked up Cole's limp body holding it close to me. Looking back at Elias, I smiled. He had done as I asked. His eyes closed, he awaited his fate that lay in my hands. Nicolai wrapped an arm around my shoulders, kissing me lovingly on the side of my head.

I looked up at the clear blue sky. "Well, here goes . . ."

I held Cole tightly against my body as I concentrated on the task that lay before me. Dark clouds began to form and thunder followed behind angrily. The trees on the edge of the clearing began to sway back and forth as the wind blew violently through their branches.

The time had finally come for me to make a choice, a choice that would ultimately lead to the person I was meant to become. Several instantaneous flashes of lightning lit up the clearing, and I closed my eyes, choosing my path, letting the light carry me away. I hoped I could live up to the potential it had just offered me.

37

Birthday Surprise

I opened my eyes to find myself sitting in the middle of a beautiful flower garden. Looking up, I could make out the image of a gorgeous woman coming toward me.

"I've waited a very long time for this moment," she commented, a smile upon her beautiful face.

"Who are you?" I whispered in awe.

"You don't recognize me?" she asked surprised.

I looked at her closely, noticing her golden eyes, long chestnut-colored hair, pale skin, and slender figure. "Are you Hecate?"

"Well I was hoping maybe you'd call me something a little more endearing like mom." She grinned.

"Is this really happening?" I asked, wondering if I was stuck in a dream.

"Of course, it is. I knew one day you would have to make a choice, and I wanted to be there for it."

"You're allowed to do that because Father said . . ."

"I know what your father said." She laughed again. "Do you really think I would miss out on my only daughter's big decision?"

I shrugged my shoulders. "Well, maybe. I mean you are a goddess and all."

"What do you think that makes you?" she

winked.

I thought about that statement briefly and smiled. "That would make me like the female version of Hercules, right?"

She let out a hearty laugh and held my hand. "You know, they call me the Goddess of the Underworld, but the real fact of the matter is I'm not dark."

"You're not?"

"No, honey, I'm not. I control so many other things, and, in a sense, I have to be both."

"Can I be both?" I questioned, looking for answers in her golden eyes.

"I'm afraid I can't answer that for you. It's something you must choose on your own."

I frowned, confused by her answer. "Will I ever see you again?"

"Of course you will, and I want you to know I'm always watching over you. I know you'll make the right choice. You've always had a good head on your shoulders."

I laughed. "Yeah, I suppose I had to get something from my father."

She pulled me close for a hug, and I breathed her in. She smelled like lilacs and roses on a warm spring day.

"Will you give your father a message for me?" she asked sitting back briefly.

"Sure."

"Tell him we did well by creating you."

She stood up and smiled again, snapping her fingers in the air gently. I was suddenly extremely drowsy, so I closed my eyes.

~ ~ ~

I yawned and opened my eyes, stretching out across the comfortable couch.

"Someone's finally awake."

I looked up and smiled at the handsome man sitting across from me, "Was I asleep long?"

"Only a few hours," he replied, closing the book he had been reading.

"I didn't miss it, did I?" I asked suddenly remembering the party.

"Maybe." He laughed.

"Nicolai, I can't miss that party! They've planned it for months!"

"Well, then, I suppose we should be on our way."

Holding his hand out to me, I allowed him to pull me up, halfway hoping he would wrap his strong arms around me and spoil me with his wonderful kisses.

Reading my mind, he kissed my face generously. "Is that what you wanted?"

Wrinkling my nose in dissatisfaction, I replied, "You know, for a mind reader, you really got that one wrong, as that wasn't the kind of kissing I had in mind."

"Well, if I give you those kind of kisses, we'll definitely miss the party." He smiled as he led me outside.

The sun was warm on my skin, and it reminded me of how much I really enjoyed being outside, especially now that I was home.

Looking around, I noticed the town I had grown up in hadn't changed much since my journey into the Crimson Forest. The 894 people that lived there still clung to many of their homegrown values. They lived comfortably with what little they had, still unaware of the many mysterious things that surrounded them. Children, fearful of the many myths they still believed in, played outside until their parents called them in.

Showing the humans the truth behind their myths and legends hadn't gone quite as well as I had hoped. We had arrived at the perfect moment, during the middle of the day while everyone was enjoying the annual Forest Festival. Though the air smelled of funnel cakes and candy apples, it soon grew sour with the fragrance of reality.

Children had watched wide eyed as their parents held them close, wondering if evil aliens had just invaded their small community. Hunters instantly reached for their bows, aiming them carefully at us, each one fighting the urge to shoot, especially after seeing Stephen, who thought it would be funny to stay in his true vampire form. Others simply watched in amazement, coming to the realization that the stories they were told as children were, in fact, true.

Though I was exhausted, I used what strength I had left to show them the realities of the world around them, including the strange beings that had fought for human existence and the monsters that wanted it to end. I revealed to them a forgotten history in order that they might come to terms with their past sins against the creatures that had walked the earth before them. Fear and anger instantly filled the crowd that surrounded us.

"Liar!" one of the huntsman had called out as he sent an arrow whizzing past my head. The other hunters held their bows and followed in unison, letting their arrows fly straight toward us. Right before they reached our soft bodies, I raised my hand, and the mass of arrows froze in midair.

Mathias turned and looked at me with sympathy. "You give humans too much credit. Their minds are clouded by disbelief at their own actions. They will never come to terms with their past sins. It's not in their nature to do so."

I knew he was right and lowered my hand, allowing all the arrows to fall at our feet. I looked at the numerous frightened faces peering at us throughout the crowd. I frowned, knowing what I had to do. No other species could ever live in peace with the humans. They would never allow such a thing to happen. In their minds, they were the ultimate species, the top of the food chain, and they would never allow anything to change that.

I held my arms out in front of me and separated them slowly, a soft white light emerging from within them. It spread across the ground and throughout the crowd like vapor. Looks of confusion appeared on many of the startled faces as the memories of what they had just witnessed began to disappear from their fragile minds. The hunters lowered their bows, and parents let go of their small children.

I looked at my companions, and each one of them nodded in agreement before disappearing into the crowd, quietly hiding their true selves from human eyes. We had all come to terms with our new purpose, and that was to keep the many mysteries and unknown beings secret from the rest of the world. If society were ever to learn the truth of what surrounded them, it would surely turn into all-out war, which would lead only to the death and destruction of many.

My companions and I never forgot the day humanity let us down. In order for my father and me to return home, I had to take away the memory of my mother's existence. That was one of the hardest decisions I'd ever had to make, but I knew it was for the greater good. I implanted my father's image in her place. Nicolai, not wanting to leave my side, decided to stay, and though he had to wear colored contacts to hide his beautiful fiery-orange eyes, I was happy with his decision. Together, we restored the bed and breakfast, returning it to the welcoming place it had once been. My father ended up moving into a small house on the edge of town. With the population growing rapidly, he decided to expand the general store by turning it into a full-blown grocery store. Patrons were grateful for the new variety of items it offered, especially the single women who used their newfound fruits and vegetables to bake him flirtatious treats.

Stephen also decided to stay and had become a favorite amongst the woman within the area. Though he hid his true self from them, he used his "powers of persuasion" to get whatever and whomever he wanted. It disgusted me, and he knew it, so whenever possible he would flaunt his many affairs in my face. I simply laughed and told him to go stake himself.

Bethani moved in with us, keeping her promise to watch over and protect me. Every time I assured her I would be fine, she just smiled her sweet smile, her lavender eyes slightly twinkling. Mathias returned to the forest but promised to visit often. His discomfort with the human world was obvious since his eye color changed every new path the humans chose. I was sad to see him go, but I knew in my heart it was best for him.

Jeremiah and Laurana ended up moving in together and were set to be married in the spring. Sadly, I had to hear the news through my father as Jeremiah avoided me, still carrying the weight of Cole's death upon his shoulders. I thought of him often, missing his sly smile and bright blue eyes.

We buried Cole next to my mother's unmarked grave in the cemetery on the edge of town. We visited them occasionally, always bringing flowers for her and a chew toy for him.

I began having coffee with my grandmother as my mother used to. She would occasionally bake me an apple pie, and we would sit for hours reminiscing of the past. She filled me in on a lot of memories that had been taken away from me. I was grateful for her patience with me and lucky to have her in my life.

Smiling to myself, I squeezed Nicolai's hand, happy with the way everything turned out.

"Ready?" he asked as we came upon a beautiful brick home, landscaped with a million beautiful flowers.

"Yes." We walked down the cobblestone path and up a short set of steps.

Nicolai raised his hand to knock on the door when it opened suddenly, a friendly face peering out to welcome us.

"Nicolai, Angelina, you're here!" Bethani greeted us, an excited tone in her voice. "Come in, come in. We've been waiting."

Walking in, we were greeted by many familiar faces, all happy to see us. Balloons and party decorations were hung tastefully throughout the home. A delicious looking cake sat perfectly on a table in the middle of the room.

My father hugged me. "Happy birthday, my dear. How's it feel to be another year older?"

"Pretty good seeing as how I didn't think I was going to live to see it."

I scanned the large crowd and was happy to see my old companions amongst everyone. Even Stephen had shown for the festivities. I frowned when I saw Marie alone in the corner. Since my return, she'd been different with me, almost angry that I was no longer normal like her. Turning her head, she caught my gaze and smiled politely. I returned the smile and turned around, focusing my attention away from her.

Hearing a slight tapping noise upon a crystal wine glass, we all focused our attention on its owner.

"We have all gathered for a joyous occasion," she held the glass high above her head, "to celebrate another year of life lived well. I, for one, am grateful to this young woman for helping me to remember just how fragile all of us are in this great big world of ours. She's taught me to treasure every moment, enjoy the small things and, most of all, she's taught me the meaning of forgiveness."

Nicolai raised his glass in the air to join hers. "Mother, you're so sappy."

Laughing, we all joined in her toast, drinking to long happy lives. I admired Ctephanyi. Her new lease on life suited her well.

Elias had been a different story, as he wasn't too fond of the gift I had given him. Instead of punishing him with a painful death, I had chosen the path of light and made him the one thing he hated most—human. Though he was grateful that I had bestowed life back into Ctephanyi's body, he failed to accept his new human form and fled deep into the forest never to be seen nor heard from again. I knew Ctephanyi ached for him and often wondered where he was. However, her brief death had given her a glimpse of the darkness that fell upon all evil souls, and it left her too terrified to return to her old ways.

I mingled a bit more, opening presents, and eating some of the delicious cake that had been prepared so beautifully. The party turned out perfectly except for one thing. I scanned the room once looking for the one face I had hoped would be there—Jeremiah. I frowned, knowing he had once again avoided me. Sensing my displeasure, Nicolai kissed me gently, reminding me that Jeremiah would one day come around. I nodded and knew I was ready to go home.

I thanked everybody for the wonderful gifts and we left, enjoying the night air as we walked home together in silence.

Opening the door, I walked in and sat down. Nicolai excused himself and took an armload of presents into the kitchen. I looked around and admired the work we'd done to the old home. We had replaced the broken chairs and tables with new, more comfortable couches and loveseats. We had moved the kitchen to a different room, making the sitting room a gathering place to make conversations.

Enjoying the quiet, I leaned my head back and closed my eyes. A soft knock came at the door, and I opened my eyes slowly, annoyed by the sound. I stood up and went to the door, opening it to find a large blanket- covered basket. Stepping outside, I picked the basket up and was immediately surprised by its weight. I glanced into the darkness, failing to find the person who'd left it for me. With both hands, I carried the heavy basket inside and over to the couch. I called for Nicolai. He walked in quickly, caught off guard by the tone of my voice.

"What's wrong?" He had a startled look on his face.

I pointed toward the basket. "Someone's left another gift on our doorstep."

"What is it?" he asked, walking over to sit down next to me.

"I'm not sure, but it weighs a ton."

"Maybe we should take the blanket off and see what's under it?"

"What if it's, like, a head or something?" I asked looking at him seriously.

Laughing, he put his arm around me tenderly. "You watch way too many movies."

I knew he was right. There were probably cookies and other wonderful little goodies in there. Of course I had to go and think of the scariest thing possible, but you couldn't blame me after everything I'd just been through.

I eyed the basket cautiously, reached down, and slowly pulled the blanket back. Whatever was underneath it moved suddenly, and I jumped onto the couch, afraid of what was in it. Nicolai laughed again and finished removing the blanket to uncover a white wolf pup. It yawned lazily, perking its ears to see who had awakened it from its peaceful slumber.

I gasped, reaching into the basket to pick it up. Tears filled my eyes as I sat it on my lap and stroked its soft fur gently.

"There's a note attached to its collar," Nicolai pointed out, pulling the note off gently.

"What does it say?" I asked trying to hide my emotions.

Nicolai opened it and read it aloud:

> *My Dearest Angelina,*
>
> *Please forgive me for my disappearance as of late. I am in desperate need of time alone to face the sins I've committed against you. I've only ever wished for you to be happy, and I know I've taken a small part of your happiness away with the loss of Cole. The only thing I can ever hope for is your forgiveness. I know this won't make up for what you've lost, but I do hope one day it can replace the small piece of happiness I've taken. Thank you for always loving me,*
>
> *Yours forever,*
>
> *Jeremiah*

I was unable to hide it any longer, so I let the

tears fall freely. I hugged the wolf puppy and wished my friend could be there with me. I wanted him to know that I'd forgiven him, and that I missed him dearly.

Nicolai folded the letter back up and dropped it into the basket. He wrapped his arms around me and I leaned into him, sobbing quietly. The puppy began whining in my arms, unsure of what was going on around it. I sat back up and wiped the tears from my face, kissing the puppy gently on its head. It stared at me, its icy blue eyes an ocean of curiosity wondering if I was going to accept it.

"You should name it," Nicolai urged. "I believe it's a girl."

Looking down at her furry white face, I could see instant love and compassion within her. She was as pure as freshly fallen snow on a winter's day. Looking back up at Nicolai, I smiled knowingly. "Snow."

"Perfect." He kissed my forehead.

Snow licked my hands in favor of the new name.

"Looks like she likes it." I laughed as she began to climb up my chest, attempting to lick my face.

"It looks like she likes you," Nicolai complimented. "Let's just hope this one doesn't try to bite my face off."

I looked at him strangely, wondering what he could possibly be talking about. He laughed and kissed me again, encouraging me to not ask any more questions regarding that subject.

I yawned and looked at the clock above the fireplace. "It's late."

He stood up and yawned. "Ready for bed?"

"Most definitely."

He scooped Snow and me up in his muscular arms and carried us upstairs to our bedroom. We had chosen the biggest room for our own and turned my old tiny room into a closet for my growing wardrobe. He laid Snow and me on the bed gently and I stretched out, pulling back the antique quilt Ctephanyi had given me. I crawled underneath it with Snow following behind me, curling up next to my legs. Her soft fur felt good against my skin. Nicolai turned off the lights and jumped into bed causing Snow and me to rise a few feet into the air. She growled, unhappy with the fact that her new master had been jolted so suddenly.

"I'm not so sure she's going to like me, either," Nicolai whispered in the darkness.

Smiling, I curled up next to him and closed my eyes. Memories presented themselves to me as I slept, reminding me of my many adventures on what seemed like an endless journey. I had come out a different person, a stronger person.

I knew one day I would venture back into the Crimson Forest to seek out the many mysteries that lay within it, but for right now, I was content. I had the love of my soul mate, I had the protection of my companions who kept watch over me, and many looked upon me curiously, wondering what I was and what part I played in the future.

They say past performance is indicative of future behavior. If there was any truth to that statement, then I knew I had to be careful of the choices I made. My decisions were much more crucial now, as they affected the entire human population. One wrong move, and I could possibly wipe out the world. That was one thing I definitely didn't want on my shoulders.

An odd, dreadful feeling washed over me. I tried to push it away, but, for some reason, it continued to nag at the back of my mind. Something in the pit of my stomach warned me that my next adventure was right around the corner, and it was going to be more deadly and unforgiving than the last. I hoped exhaustion was playing its cruel tricks on me, because in my opinion, I didn't know how anything could be worse than my last experience. I mean, was that even possible? Time is the keeper of all secrets, and in the end, only time will tell.

Epilogue

Bright green eyes peered through the window as they slept. He had watched Angelina crawl into bed with her new wolf pup and the man she would soon marry. He didn't like the fact that she was with another man. He had known immediately who she was the day he had seen her inside the quaint little general store. To his surprise, she looked very similar to her previous self, only much more beautiful.

He had seen the way she looked at him, the way her cheeks flushed when he smiled at her. There was even a moment when he felt a strange sensation run through his body. He was sure she felt it too by the look on her pretty face.

He didn't know much about the man she was with, except that his father had gone into hiding due to some sort of betrayal. The man's mother had moved into town a short distance away but mostly kept to herself.

He also knew their family was from some ancient race that worshipped the Goddess Hecate.

He cringed at her name. Hecate had brought so much pain to his own family, and once he found out that Angelina was her daughter, he had even more reason to take her away and make her his. Everything he loved had been taken away from him, and he would make them all pay for their sins. He had spent years planning his revenge, and with the help of just the right person to make it all come together, he knew he would succeed.

He jumped down from the ledge and walked quietly down the street. He had something big planned, and it would all begin tonight. He made his way through the darkness and walked up the gravel driveway to a small house that sat on the edge of the woods. He peered into the dark window before slipping in unnoticed. Tiptoeing through the house, he crept into the bedroom where the pretty blonde rested quietly. He had been watching the house for some time now and knew Jeremiah left shortly after she fell asleep to take his nightly walk in the woods.

He smiled to himself as he pulled the sharp dagger out of its holster. Standing next to the pretty blond, he lifted his arm. Suddenly, she opened her eyes and let out a startled scream. He covered her mouth with his hand as she struggled to free herself from his grasp, but she bit down. He yelled out in pain. He drew back his muscular hand and hit her hard enough to knock her out cold. He didn't have much time. Jeremiah would be on his way back if he had heard her scream.

He picked up her limp body and left the house quickly, disappearing into the dark forest, a smile upon his wicked face. Jeremiah would go to Angelina for help, and she would help him. Things were beginning to fall into place. He would wait patiently for them to come and find him, but soon, he would have her all to himself. Soon, she would be his and that was definitely worth the wait.

Coming soon!
"The Crimson Chronicles—Crimson Moon"
by Christine Gabriel

Acknowledgements

There are so many people I would like to thank for helping me make this book become a reality. Without any of them, this would never have been possible.

I would first like to thank Zara and Allan Kramer of Pandamoon Publishing. They took a chance on this small town girl from Ohio with a big dream and helped make it become a reality. I will forever hold you both in my heart, and you have become family to me. Thank you.

Stephanie Gerold, Angela Pack, Bethany Perry, and Jeremiah Calderon—you guys were my character inspirations and believed in me from the start. You told me I could do it and helped me prove it to the people that didn't believe in me. I will forever be grateful for your friendships. Thank you!

I would like to thank Matt Gabriel. Though it was a long, rough road, he stood by me through every bit of it by bringing me chocolate ice cream, bottled water, my headphones, and even reading my rough drafts (pretty nice for a guy that hates reading).

Elgon Williams, my marketing partner-in-crime, has stood by my side through all the ups and downs the publishing world has thrown at me. Thank you E. It'll forever be the E & C team!

Diana Jones and Deborah Deforest for staying up late to read all my rough drafts and being <u>extremely</u> honest with me about the parts of the book that sucked and the parts you absolutely

333

adored. Thank you!

I would like to give a special thanks to Tom Suder, my boss of eleven years who thinks I'm good enough to sell a million copies of my book so I can quit my job. Thank you for believing in my ability and believing that I have what it takes to make my dreams come true, though I'm not quitting my job—not yet at least. ☺

Regina West, Steph Post, and Michael McBride. Let's just say they're the best editors ever! Thank you for being so incredibly awesome and fixing all my run-on sentences. Ha ha.

John Fulton, the one person who has the real first edition of Crimson Forest, and who told me that with my imagination I could do anything and be successful at it. Thanks for holding on to that original manuscript. Perhaps one day you'll actually get around to reading it, or you could just wait for this really cool version in paperback. Just remember, if you sell that original, I get half the money!

Josh, Tiffany, Stephanie, and Ashley Perry, my awesome siblings who put up with my craziness. I love you all!

I would like to thank my parents, Steve and Julie Perry, for raising me to be the good person I turned out to be.

Lucas, Lily, Lylah, and Kirra for staying out of my hair while I wrote this book. Your momma loves all of you very much!

Finally, I would like to thank all those who doubted my creative ability. You pushed me to want it more than I've ever wanted anything. With all the negativity you provided, something beautiful and positive was created for thousands of people to read and enjoy for many years to come.

Oh! And on one last note, I would like to also give a special thanks to all my Facebook, Twitter, and Google+ friends. Though I've not met many of you in person, you've all believed in me, and many of you have become close friends. You've all proved that you don't have to physically meet a person to know that in some way, shape, or form, you're connected with them. Thank you!

Made in the USA
Middletown, DE
11 September 2015